Lawrence Williams lives in West Sussex, and has written over thirty books.

THE FATE OF WOMEN

Every police officer has a case that will haunt him. For Detective Sergeant Jack Bull it is the case known as the Fate of Women. Someone has developed a solution to the problem of responding to violence against women. That person is murdering rapists discharged from prison after serving derisory short sentences. For Detective Sergeant Jack Bull, the stress is partially caused by his ambivalence towards wanting the serial murderer caught. But greater worry comes from the possibility that he too will be murdered . . . Jack is pushed to his limits as the investigation leads to its tragic conclusion.

Books by Lawrence Williams
Published by The House of Ulverscroft:

THE MURDER TRIANGLE
IMAGES OF DEATH
A COPPER SNARE
THE WOLVES

LAWRENCE WILLIAMS

THE FATE
OF WOMEN

Complete and Unabridged

ULVERSCROFT
Leicester

First published in Great Britain in 2007 by
Robert Hale Limited
London

First Large Print Edition
published 2008
by arrangement with
Robert Hale Limited
London

British Library CIP Data

Williams, Lawrence, *1915 –*
    The fate of women.—Large print ed.—
    Ulverscroft large print series: mystery
    1. Police—Great Britain—Fiction 2. Rapists—Crimes
    against—Fiction 3. Detective and mystery stories
    4. Large type books
    I. Title
    823.9'14 [F]

    ISBN 978–1–84782–065–5

Published by
F. A. Thorpe (Publishing)
Anstey, Leicestershire

Set by Words & Graphics Ltd.
Anstey, Leicestershire
Printed and bound in Great Britain by
T. J. International Ltd., Padstow, Cornwall

For the one in ten women victims
who fights back

CONTENTS

PART ONE

Home is where we start from.

Donald Winnicott

Home Is Where We Start From
Published by Penguin

★ ★ ★

Always anticipate the menace of strangers.

Louise Welsh

The Cutting Room
Published by Canongate

1

Daybreak. Pale mist wreathing down through the hanger wood on the chalk hill, bleeding out the late summer colours, subduing vibrancy; a moment for pretending no one is being murdered, raped or robbed. I feel the power of it like a respite from grief, but feel also its remorselessness: my life as nothing when embraced by this daybreak.

And I have known such a day before: the rush through grim adult silences to a hospital where I was only just tall enough for my head to be level with that of my dying foster mother. Standing, my eye line had been horizontal; lying down, her eye line vertical. Our faces had groped for a purchase, an alignment with each other. And she repeatedly and increasingly softly, like a battered old alarm clock running down, apologizing for her imminent death inflicted by a stranger. My only desire then to be out of that death place, out in the pure misty dawn and awaiting the view to distant grey hills. And perhaps a bird singing louder than any coughing death in a pale and shadowed room.

Now, as then, there is that same suffocating sense of threat. But birdsong has this time been ruptured by the tearing sounds of gunfire. My hands are cold on the steering wheel, my silent weapon-bearing colleagues hugely menacing.

'Ready, Bull?' demands Chief Instructor Sergeant McClaren.

Speechless, I nod. But he will reinstruct; silence implies redundancy. 'Keep the speed up. No cadence braking passing the targets. And — ' Not listening, I stare ahead through the windscreen of the Toyota pickup. In front of me like a sneer lies the floodlit ensnaring sheen of the skid pan. Behind, strapped and wedged in the open body of the truck, is Jimmy Pearson cradling the Belgian F2000; weapon of his choice, but not mine. With him is one of the armourers temporarily his supervisor. All three of us are linked to Pearson's throat mike. McClaren finishes telling me. Today is the fortieth of ninety days of being told and retold, tested and retested. Hell! We're not halfway yet.

'Go!' says McClaren.

I turn the key. The engine fires. Behind me Pearson is bracing himself tighter against the bodywork, the armourer next to him but well out of his way. McClaren is tightening his seat belt. Scattered on the grass mound in the middle of the pan, insubstantial in the dispersing mist, are our wearisome assessors, come to see if Detective Constable Jack Bull can get this right. Me, leader on our course, fitter than I have ever been but already exhausted by the relentless pressures of the training. And troubled, not about my competence but by a sensing, more grounded than intuition, of some kind of running sub-text beneath our training which is specifically about me. I am currently top dog of six survivors from an intake of twenty-four and am so on merit. But something else is happening around me and I don't yet know what it is.

I roll the truck forward, flick through the low gears. I have to pass the first traffic cone at twenty miles an hour or face the humiliation of being branded timorous: sent back to start up again. I transfer thirty-nine days' frustration down through my right hip, thigh, knee, calf, ankle, foot to the accelerator. The front wheels bounce slightly on the edge of the pan. I hear McClaren catch his breath. Everything is sliding slightly too fast. Clockwise round the central grassed mound, steering into the skid, not braking, touching the accelerator. Coming round the mound. A slight misjudgement: seeing in the mirrors a traffic cone displaced and toppling. Then into the oiled straight. Part of the test is to give Pearson a stable platform as we slide past the target figures on the outer edge of the pan. But the speed must not drop off.

Crackling gunfire. No shock, not after all that has happened, been inflicted. Ignoring the targets, I am entirely focused on tracking into the next inevitable skid when cornering the mound. Pearson stops firing; saving the remainder of his ammo for the second pass. I am halfway through the first circuit, keeping the speed up. Any fool can do this at walking pace. I know that round the curve lies the self-created hazard of the displaced traffic cone. Momentarily straight, no slide; brake touch, the only one. Into the bend, into the skid round the mound.

The displaced traffic cone is not there. Someone has — no time to think. Into the straight. Pearson firing again. Has to use all his allocated rounds. Me giving him the platform needed, as he did for me yesterday. Then the last bend, slowing for the stop. I switch off.

'Clear round,' lies McClaren. He avoids looking at me by getting out of the cab. I do the same. We walk to the back of the truck. Suddenly birdsong is restored, radiating out of the enfeebled mist. There is hint of muted sunlight on the hill crest. I will not contradict

McClaren. If I've learned only one thing in the past six weeks of mayhem it is the value of silence. But someone came down from that grassy misty mound in the centre of the skid pan and removed a dislodged traffic cone. To encourage Pearson and me as a team? I think not. No, something about me. That subtext: DC Jack Bull is not only the proven best, there has to be insurance. Excellence alone is not quite enough. But if I am right what is it they need me for *that* badly?

Pearson hands his weapon to the armourer who clears it; confirms to McClaren that all the allocated rounds were expended. Then Pearson and I are dismissed. We walk next to each other but wide-spaced, neither anxious about Pearson's score, which will be conveyed to us later. We both anticipate it will be slightly lower than mine yesterday. We walk as companions only because we have the same car waiting. And waiting in it are Paul Henderson and David Thomas, who had driven through the skid pan before us. It was Henderson's favoured Heckler and Koch 36 which had first silenced the dawn chorus. Paul I like: dependable rather than imaginative, a man to guard your back. About David I'm not so sure: a red-haired Welshman and excitable.

'Breakfast,' says Pearson, anticipating. The

man has become a foodie during the course. Why not? All six survivors have found coping mechanisms; mine more private than Pearson's. We slide into the waiting black Mercedes, are chauffeured smoothly by Henderson down into the coombe and along a gravel track which is raked every night. Through rising mist, the dew-smirched car glistens down the gravel, jolts on to a broken concrete strip that winds through the disused cement works built in an abandoned quarry. I look sideways at Pearson. The man is disgusting. Breakfast fifteen minutes away and he is already licking his lips. He is becoming one of the fittest men in the country but will be paunchy before he is forty.

Today is mainly one of lectures, and the only participating activity will be a visit to the underground range. It will be so much less stressful than the next confrontation with the members of the SAS training team: more assault course, combat tests, and more of being ripped out of sleep by gleeful sadists who know their malice has official approval. To think that I, and all the others — most of whom have been chopped: faces a blur of pain, names forgotten — were volunteers! No wonder I am being reborn as a morose antisocial yob: speechless with offence — and in defence. And, like the other survivors, utterly divorced from any sense of humour. How soon before a joke can once again be something better than abuse on a parade square, a wilfully misdirected night march, a sly punch in the kidneys while climbing a wall?

We had all volunteered for similar reasons: a fresh start, chances for more demanding work, an opportunity to break out from the restrictive patterns of ordinary police work into something more challenging. We had trotted out all the phrases Mr Frimmer, Director of the Serious Incident Unit, had anticipated. His cynical smile had been much in evidence then. (None of us had ever seen him again.) The irony was that had we known just how challenging the training was going to be, a lot of applications would have been withdrawn. All this Frimmer undoubtedly knew. Equally well known to him, but unspoken were all the negative reasons we shared for wishing to join his outfit: all the disillusionments of our ordinary police work.

Our Chief Constables had justified our attempts to get out from under with the flabby cliches of 'healthy ambition', 'desire for a greater challenge' (that word again!) when we were really escapees from pressures we had been powerless to change. We were sick

9

of a job where senior officers got blisters on their arses and not their feet, where computers wore out before boots, where cost not effectiveness was the chief parameter, where ability to take a degree counted for more than ability to take a thief. And where truth was forever politically incorrect. And all that shit shovelled on top of policing an increasingly violent and resentful public that branded us racist fascists until the day they grovellingly sought our help.

After the morning lectures we have an excellent lunch, then go to the basement range, we six surviving hard men: Pearson, Henderson, Thomas, Jakowski, Tenby and me. I suspect our hardness would melt away if offered an afternoon sleep in a freshly made bed. What we get is six rounds in our own time and then six rounds rapid.

In our own time Pearson, Henderson, Thomas and me go clear; Jakowski and Tenby each drop a point. McClaren gets us set for the six rounds rapid, but before he gives the order to shoot I resolve to put my last shot wide. We shoot. Then we are clearing our guns, stepping away, and McClaren is winding in the cards. We don't see our individual cards, but then we never did unless we scored low.

'Good set, lads,' says McClaren. 'Everyone

shot maximum. Verry, verry satisfactory.' That Scots burr indicative of approval. Then the liar is away up the steps ahead of us, and I, bemused by deceitfulness, am the last to leave.

More than twenty years ago a lying, bright-faced nurse had told me my foster mother was doing well. Now, as then, I wait for a plutonic truth to reach me. Perhaps this time it will not overwhelm.

2

The ninety days have passed and I am still top student. Now I wait to be interviewed by Frimmer himself, an accolade not offered to others. But I sit uneasy in his waiting room believing I have been called here for reasons other than success on the course. My only companion is a woodlouse who has been making good progress (for ninety days louse time?) along the valley between skirting board and fitted carpet. But now he has a problem. There is a telephone lead lying across his route. I don't want him to be turned aside by the obstacle but go straight at it and climb over. Deflection will take him halfway across the room to the point where the lead rises off the carpet and up to the telephone on the desk. Then he will have to chunter all the way back to the skirting board, to the woody world that is his. What his decision is I am never to know. The red light over Frimmer's door has switched to green. There is just time for me to wish good louse luck before I knock on the door.

A metallic voice orders me in. I push the door and realize the wood facing conceals steel. I am entering a bunker. As the door clicks shut behind me I am temporarily separated from pain, rage, gunfire and screaming tyres. But how temporarily? What I know instantly is that the wall to my left is completely covered by huge photographs of myself. A few are full-length pictures but the majority are portraits, the largest of which is a metre square. More disorienting is that several of them have been defaced with coloured inks.

'Well done, Bull!' Frimmer extends his right hand. I realize he is referring to my success on the course, not my capacity for making a good photograph. 'Meet my colleague, Mr Stone.'

Of Stone I have heard only the rumour of an arm missing. This is confirmed as he steps forward and offers me his only hand, his left. Oddly, his deformity is the more horrible because he wears an immaculately cut suit. Both men are taller than me but as I look up at their faces all I see is the replacement steel hand. Is this the price Stone paid for working with Frimmer?

Frimmer's jumble-sale costume I remember from our one previous meeting many months ago. It is a map of indifference: creased, a button missing, and what resembles old scorch marks or gravy droppings down the front of the jacket. The huge and close-cropped head rising out of the suit is almost an anachronism: Bismarck as pauper. I look back at Stone. His face has smoothed out, the smile replaced by a look of hawklike intensity. Not a man to lie to. But I haven't come to lie, rather to fight. Intimidated by the pair of them, even more so by the photographs, I know resolve is weakening. They are the perfect double act for creating alarm in a third party.

Feeling distinctly third of three, I allow them to manoeuvre me into a wooden carver facing them across a paper-littered desk. I collapse. They sit some distance apart from each other in large leather armchairs. I foresee getting a stiff neck looking from one to the other, the more so if I am also asked to look at those photos. Frimmer creates a theatrical moment of cigar lighting. This gives me time to see the room more clearly; maybe his intention. All the other walls of this large windowless room are covered with graphs and charts. Illumination by overhead spotlights gives this display an air of seedy glamour, as if someone has not quite succeeded in creating a film set of a military operations room. High in one corner, glowering like an angry infected eye, a large TV monitor stares down at the three of us. The room has only two doors: one by which I entered and one I know better than to ask about. I attempt to stifle rising anxiety by acknowledging to myself the excellence of the air conditioning. Frimmer's cigar smoke does not offend.

'The charts remind us of where we've got to,' says Stone, peaceably.

'And where we're going,' growls Frimmer. 'Talking of the future, I can confirm you in the rank of Detective Sergeant. You will, however, be paid as Acting Detective Inspector from the beginning of next year in recognition of what we'll be asking you to do.' He gives me a blast from his cigar. Something in his facial expression hints that his feelings include regret. I suspect he is displeased that I personify extra cost.

'Thank you, sir,' feebly. I feel it is not the right time to question his sinister remark about pay. I move my chair further back.

'No trouble from your burns?' He doesn't like fidgets. 'Pity about that business,' he says. I guess he is not sorry about me getting burnt dragging a lover out of her arsoned flat. What really bugs him is that he has acquired damaged goods: my body can be too easily indentified. An additional irritation for him is that the incident occurred *after* I had been offered a place on his course. He could have cancelled that offer but the photographs of me on his wall imply something else.

'Obvious only when naked, sir.'

'You and your women,' says Frimmer, obliquely. There is a silence while we think about my women and how they have scarred me.

'Right, Bull. Outstanding on the course you may have been but we had a good enough reason to insure against any last-minute slip-ups either by you or our nit-picking assessors. So don't start a fight about being fitted up. If you think we've got your photos on our wall, been doodling on 'em because we've not enough to do, then think again.'

'We have an interesting case for you,' says Stone. 'Involves women.'

'Start from the beginning, I think,' says Frimmer, weightily.

'Sir.' Stone knows obedience pays. (I'm not good at obedience. My former guvn'r won't be missing me.) 'The Serious Incident Unit can be called upon by any local police force that is either stymied on an old case or making a pig's ear. That doesn't make us exceptional. We're just part of the thin edge of the wedge moving towards a national force. You know how resistant we are to change in this country.'

'And especially the police,' says Frimmer, waspish.

'Yes,' says Stone. 'Well, what makes us exceptional — apart from underhand methods — are two aspects of our brief. First we can refuse to respond. We protect our reputation by refusing the no-hopers.'

'That term refers not only to cases but also to our judgement about the police force in question. Offering assistance is one thing; shovelling other people's shit is another. Oh, sorry, Stone.' Frimmer obviously isn't sorry about interrupting, but chooses to acknowledge the faint sigh that is Stone's parallel to cigar smoke.

'What goes with this is that our successful interventions are confirmed only to Whitehall. All public praise is directed to the local force we have assisted. That cheers them up and gets us more referrals.' Stone flashes a quick look at Frimmer as if daring him to intervene again. 'But we have a second role which is very much more undercover than helping inadequate anxiety-ridden Chief Constables,' continues Stone. 'Our brief includes searching out undiscovered crime and, in some cases, dealing with it undercover.'

I wonder what 'dealing with it' might mean. Fantasy of joining an assassination squad? 'Now here's our current research.' Stone rests his left hand on the papers covering the desk. His steel claw is pocketed.

'We've been making a statistical analysis of what's happening to ex-convicts. Won't bore you with details about why we started this. We identified a group of thirty men who have died in the last six years and for whom all the inquest verdicts were either misadventure or accident. None of them died during a criminal act and most did not die at home. The next coincidence for our particular sample was that for all of them their last previous was either for rape or for GBH against a woman. Now that's *really* odd. You might expect a significant proportion of recidivist cat burglars to die in falls from roofs and balconies, but rapists dying? Even more extraordinary is that for nineteen of the thirty deaths there were no witnesses. That's a higher proportion than for road accidents. So we've stayed with those nineteen for the moment. They include eight drownings, four falls from high buildings and seven domestic accidents involving electrocutions, gas leaks and fires. What's your reaction, Bull?'

'Nineteen's quite a fat number.'

'Not after Shipman, surely?' Frimmer is even less appealing when smooth. I watch him fondle his cigar back into shape. 'Anything else?'

'Yes, sir.' I pause: a man feeding tidbits to a tiger in the hope he will not pounce. 'Your sample includes rather a lot of non-swimmers.'

'Good man!' Stone's enthusiasm prevents reply from Frimmer. 'We're prepared to believe the various domestic accidents, particularly in view of the mental derangement or low intelligence of some of the victims, but eight drownings — never! I can't think of any criminal group in which more than a third of the members are drowned in six years — nor any non-criminal group for that matter. Just to check, ran a programme on all British merchant seamen with criminal convictions. The percentage drowned over six years was nought point nought seven per cent. The next question was obvious.'

He expects me to ask it but I take a moment to consider the value, or lack of value, of his maritime statistic. 'Who's doing it?'

'Not for me,' says Stone. 'That's a question for our fieldmen. No, what I got into was: Why those nineteen? Got a possible answer almost at once.' Stone pauses dramatically. Even Frimmer, who knows the answer, is staring at him. 'All nineteen men got sentences leading to complaints about leniency. In some cases juries had difficulties reaching a verdict. In others, defence lawyers cast doubt on the veracity and morality of the victims. And don't waste your breath telling me that shouldn't affect sentencing! We all know that it does.

'By this time we were getting a bit punch-drunk with coincidences. And the odds that all these coincidences might come together *coincidentally* are about the same as you winning the Lotto jackpot.'

'There's another coincidence as well, Stone. Maybe not so clear cut but it's in there. I wonder if Bull has worked it out?' I allow myself a moment to watch the smirk fade on Frimmer's face. After all, they are my photos up there. But he knows I've spotted that other coincidence. I decide to summarize, if only to convince myself I am recovering from the shock of the photos.

'The coincidences are that all these victims died accidentally, that there were no witnesses — or none came forward — that a surprising number would have benefited from swimming lessons, that they had all committed crimes against women, that in every case the sentence given had been criticized. But there is yet *another* coincidence. For most of these deaths forensic could be pretty sparse.'

There is a moment of mutual smugness between the three of us which in other circumstances might have been bearable verging on pleasant. It is possible to drown someone without them necessarily touching you in a way that is helpful to Forensic. Ditto for being pushed off roofs and for certain types of domestic 'accident', especially electrocutions.

'The best Forensic can offer is that in two drownings the victims may possibly have had contact with someone's wetsuit. In one of the fatal falls the deceased had hit the ground face down but also had bruising on his back.' Frimmer grinds out this information as if insulted by it.

'Does geography help, sir?' I aim this one at Frimmer.

'No, Bull, it bloody don't. The only specific connection is with the motorway network, and that doesn't mean much with most of the UK connected. And we can't expect much help from local forces, not with corpses scatted countrywide. And they've not the manpower to query coroners' accident verdicts. Some don't even have the resources to fully investigate open verdicts.'

'And time doesn't help either,' said Stone. 'No significant order in prison discharge dates and death dates. They were not killed — er, did not die, I suppose I should still say — in the order in which they were released. And if there is a link between the rape date and the death date we are dealing with a long time span in some cases, but short in others.

For some of these cases we are proposing links between deaths and crimes committed in different decades. And, before you ask, no link between the prisons they were in; for example, only one of the drowning victims was held in Parkhurst. Only three of them might have met briefly while being moved between prisons and/or remand centres. It is almost certain they lived and died strangers to each other.'

'And what do the profilers say?' Even as I ask I know the question will make Frimmer grit his teeth. Fortunately, Stone goes for it.

'Favour a man — or team of men — rather than women. Not sure I take that. But they see significance in the DIY element behind domestic accidents, the possibility we're looking for a powerful swimmer, amount of physical strength required in some cases.'

'Partner or ex-partner of one of the rape victims?'

'Could be,' says Stone, almost glumly. 'Could also be a team. The psychologists certainly don't dismiss that. Either way the implication is a lot of messy prodding around in old cases and with distressed people. That's just one of the things you'll be involved in as soon as you get back from leave.' Pleased as I am to hear about leave I also note the phrase 'just one of the things'.

So what about these bloody photos?

'Now a big question, Bull.' Frimmer pauses, gives me a generous share of his cigar smoke. 'How can our killer, or killers, guarantee either event or outcome? How does he/they get rapists to the lakes and rivers where he drowns them? What's the inducement?'

'Sex or money, sir. Not power, not for a share in some lucrative crime, not for deadbeat convicted rapists.'

'How's that work, then?'

'They have to have had a very persuasive introductory offer. Any indications of sudden wealth just before they died?'

'No,' says Stone, pushing both claw and hand under the desk.

'Right, sir. Your team of killers may include a woman. But not many men will travel to meet a stranger solely on the strength of a telephone offer of sex or money from a woman they've never met. So there must have been a previous meeting. Maybe she's a hunter, travels to them, perhaps becomes a neighbour, even a temporary friend. The only certainty is none of them was murdered by the person they had raped. They wouldn't go near their former victim — for love or money.'

In the long silence that follows, I recognize

23

a new element in the room. Very slowly but inexorably I am beginning to become afraid.

'That's pretty sick, Bull, What sort of woman or women would — ?' asks Frimmer.

'Not sure many women could answer that. I know I can't.'

'Interesting you chose to say *that*, Bull. Our profilers see an overlap between their views of our killers and of yourself: a propensity for violent action.' I feel a stiffness in my neck. Not only is it clear there's nothing new I can give these two, it is also clear they've been leading me by the nose. 'Another relevant fact, Bull, is that the elapsed time between prison discharge and death of these rapists is getting shorter. That could reflect it's easier to track down men recently released than those set free many years ago. Some are easily traceable because they return to sympathetic relatives who have continued living quite close to the scene of crime. Like dogs to their vomit. It's their poor bloody victims who moved away. Or maybe our killers are just getting more confident. Had plenty of practice and no one's noticed — or so they believe. So we're setting a trap. We're anticipating them. We've found a rapist who fits all the criteria we've discussed and we're making him a tethered goat for her, him or them. Switch on the TV, Stone.'

The picture on the screen is of a man I've never seen but feel I know. He is dark, swarthy, black hair, black moustache, long sideboards, Mediterranean appearance. Wears rimless spectacles. Dark eyes with dark circles under them, broad forehead and straight nose. Stone moves his real hand over a small keyboard. The screen divides and a photograph of myself appears next to that of the swarthy man.

Split like the screen, I both deny what is happening and fearfully accept it. Then Stone is painting in the hairstyle, the sideboards, the moustache on *my* face. Then my cheeks are slightly dragged down, my eyes shadowed a little. Both men turn away from the TV and look at me. I look at them in turn while at the margin of my vision I see the rimless spectacles forming on my face on the screen. I can't speak. I had always believed it was my own positive choice to escape routine police work by applying to join SIU. Now, and too late, I know that tentacles have long been silently reaching for me, but without alerting me.

'You see why we had to be absolutely sure you passed the course. To some degree your psychological profile parallels that of the killer, and you physically resemble the man we hope is to be the next victim. He's Jake

Corelli, due out next April. You've plenty of time to prepare.'

'I don't look much like him.'

'Don't have to. He's no relatives, and in the last three years only his warders have seen how he has changed. Being the same physical type is likeness enough — plus a bit of make-up!'

None of us questions the adequacy of my qualifications for this operation. Will a slight resemblance to a rapist plus a reputation for toughness be sufficient?

'This could be bloody dangerous.' The stupidity of my remark betrays more than my doubt.

'Indeed it could,' says Frimmer, coldly. 'That's why you're here, Bull. We reckon you can cope. Now if you'd rather be directing traffic, don't sign this paper.' Left-handedly, he slides a form across the desk towards me. With his right he offers a cheap biro. The only way for me to assert independence is to take out my own pen. With that puerile gesture of defiance, I plunge into an oceanic deep.

PART TWO

You have to protect yourself from sadness. Sadness is very close to hate. Let me tell you this. This is the thing I learned. If you take in someone else's poison — thinking you can cure them by sharing it — you will instead store it within you.

Michael Ondaatje

The English Patient
Published by Bloomsbury Publishing

3

I sat in the tatty car SIU had provided. Being gridlocked fitted my mood, as did the drizzle wearing away the remnants of November. In the mirror I saw the new temporary version of myself. Arthur Snell I had become, DHSS representative: investigator of compensation terms for raped women. A job as ugly as it sounded, ugly as the face in the mirror: sallow complexion, long, blonded hair and moustache, heavy dark spectacles. (Absolutely unlike Corelli!) Equipped with leaky raincoat, damp trilby, and a scuffed briefcase full of convincingly designed documentation, I was on my way to visit the fourth of the victims on my list of eleven.

I had wanted to protest the role play, to proceed as Mr J. Bull. But more than rank had silenced me. I was also hamstrung by the possibility Frimmer knew of horrors ahead that were beyond anything I could imagine. As an exercise in practicalities the role play was simple enough; good experience even though the role awaiting me next spring would be very different. Secondly, I was meeting with victims and their loved ones as part of a process of 'getting inside' the case, as Frimmer coyly expressed it. Stone curtly: 'Total immersion.' It had also seemed a sensible decision that I should recheck eleven cold cases and not yet be exposed to those on Stone's hot list. Now I knew all that stuff was merely words surrounding a hideous reality, but had no intimation of that from my first interviewee.

Her name was Molly Poling, innocent victim of a brutal rape and of unscrupulous defence counsel who had managed to raise doubts about her character. He had wished the court to believe that, because Molly had had several sexual partners by the time she was raped at age twenty-two, she must have been giving out certain signals which his client had understandably misinterpreted. Molly had found some kind of acceptance of her tragedy by the time I arrived on her doorstep some eight years after the event, two years after her attacker's death. She had rebuilt her life, got a flat, a lover and a job. Her lifestyle, her recovery and her matter-of-factness had deceived me. Later, I was to wonder if that deception was partly an outcome of the contrast between us: she the smartly dressed businesswoman, dark-suited over a white sweater, gold ear studs her only jewellery, and I epitomizing the seedy, unkempt government functionary.

My second interview had come close to unnerving me. Sounds odd, that phrase from an experienced copper. But words fail, especially now I have to justify to myself what I am doing. (I have wasted no words on Frimmer. His response would be one I had come to accept as a mantra: 'Ends and means, Bull. Ends and means.' My reports to him are models of unfeeling clarity.) Her name was Rosie. Her spirit was snapped and her life unspeakable. Her husband had been unable to get clear of innuendoes uttered in court by her attacker and his defence counsel. Divorce followed. She had collapsed into a lonely sluttishness. Her home stank and so did she. In my male arrogance I had looked for a redeeming spark in her, for any sign she might emulate Molly Poling. Fool that I was.

Molly personified recovery but Rosie lived a different version of reality: the endless solace of self-pity. And that was when I knew rape could be worse than murder. The murder victim knows no consequences; the rape victim lives them for ever. And, yes, I knew the futility of these thoughts and words. If there is a language about rape I hadn't learnt it. But what words could ever fit? I seemed to hear only the sounds of rage, despair, self-pity, irredeemable loss.

I have never understood rape except from the protected stance of an investigating officer who never doubted it was a major crime 'against the person'. Even our methods had given me a protective distance; it had been my women colleagues who ran the intimately detailed interviews, and who, at times, shared in the healing consolation of embracing the victim. Not that I thought any of that was wrong but it had shielded me. Trying to find some help in honesty, I acknowledged I had never felt the desire to rape. I wanted to possess, to master, to take the lead — of course. But never that other thing. And women have always received me with such generosity and frankness that sexual pleasure has been not only available but also a mutual delight. In rape there are none of the colours of desire. Now, in this work, my good fortune felt like a disqualification. How could I ever understand?

The traffic lurched again, edging me towards another interview I didn't want; the certainty it would contain more terrible and disgusting surprises. But I also knew something was changing in me that went beyond destroying my ignorance. Somewhere inside me — and I am in such despair at the futility of words I cannot precisely name that place — an anger was fermenting, and it carried with it a kind of relief because I trusted it. It was not the recurring futile rage that goes with a more common helplessness: the rage over the roadside corpse and the voluble protesting drunk driver. It was more purposeful than that; had an intentionality which I didn't understand but to which I clung.

It would be easy to make too much of all this and so lurch into a kind of maudlin regret for the victims, and into a shabby self-pity that I was now obliged to face them. But the harsh truth was that I, a copper with nine years' service, four commendations for bravery, two negative assessments — both for the use of unnecessary force — was out of my depth in an area of crime where I had thought myself both hardened and familiar. Not even reading the trial transcripts provided by Stone had fully alerted me to my shaming ignorance.

My third interview had been with Miss June Wiston, a victim of GBH. The bodily harm had been so grievous she was permanently facially disfigured and confined to a wheelchair. Yet her mother had almost gloatingly assured me all would be well. At least her daughter had not been raped. Because the man had not done *that* there was not much to worry about. What made the mother's attitude all the more horrible was the reflection of it in the words of the defence counsel. In court he had tried to imply that the lack of rape might be regarded as a *mitigation*. I had looked into the victim's crooked face and she had looked into mine. My merely male bewilderment had seemed shared. Was rape really so horrible if afterwards there was still walking, dancing, swimming; still possibilities of love with a man?

Someone gave the South London traffic an enema. I risked a quick glance at the A *to* Z on the seat beside me and swung the battered Ford left at the lights. I found Ridout Crescent and parked a few yards from number 22. I listened to the rain drumming on the roof of the car. I was going to get wet again; my damp and inadequate costume would suck in the rain. ('What social workers wear,' Frimmer had said.) I splashed to the house: pokey 1930s Tudor. The door was opened by a very large black man dressed in a violent tartan shirt, black jeans and white trainers. There was a joke in there about the Black Watch but I wasn't making it. I looked up from the straining waistband of his trousers. He slightly inclined his head, the discoloured whites of his eyes the only contrast inside the black face. He had no gleaming teeth with which to impress.

'Mr Snell.' I presented my card, which he ignored. I tried again. 'Department of Health. Brigadier French is expecting me.' He stared at me. I opened my mouth to try again but he forestalled me.

'He was. But you's awful late, man.' In other circumstances his high-pitched voice might have provoked laughter.

'Er — yes. Sorry. Traffic's bad.' Maybe semaphore would be quicker.

'Wait.' The word was a squeak. I waited for some time. 'I'll see if you can be seen in the study.' Quick footwork thwarted his attempt to shut me out in the rain. He glared at me, perhaps speechless at my affrontery. I never doubted his ability to put me out like a damp cat. 'Man. You is *wet*.' Another wait: I was getting the hang of things now. 'Stay on that mat. You dry off a bit before you gets on my floors.' He snatched my card and went away: the great mound of him, mostly muscle.

I looked round the tiny, panelled hall, cluttered with mementoes of the brigadier's career: photographs, citations, animal heads. None of the rapists had been shot. Had he used retirement to learn new ways of killing? 'Anything's possible in this case — even that.' The head of the gazelle addressed stared down at me with a contemptuous expression.

After a long wait the retainer returned. He had used the time wisely by putting in his teeth. His sneer, as he relieved me of my sodden raincoat, was now something wonderful. He looked down on my faded jacket and wet jeans, and then revealed his choppers again by ordering me to rewipe my shoes on the mat. As I followed him to the study I acknowledged that more than his teeth might be false.

'That Mr Snell,' he muttered, and shut me in with Brigadier French.

'Good day, Mr Snell,' said the Brigadier. He did not offer to shake hands but stood and looked at me across the darkly patterned carpet. A small, upright, slim, white-haired man: taut as a stressed steel wire. He was wearing a black pinstripe suit with a white shirt and pale blue tie.

'You appear to be rather wet,' he said, blamingly. 'Sit here by the fire.' I sat. 'Understand the traffic's bad.'

'Yes, sir. Sorry I'm late.' Steam was already rising from my jeans. The blazing fire was bitingly hot and I would soon need to move away.

'Think you need a drink, Snell. Best defence against this weather.'

'Er — thank you, sir.' To hell with role. Snell might be a dypso.

36

'Whisky, I think.' He opened the cabinet under the window. The room was so small I could read the labels from where I sat. His hand hovered over two bottles. Then he made up his mind. It is not everyone who offers his better whisky to a stranger; perhaps he was apologizing for his curtness — or for his retainer.

I looked round the room: only a small suburban sitting-room but the book-lined walls justified the title of study. What it had in common with the hall was inappropriateness of scale, a claustrophobia. Just as the hall was overfull with decapitated beasts, the study was too crammed with bookshelves and a grotesquely large fireplace. It was as if the Brigadier had been unable to slim down his service life to fit with his pensioned state. And he had chosen a manservant on the same overblown scale. And *that* choice was the one that interested me.

Stone had allowed French to drop off his list of 'most likelys' because the Brigadier was considered too frail to be the murderer; additionally, his only murderous skill was as marksman, and none of the victims had been shot. But that large slow-speaking black was capable of throwing someone off the roof of a multi-storey car park. And the thought of meeting him in deep water! There had been the briefest mention of a servant in the French files but nothing about his dimensions. Was it possible that these two men, both devoted to the daughter, Isobel, were the team of killers the profilers had postulated?

'Your manservant is a big chap, sir.'

'What? Oh, Atkins. Suppose so.' I'd missed out on the Black Watch joke but this one I decided to follow.

'Tommy, sir?'

'Lord, no. No army background there. Name's Samuel, as a matter of fact. Took him on when I retired. He'd not had much luck in life up until then. He does the heavy work. Comfort to the ladies having him about the place. Especially after what happened.' In the following silence I moved my chair back from the fire. It felt a bit like sitting too close to Frimmer.

'Very surprised to receive your letter,' he said, abruptly sitting to attention. 'Precisely what is it you want, Mr — er — '

'Snell, sir.' He knew my name well enough. How many times had he read Frimmer's faked letter before agreeing to see me? 'Neither I nor the Department *wants* anything, sir. It is simply that new legislation empowers us to offer help to the victims of criminal assaults in those cases where

considerable medical treatment was necessary.'

'Bit late, isn't it? Isobel was attacked eight
years ago.'

'It must seem like that, sir. But the
legislation is new and we are now empowered
to seek redress from your daughter's — er-
assailant.'

'Can you imagine a — a rat like that having
any assets? And can you imagine for a
moment that Isobel or I would accept money
from him?'

I sipped my drink. Was he just angry or
covering his negotiation of the first hurdle?
He had not revealed he knew the man was
dead. But the language was not quite right.
'Can you imagine a rat like that — ' A
dissonance there. Try again.

'I understand your feelings, sir, but — '

'But nothing! You can have no idea of my
feelings. No idea!'

'Right, sir. But I have been doing this job
for some time, and have met a number of
women who have suffered the same kind
of experience.'

He avoided my eyes, gazed into the fire for
several seconds. Then he spoke sadly, not
aggressively: 'How can you bear your work,
Mr Snell?'

'Because I can offer help.'

'They accept? The help I mean?'

'Sometimes. For some people the help is in talking about an experience they are generally unable or afraid to talk about. For others the practical help is more important.'

'You offer money?'

'Tactfully, sir, tactfully. Sometimes the help is to put them in touch with new facilities within the Health Service.' (If only you could hear me, Frimmer: as despicable as yourself!)

'Shrinks, you mean?'

'Maybe. In some cases the help is to cope with physical disabilities.'

'Cases? God! We're a case now, are we?' Another pause. 'Mr Snell, you must excuse me. I get very angry. All this belated concern, but they let rapists off.'

'Well, I don't know the legal ins and outs.' Keep prodding.

'Four and a half years for rape doesn't require you to be a lawyer, Mr Snell. And at least a year off for good behaviour!'

'I suppose that depends — ' But he wasn't going to let me talk about circumstances. That might imply Isobel had contributed to her own fate.

'Depends! Depends! D'you think I don't know what my daughter has suffered? Execution would've been too good for that animal.'

40

'Execution, sir?'

'Yes, Snell. If he ever comes near us I'll certainly kill him.'

'Please, sir, please. Interviewing you and your daughter will not lead to that happening, I assure you.'

'And I assure you, Mr Snell, you'll not interview my daughter.'

'She is of age, sir,' I said, switching to soft pedal.

'Then why interview me? Anyway, she's away.'

'I often interview a relative first, sir, because we have learned from experience that is sometimes a tactful way to begin.' No reply. I stood up, pushed my spectacles back on to the bridge of my nose. Mr Snell was feeling embarrassed and affronted. (Detective Sergeant Bull was feeling something else.) 'I do assure you, sir, that — '

'Sit down, man! You must excuse me. Living with Isobel every day — '

'I think I understand, sir.' I walked to the window. 'She's down in Bournemouth, is she, sir?'

'Bournemouth?'

'You said she was away, and you have a second home there, sir. Our records show — '

'Your records are out of date. I sold that property some years ago.'

'Oh, did you, sir?' And did he know he had sold it only weeks before his daughter's attacker was released? And did he know the rapist had elderly parents in Bournemouth and no other home to return to? I hunched my shoulders, peered out into the garden. The link was more tenuous than the spiders' webs glistening in the rain. As for the lie about Isobel being away, that might not be significant; merely a father being protective. But I knew from surveillance reports that his daughter no longer ventured beyond the local shops, and even then always with her mother.

'All I can say is your daughter is entitled to the same rights, the same help as anyone else if she wants it. That decision is legally and morally hers. It is also a matter on which she can take advice from you.'

'I will discuss the matter with her. Now if you will excuse me — ' Brigadier French looked at his watch again. My late arrival was leading to late departure, and he was expecting wife and daughter back any minute. I wondered how he had persuaded them to go out on such an unpleasant morning. Very slowly, I walked back to my seat but finished my whisky while standing. The heat from the fire was intolerable.

'You understand, sir, your daughter has to make the final decision?'

'Yes, yes.'

'Perhaps you can suggest a day and time I can call again?'

'I'll telephone your office. I've got the number on your letter. Now please — '

'Thank you for the drink, sir.' I picked up my briefcase. 'I have a coat and hat.'

'Oh, yes. I'll get Atkins to find them.' He almost ran from the room.

Movement in the garden caught my attention. Someone was opening the gate in the high wall. I stepped close to the window so the light fell directly on my face — Mr Snell's face. Two women carrying shopping bags, dripping umbrellas clashing, entered the garden and walked along the path towards me. Even though I knew what to expect, I still caught my breath. Now I saw the burdens of the victim personified in the flesh.

Isobel French had more than doubled her body weight since the rape. Maybe she believed herself safe from every man behind her self-containing wall of fat. Her shapeless clothes held her flesh against her skeleton, but where that support was absent folds of flesh hung loose. A great muffler of chins dragged her head down at an unnatural angle, and the original fine lines of her face were swamped in pallid fat. Below her wet raincoat her bloated ankles overhung the edges of her flat-heeled shoes. Impossible that this gross body contained the same spirit that had lived in the smiling girl in the photograph on the window-sill beside me. Or was it?

No possibility Isobel French had revenged herself. It was only the wiry strength of the sparrowlike woman she leaned on that enabled her to leave the house. Mrs French looked through the window at me. Panic distorted her face. Hurriedly, she steered her enormous child away. Isobel French did not even see me. Perhaps she was no longer permitted to see; some victims' mothers rejoice in their child's captivity. Isobel was twenty-nine years old. Beyond her, and Rosie and Molly and June, towered the appalling statistic of ninety percent of *unreported* rapes and beatings endured by women. I turned from the window.

Atkins was standing behind me. I had been too distracted by distress to be aware of him entering the room; a man big enough to throw me off a roof. Scowling, he thrust my hat and coat at me. He knew what I had just seen.

'Er — thank you, Atkins,' I said, trying to restore my balance. He made no reply nor any effort to help me into my damp coat. 'You worked for the Brigadier for very long?'

Then, almost as if reading my mind, he smilingly flashed his teeth at me before giving the answer that might nullify my conspiracy fantasy.

'Two years this comin' Christmas.' As I followed him across that cluttered hall, the claustrophobic, overheated house felt it was on the point of exploding.

Sitting in the car, watching the rain, feeling even worse after the interview than before, I recognized for the first time another cause of shame in me that outstripped even that rooted in my incomprehensions around rape. I was getting *better* at this disgusting work: better at pretending, questioning, shamefully ferreting in griefs. A twinge of shame also in my recollection of the innocence with which I had taken out my pen and signed that paper Frimmer had slithered across the desk at me under the collusive gaze of Stone.

4

Dressing in the dankness of my rented room at 01.15 on a cold, damp, early January night, I allowed my mind to swerve swallowlike, to distract me from the impact of the message on my mobile, and my reply which had been loud enough to wake my landlady, Mrs Giles. As I pulled up my trousers I could hear her coughing and snuffling badgerlike down the stairs to her kitchen. My telephoned identification as Arthur Snell DHSS 2937 had sprung a troubling reply.

'Duty Officer Jim Douglas here. Time to pretend your auntie's died. There'll be a car at the door in thirty minutes. Got that?'

'Yes. Thirty minutes. What's up?'

'Wait and see. But a word, Jack. Frimmer'll be in the car.'

As I dressed I let my mind carry me first to my greatest help: that my listed interviews had dwindled to the last one, and it was likely to be the most straightforward. Soon to be free of this perpetual wail of grief.

My second help had been my determination to maintain the level of fitness developed on the SIU course. As soon as I was set up in my rented room I had joined the nearest gym where I worked with a ferocity that probably alarmed the staff. But then they had no inkling of the body-mind link with the mental fitness I was struggling to maintain.

It was at the gym I met my third help in the form of Jayne, a plain but very fit woman slightly younger than me, proud possessor of both a very good body and a delightful flat within walking distance of the gym. Being two healthy, unattached animals meeting three evenings a week and twice every weekend in the glare of body-consciousness, the result had been predictable. The cathartic value of athletic sex for Arthur Snell was all the greater because of its contrasts, literal and implied, with his miserable work. Celebrating our bodies together was not only delightful for both of us but, unknown to Jayne, was also healing for Arthur Snell.

In that phrase, 'unknown to Jayne', lay the potential maggot in the apple. How much *was* unknown to Jayne? I never lost sight of the possibility she had been positioned in my undercover life by Frimmer. The man must have had some idea what the work was costing me, knew that neither my previous experience nor his training course had prepared me for the demands of the last three months. Weekly reports by my lover might be keeping him in touch with how I was coping. Frimmer and I both knew my potential worth. Where would he find another officer who so much resembled Jake Corelli?

I had also drawn on another long-held secret — secret even from Frimmer's professional ferrets. About six years ago, while still a uniformed plod, I had been part of the team that swooped on the Romford armourer. There had been a lot of confusion during the raid, partly because we had chosen to arrive while he was parcelling up guns for two well-known hoods. In the melee, with its scuffles, shouts of protest, bellowed commands, I had been shoved up against a workbench on which lay a loaded Webley. I had immediately put it in my pocket. I have never really understood what motivated me to do that, any more than I understood why I had kept the gun. At the time it felt like an act of defiance; almost like scrumping inedible apples when I was a kid on the run from the hostel. There was also a parallel in that the gun I had lifted was one I didn't much like, like the theft of sour apples picked merely because they were there.

I had retrieved the revolver from its hiding place and rehidden it a short distance from Mrs Giles's front door. My reason was obvious enough. I was soon to be set up as

48

bait for a killer or team of killers still unidentified. And, as far as I knew, I would have no back-up. Then there had been that meeting with Samuel Atkins. I had more than once imagined circumstances of pitch darkness, and of that black giant sidling up behind me and throwing me off a roof. That I had smiled at the joke about him taking out his white teeth to make himself less visible had not reduced my wariness. Maybe I was arming myself against a whole range of possibilities both real and fantastical. And I guess we all need a secret to confirm our identity.

Tying my shoes and shrugging into my coat moved my mind forward into the active present; the present in which being accompanied by Frimmer implied I had no need to be carrying any weapons other than my wits. Mrs Giles, knowing of the ailing aunt but not of Frimmer, had her own ideas about what I might need. Wrappers swirling, she pounced as I reached the bottom of the stairs.

'Your auntie, is it, Mr Snell? I guessed when I heard your phone go. Woke me *at once*. Gave me time to get this for you. Seeing it's so early on a nasty cold morning. Coffee, no sugar, dear. Just as you like it.' She thrust a vacuum flask into my arms. 'Far to go?'

'Yes, Mrs Giles. That's why a car's being sent instead of me driving.'

'Least they could do, dear. And you so busy with your job, out all hours and several nights as well. Now you take care. Don't bother to phone. I'll expect you when I see you. My old mother took two days to die so — ' Knowing how much Frimmer prized punctuality, I cut across her chatter with muttered thanks. I had only just shut her front door when, from round the corner, lights struck at wet walls, at the road nameplate, the blind windows of silent houses. Then the headlights were switched off. A black Jaguar, rain-studded, parking lights only, came silently into the street, edged over to my side. A single gunshot could have ended my life but instead the car came to a murmuring stop directly outside Mrs Giles's gate. As if to reassure further, the driver got out and opened the nearside rear door.

'Be brisk, Bull,' hissed Frimmer from within. 'What's that?' he demanded as I lurched against him on the back seat.

'Morning, sir. Sorry. Flask of coffee. Mrs Giles is worried about me.'

'Christ Almighty, Bull! How do you do it? When they're not dropping 'em for you they're giving you meals-on-wheels.

'What are you sniggering at?' This to the

driver. 'You know the way. Get on! Get on! We'll talk privately. You drive — fast.'

Frimmer leaned forward, pressed a button. A glass screen rose between us and the back of the driver's neck. I was more than ready to enjoy being on the right side of the glass. 'Holloway's a bit of a comedown for you after Hyde Park, ain't it?' He peered out of the window. He knew well enough my former lifestyle in a sixth floor service flat overlooking Hyde Park. Fortunately, he knew how I had got it; no question of me being a bent copper.

My maternal grandfather's self-interest had been flavoured with a kind of guilt just before he died. Having disowned both my mother and myself, his bastard grandson, he had belatedly realized that my mother's brother was gay and not going to provide him with an heir. If his dynasty was to survive, I was it. So he left me his flat plus a huge sum of money. Despite his protest, I kept the name Mother had told me was that of my vanished father. Nor did I respond to Grandfather's wish that I follow a career 'more seemly' than policing. Those were not merely gestures of defiance but responses to the fact that when he might so easily have done something to spare me and my mother the griefs of separation, and the abuses that followed, he had not acted.

And I had genuinely wanted my career as policeman with no place in my life for a family.

'Right, Bull. Tell you where we're going presently. Some updating first. We took your idea about Brigadier French and his manservant on board. Also see why you think they might only have knocked over his daughter's rapist rather than setting up a multiple murder scheme. One possible problem: Samuel Atkins became French's batman, bodyguard, whatever, three months after the daughter's rapist was murdered.'

'Not a problem, sir! 'You wipe out this scum who raped my daughter and you'll get a job for life, guaranteed pension, etc.''

'You read it like that, Bull? Well, why not. Now you're into this work I guess I don't have to tell you about depths and strengths of feelings.'

'No, sir.' I hesitated then plunged in. 'I don't feel I can carry on with this — with this line of inquiry.'

'That's fuckin' nonsense and you know it! All this was bound to get to you but we needed you to be as tight inside this case as possible. And not just for bloody background. Don't you forget young Bull, that all you've been immersed in, all the grief and rage of it, will be directed straight at you as soon as you

52

become Corelli. We're giving you a damn sight more than just practice at assuming an identity — useful though that is.'

'Not quite what I meant, sir. It's not an issue of my toughness. I'm beginning to doubt I *want* the killers caught.'

'And you fuckin' well know neither you nor I nor any other copper can go down *that* road. We all took the same oath, remember? We uphold the law at whatever cost to our personal feelings however strongly held. I'm going to pretend I didn't hear what you just said and you're not going to repeat it — ever. That clear?'

I stared through the rain at the road signs. Soon we'd be turning onto the M1. And he accepts I know about depths and strengths of feelings. How very good of him.

'If you want to protest about the rotten way society deals with rape that's OK. But not that other thing: that corruption. God knows there are enough ambiguities about these cases already. That clear, Bull?'

'Yes, sir.' I wondered which of us loathed the other the more.

'Right then, Bull. While you've been Arthur Snelling around, others have checked other cases that first interested Stone. Outcome remains much the same; about a dozen survive as 'hot' from his original listing. But no one fingered as 'most likely'. If anything breaks on *that* you'll be first to know. Being first is one of the reasons I've disturbed your beauty sleep. I'm not keen on widening the scope of our inquiries, re Brigadier French etc., because they're already a damn sight too wide. SIU is bloody stretched, Bull. Trouble is there's a helluva lot riding on this one. If our theory is right then catching the killers might solve more than a dozen murders. All those Chief Constables delighted at one and the same time. Kudos for SIU. And that means big financial rewards, Bull. Guarantees we keep heads above water for a long time.'

'You know the right people?'

'Yes and no. Part of the secret of success in this business is knowing the wrong people. *And* fortunately, for-tun-ate-ly, for them I'm not into blackmail. More a kind of gentle business pressure.'

'So why SIU? Not a very original name.'

'A catch-all. Means we can investigate anything we like.'

'Sir. So what's your rank, as a policeman, I mean?'

'What else could you possibly mean, you cheeky sod? I answer to Commander if and when that suits. I'm legit as a policeman — but that goes back years. I'm most often seen as a crack civil servant who used to wear those big vulgar boots no one dreams of wearing in Whitehall.

'But back to this journey north. You'll not be surprised we've been keeping an eye on half a dozen villains who deserve our interest because of the disgustingness of their crimes, some of them worse than Corelli. Now one of them has given us the slip.'

'You mean he *knew?*' A chance to let out resentment.

'Doubtful. Anyhow, we put out an alert, and his car's been found up here outside a large park.'

'And in the park there's a lake.'

'Right, Bull. While we were coming to pick you up the locals were breaking down a fence; all the park gates padlocked, of course. They found him in the lake just before I got to your front door.'

I didn't say anything. Had he been running on intuition when deciding to involve me even *before* the body had been found?

'Want you in on this one as early as poss. Remember: this could be you in a few months' time.'

'Thank you very, very much indeed — sir.'

'Right-ho. You have a sulk while I have a snooze.' (In the future I would wonder if that was the moment antipathy tipped into hatred — on my part at least. I doubted Frimmer

55

would have bothered — not with someone he believed he could swat like a fly.)

An hour later we were forcing our way through a hole cut in the park fence. As we ploughed across the saturated grass we were joined by a uniformed Inspector with whom Frimmer began a muttered conversation inaudible to me. I walked behind them to the lake.

'Peter Abercrombie, rapist, late of Leicester Goal, formerly resident in London.' Frimmer sounded angry.

I looked down on the grounded corpse, one of its legs still trailing in the shallow water of the lake edge. I shivered inside my damp raincoat. Isobel French was more bloated in life than was Abercrombie in death. Our killers were continuing the good work. I smiled ruefully.

'OK, so we boobed,' snapped Frimmer, misinterpreting the expression on my face seen through the near darkness. 'We had him covered until about eighteen hours ago in Luton. Then he slipped us. We discovered he had a contact up here so we switched the search. What bloody use it was!'

The Inspector bridled but had the sense to keep his mouth shut.

'What was he doing in Luton?' I asked.

'Staying with Mum. Told us where he'd

gone for 'a job offer' only after we convinced her he was in danger. Too late to prevent this.'

'And how did he give your tail the slip?'

'Dodgy running in the Arndale shopping centre.'

'So he *did* know he was tailed?'

'Raises questions about the 'job offer' up here, don't it, Bull?'

'Yes, sir. Possible someone knew enough or guessed enough to *warn* him he was being tailed. Maybe they know we're closing in on them.'

'*They* might know that. Wish we did.' Irritably, he smoothed his wet hair. I had nothing to say. 'You know the other reason I called you out?'

I looked through the dying night at the assembled forces, the waiting body wagon and crew, the impatient police surgeon.

'Not short of help here,' I said, also irritable.

'No. But you need to get inside this one. Remember what I said. This could be you. Get to know this case inside out: might be valuable life insurance in that weird zone where rage and madness overlap.'

'Can we proceed, sir?' The Inspector was polite but impatient.

'What?' said Frimmer. 'Oh, yes. Make sure I get the medical report soonest. And tell your doc not to assume it was a straightforward drowning. I'll leave my man here with you.'

'Sir.' The Inspector was not happy. He turned his back on me, walked away, spoke to the doctor.

'Look,' said Frimmer. 'Past that clump of willows. Small island with summerhouse of some sort. Maybe he set out for it in the rowing boat found drifting upside-down. They've tied it up round the corner.'

'Why would he be going there this time of year and night?'

'Dunno. Nor does anyone else yet. One of the reasons I'm leaving you here. Obviously pinched the boat this night. Not sure how long he's been dead but looks pretty fresh to me.'

'Could be at least one other person who knows that,' I said, watching the body being pulled clear of the black water, almost feeling the dragging weight of it. (When Mr Stone had spoken of 'total immersion' at my interview with him and Frimmer, was he anticipating something like this happening to me?)

'And since neither they nor the victim are telling, we'll rely on the doctor. You go over this site with the local SOCO, then report directly to Stone. Christ! If we don't get a break soon the buggers inside'll be refusing their discharge!'

'You're sure this is another for Mr Stone's collection?'

'Bloody hell, Bull! Yet another drowned rapist! Whaddya think?' snarled Frimmer. 'Now you carry on here. I'm for early breakfast with the Chief Constable up here.' The yob stalked away, leaving me with Mrs Giles's Thermos of coffee. I wondered what compensations Mr Stone had found to justify working closely with the man.

'Detective Sergeant Bull,' I said to the Inspector.

'Hinchcliffe,' said the Inspector, curtly. 'You with his team?' He jerked his head towards Frimmer struggling through the hole in the fence.

'Yes, sir.'

'What's all the interest?'

'Not the first case like this, sir. Maybe some tie-up.'

'Inspector.' It was the doctor, who was crouching beside the body, now on a stretcher. 'Looks like drowning but he knocked his head. Contusion behind the right ear. Could be he fell in unconscious. Let you have a full report in due.'

'Yes,' said Hinchcliffe. 'It could happen. Could've stood up to pole himself clear of the bank, slipped and fell in, hitting his head on the gunwale as he fell. You taking him now, Doc?'

'Soon as poss. Don't want any more

hanging about in the rain.' The doctor gave me an unfriendly look, which I accepted on Frimmer's behalf.

'Where's the boat, sir?' I asked.

'This way,' said Hinchcliffe. The small rowing boat was tied to a willow tree, and guarded by a rain-caped constable who appeared to be about four times my age. There was only one oar in the boat. 'This is DS Bull, Constable,' said Hinchcliffe, curtly.

'Haven't found it yet, sir — er, Sergeant,' said the constable, answering my question. 'Probably drifted into the reeds somewhere.'

'Where did he get the boat from in the first place?' I asked.

'Along here, Sergeant,' said the constable, leading the way along the muddy bank. 'This lake's a popular recreation area. The boats are tied to each other until the start of the season — end of March.'

We came to a small pier with a shuttered kiosk at the landward end. Nine rowing boats nudged each other in undulating line abreast. At the end of the line the rope that held them all together trailed in the water.

'All he had to do was untie the last boat,' I said.

'Yes, Sarge,' said the constable.

'The boat was first seen floating upside-down in the middle of the lake. By the time I got here it had drifted to the side and been righted,' said Hinchcliffe.

'Really?' I turned to the constable. 'Did that yourself, did you?'

'Er — yes, Sergeant,' he said, looking anxiously at his Inspector.

'You had to, of course,' I said. He relaxed slightly. 'Was it easy?'

'Oh — no. As you can see, the boats are very broad.'

'Right. Now if you climbed down into one of these boats would it be as hard to reverse the job, overturning it?'

'I reckon it'd be even harder, Sergeant.'

'Yes,' I said. 'Perhaps easier if standing *in* the water?'

'You're not suggesting — ' began Hinchcliffe.

'Not yet. All the same, it makes you think.' We stood and thought.

'It seems,' I said, 'that Abercrombie was either barmy or very keen to meet someone on the island. Can we go there now, sir?'

'Doubt it,' said Hinchcliffe. 'Our SOCO won't want anything disturbed. Not when a drowned man has a bruise behind his ear.' As if to confirm that opinion, a generator started up and the lakeside was illuminated by arc lights. Disconsolately, the three of us huddled together against the front of the kiosk.

Pressure against the constable's rain cape produced sinister slithering and cracking sounds as if some bestial creature was struggling to emerge from the lake. I stared out into the raining dawn, asked the constable his name.

'Parks, Sergeant.' None of us smiled at the geographical joke.

'Right, Parks. Tell me what you think of this. You've been out of prison some time, unemployed, no friends in the district where your mum, your only relative, has moved to. OK?'

'Er — yes.'

'While staying with mum someone contacts you with the offer of a job. The job's crooked so you have to be sure you're not followed when you set out. You are told to come to this lake to get instructions and a big wad of notes to get you started on the job. You're told it's urgent. This park was chosen either because you know it or because it's very easy to find. When you get here it's dark. You've been told to row out to the island to meet your contact. How d'you feel about that?'

'Do I know the person who phoned me?' asked Parks.

'Probably. Likely they met you at least once before they phoned. Maybe they've already given you a generous sub for travel expenses.'

'Then I'm not frightened,' said Parks, thoughtfully.

'So what do you need?'

Parks thought for some time. Hinchcliffe moved restlessly. 'I need to know — ' began Parks, nervously. 'I need to know the other person's already there on the island before I'm willing to start the miserable job of rowing across in the rain.'

'Good man! That implies a signal from the island or a message at this kiosk. Now let's assume a light was flashed from the island. Feasible?'

'It is,' said Parks.

'But they could have left a message here, pinned up on this kiosk,' said Hinchcliffe, impatiently. I stared at him until he flushed with anger.

'No, sir,' I said at last. 'They didn't leave a message at the kiosk just in case someone else saw it or Abercrombie missed it.'

'Because the job they wanted him for was crooked?' asked Hinchcliffe.

'No. Because they meant to murder the man by drowning him.' My companions glanced at each other. 'You see, my murderer was determined to leave no clue as to his presence. That's why there was no message just in case, even on this godforsaken night, someone else came down here.'

'So how did it work?' demanded Hinchcliffe.

'I think the light was flashed from the end of the landing stage at the island. From here the signal would have appeared to come from the middle of the island.'

'You mean no one ever landed there, Sarge? The murderer was in another boat?' asked Parks.

'I think not. Another boat might betray him or her. Say the boats banged against each other, then the damage might be a give-away. Or forensic might find some significant fibres, or even DNA material, in the second boat. No, he/she was probably in the water in a wet suit.'

'Your trouble is your imagination is creating a case we can't possibly solve,' said Hinchcliffe, almost pleased.

'Not down to me, sir. It's the murderer's imagination, and he/she might be expert by now. And think of the advantage of surprise over Abercrombie.'

We looked out on to the rain-rippled, wind-flecked water, imagining the moment of surprise, of terror. Black-gloved hands out of black water wrenching on the side of the boat; Abercrombie off balance, his own weight helping to overturn the boat. Or the victim was stunned first, perhaps with one of his own oars which he thought he had lost by

64

snagging the bottom of the lake; a lake so shallow his murderer was able to stand on the floor of it as he pulled down on the boat edge.

'Pretty hard to bruise yourself behind the ear when you fall,' stated Parks thoughtfully.

'Maybe so. But what do we do now?' asked Hinchcliffe irritably.

'Well, sir, there was one thing my murderer would not be certain of concealing, especially as he could not be sure it would continue to rain.'

'And that was?' asked Hinchcliffe.

'He had to get into the lake — and out again,' exclaimed Parks.

'Good man, Parks,' I said. 'Go talk to Scene of Crime.'

5

Until the last Monday of that January, driving on the A303 had always been a pleasure for me. The road swoops and swerves through some of the most beautiful scenery in England. Even in winter it is appealing with its patchworks of fields, brown or chalky from the plough, subdued greens of the autumn-sown wheat and winter-hardy vegetables, greyness of leafless woodlands and the rustic colours of the half-concealed villages. Driving over chalk uplands, then cutting across the grain of the Somerset country, it is easy to feel oneself a swallow dipping and diving over the landscape. But that particular day I carried with me a new sorrow that held me earthbound. I had just heard via my mobile that Molly Poling had killed herself. She had been the only victim of the ten I had interviewed who had apparently risen clear of the trauma. But not even Molly had made it; whatever 'made it' might mean in the cosmos of an ignorant male. The news was some kind of horrible contradiction, not just of my belief in her, but also of the life I had seen in her pale creamy face, in the dark eyes beneath her smooth forehead and black curly hair. I felt as if someone had swung a razor-sharp axe through both my ankles. Relief I had felt on going to my last interview now drained out of me like blood loss from my legs.

Also lost to me in the sadness about Molly was any satisfaction I might have felt at progress in the Abercrombie case. PC Parks had been right. There had been some evidence, blurred by rain, that someone had entered and exited the lake at a point not far from the boat jetty. But there had not been much to go on except that the killer had deliberately brushed over the mud in an attempt to conceal the evidence. The wet grass of the park had revealed nothing. It would have been easy enough for the killer to change into wellies, conceal the wet suit under a long raincoat and, choosing their moment, exit the park unseen.

There had also been speculation about how and where killer and victim had entered the park if all the gates had been padlocked at dusk. Forensic had followed that up and now suspected that one of the gate padlocks, all of common design, had been unlocked and then relocked that night. This was suggested by the amounts of both oil and rainwater inside the mechanism of that padlock compared with those on other gates.

Forensic had proposed this as a 'possibility' but wisely refused to advance beyond that. Also pertinent was that the gate in question was the one regarded locally as the rarely used 'back gate', being furthest from both the car park and the few attractions inside the grounds. What gave significance to local opinion was that the gate was opposite the end of Victoria Street.

During inquiries a local taxi driver had identified Peter Abercrombie as a fare he had taken at the station that night. He had asked to be taken to 78 Victoria Street — the last house in that road and the one nearest the park. The driver said that when he dropped Abercrombie outside the house he had made no attempt to open the front garden gate but had just stood on the pavement in the rain. The last the driver had seen of him he was still standing there. Taxi drivers see much stranger behaviours than that, especially at night, but he had remembered it because of the rain. He had not seen Abercrombie walk to the end of the pavement and cross over to the park.

'Not worth a bag of beans,' Frimmer had said, disgustedly, but had not disagreed when Stone and I pointed out the implications. But we were all experienced enough to know that by themselves these fragments would never

constitute evidence. They were merely point-
ers toward a hypothesis; just as Molly's
suicide might now point to the even more
unlikely hypothesis of her murderous guilt,
of her panic as SIU closed in. To become
suspect because she had made a brave
recovery!

I arrived at my destination wishing for
anything other than what I had: a duty to
listen to another's grief and rage.

'We had very little warning of your coming,
very little indeed, Mr Snell,' said Mrs
Athelsteyn-Platt, a touch petulant.

'The Department did write, and more than
once,' I said, defensively.

'Writing to Ms Grey did not automatically
ensure that the staff knew of your intentions.
Peacehavens is a private nursing home, you
know.' She shifted her handbag across the
bulge of her belly from left hand to right. I
looked at the broken veins in her cheeks, the
red-rimmed, pale-blue pebble eyes. I wondered what she was on — apart from
self-importance, although that's a powerful
enough drug.

'You left your car in our outer car park, I
trust, and not in the lane?'

'Yes, ma'am.' Toadying a little.

'Then let us walk down the avenue
together. Thank you, John.'

John the gate-keeper swung the great wooden gates together behind us. Odd effect: we were imprisoned in open country. To left and right a three-metre-high wire fence separated our landscape from all others. Wire fences are metaphors for guilt, and I felt the full bitterness of that. Inside the wire was the haven not the prison: here people were supported, nurtured. Molly had died outside the wire, and I would never know if it had been my visit and clumsy questioning that had tipped her into suicide. Ahead, under a cloud-blanked sun, the leafless tree-lined avenue was noisy in the cold breeze. In the far distance, framed by the plane trees, stood a grey, stone-clad mansion. Within its bleakness yet another distressed woman awaited my lethal intrusiveness.

The gravelled avenue was like a dry stream bed in a narrow valley. To the right there sloped up unkempt fields, post and wire edged; north-facing, the sullen, tufted grass-lands studded with frost which had not succumbed to winter sun. On the left the slope was gentler, south-facing and patchily cultivated. The pattern of cultivation was of scattered allotments interspaced with small huts, and failed rectangles of weedy grounds where enthusiasms had not survived the realities of gardening.

'Up there are our friends' vegetable gardens,' said Mrs Athelsteyn-Platt, swinging her formidable handbag against the breeze. 'Gardening is *such* a blessing for them, so therapeutic, you know.' I might have qualified her remark in the light of the many abandoned patches but my attention was distracted by a sudden movement on the avenue ahead of us. Someone had just looked out from behind a tree and then dodged back again. I felt a slight twinge of alarm, never having been ambushed inside a psychiatric unit. Then I wondered if my guide had read my mind. 'You understand, of course, Peacehavens is absolutely not a mental hospital.' I nodded my agreement. The man behind the tree had emerged and was scuttling up the south-facing slope into the allotments. 'We think of it as a respite home to which distressed people can come for a period of recuperation. Although helpers like myself donate seeds and tools, interested friends are encouraged to cultivate their plots quite independently of us. Unfortunately, some lack the necessary persistence.'

'Is he a friend?' I asked, pointing up the slope at the scuttling figure.

'Mr Henry Johnson? Well, yes and no.' My guide's pursed lips, the gesture of clasping her handbag with both hands, implied that while he might be a 'friend' in the institutional sense, she felt no personal attachment. To my surprise she asked if I would like to meet him. I nodded; anything to delay arriving at the house. As she began to toil up the slope ahead of me, my eye level on that of her large buttocks, she explained her ambiguous answer. 'Mr Johnson was a patient — er — a friend initially, but then applied for a part-time caretaking post here. The medical board decided in its wisdom that his application should be considered. Can't get staff here. Well, no one else wanted the job so — he — got — it.' She was beginning to find the slope too demanding. 'Gets on with our — guests. Keen — garden-er.' Then she abandoned speech in favour of breathing.

Surrounded by patches of bedraggled cabbages, and of a shaggy green plant I could not identify, we swung right and traversed along the slope to join him. He was a small, grey and grey-eyed, grief-smitten man with the general appearance of a very slow greyhound. I doubted I would ever guess his age. He wore a cloth cap, brown overall and amazingly large boots for such a small man. In his right hand he held a long-bladed flick-knife, in his left a straggle of green twine. At his feet were scattered numerous tools including spade, fork, wire cutters and theodolite.

'Hello, Mr Johnson,' bawled Mrs Athelsteyn-Platt.

'Watcha want and look where you're walking, Mrs Pratt,' said Mr Johnson, curtly.

'Thought you might like to meet our new visitors. This is Mr Snell who has come to see your good friend Ms Grey. He's interested in gardening, I believe.' This was as much news to me as to Mr Johnson.

'Bet he ain't,' said Mr Johnson. 'And mind your great feet,' he added, glaring at me. I looked down at the theodolite balanced on wedged bricks. 'Jest got it set level. That third cabbage along's bin giving me trouble.'

I looked across the plot. No naturalness was permitted in cabbages. Each row was appallingly straight and every cabbage had its outer leaves tied in, except for the one troublesome plant at which the theodolite was presumably aimed. I was looking at a physical representation of madness: *endeavour pushed beyond all reason.*

'Move on, woman!' snapped Mr Johnson. 'Too cold to hang about chattin'. I've got work to finish if you haven't.'

'Oh — yes,' said Mrs Athelsteyn-Platt, blushing slightly. I turned to follow her down the slope but was detained by Mr Johnson seizing my left arm in an enfeebled but still spiteful grip.

'Careful of her, youngster. Not safe with us fellas, not with a name like Pratt. Why d'you think she calls us all friends? Now that Miss Grey — '

I stopped shuffling my feet. 'What about her?'

'Real lady *she* is, not like this cow. Ever so kind to me. I'd do anything for her. Not surprised she don't live here full-time. She's too good to be shut up in this place and with people like us.'

'Kind to you?'

'Brings me little presents when she comes back. Wonderful woman, 'specially when you realize what she's suffered, including from her rotten religious family. Bastards dumped her after the rape, moved away, no forwarding address, just when she needed 'em most.' He rubbed his hands over his face, leaving a muddy tear stain on his right cheek. 'But she's here to be away from your sort!' He was beginning to shout. Mrs Athelsteyn-Platt intervened.

'Come away,' she called up the slope. 'You'll be late for your appointment. And we mustn't get Mr Johnson excited.'

'Piss off, Pratt!' he shrieked, so we did. But as I hurried after my guide I looked back over my shoulder. Mr Johnson spat words down-slope at me but I heard no intelligible sound.

'Mr Johnson is a little strange at times,' said Mrs Athelsteyn-Platt, as I joined her on the avenue. 'But I suppose we must be charitable. He's been here a very long time. Don't know how he manages the fees. His wages as part-time worker can't possibly be enough.' I wondered how charitable she would be if she had heard everything he said.

When we entered the house she pointed to a row of chairs at the side of the large entrance hall. 'Wait here, Mr Snell. I will inform Ms Grey of your arrival.' Then she began to puff her way up the broad staircase, leaving me to inhale the institutional haze that afflicts all great houses subverted for charity. I sat down facing a full-length wall mirror. I had long accepted my facial disguise; it was the costume of the day which offended. The worn, pale-grey, ill-cut suit was the least offensive part. I averted my gaze from the Fair Isle pullover worn with a cerise tie and a blue and white striped shirt. Then I watched Mrs Athelsteyn-Platt negotiate the stairs downward; she was having a strenuous and alpine afternoon.

'Our friend, Ms Grey, will receive you, Mr Snell,' she announced. 'Her room is Room 14, on our first floor and to the right. Just knock on the door. I shall remain here. This is where I usually sit until afternoon tea; in case

I can be of service.' She opened her capacious handbag and pulled out knitting. She was working on a Fair Isle pullover. Sounds of her continuing struggle to regain her breath followed me up the stairs.

On the first-floor landing was another full-length mirror. A young man with snow-white hair talked softly to his reflection. I edged past, wondering if mirrors were believed to have therapeutic value. The door of Room 14 stood wide open. There was nothing institutional about the interior: attractively furnished with comfortable arm-chairs standing on a dark brown carpet. The flower-print curtains matched the wallpaper, a pot of early daffodils stood on the small occasional table, and a modern gas fire hissed gently in the far wall. Something about a feminine well-cared-for home. Home? Feeling both foolish and shabby I hesitated; hesitated also for less superficial reasons. I tapped on the open door.

'Come in, Mr Snell.' She spoke from behind the door. I peered round the edge of it as she rose from a little writing desk and held out her hand.

'Ms Grey, Ms Madelaine Grey?'

'Yes.'

I recognized her from the files, from the merciless photo record of her battered face and body. Her eventual submission to rape had probably saved her life. I had thought I knew her, almost her tone of voice, from those same files. But no, not *this* woman standing before me *now*. If other victims had left me confused, this one was about to push me over the edge into some kind of fathomless ignorance.

I was stunned by some kind of spine-snapping collision unlike anything I'd ever experienced. Unbidden came the metaphor for the feeling words could never frame. Many years ago at Moorgate Station in London a driver lost control of his underground train and smashed at full speed into the wall at the tunnel end. The front carriage and its occupants were instantaneously compacted into a space three metres long. It took several days to separate most of the flesh from much of the metal. Something like *that*! She stared fixedly at me; no indication of what she felt in that petrifying moment.

She was tall, elegant in a high-necked grey wool dress and pearls. A lissom woman, not beautiful but having that aristocratic cool style: fine skin, broad forehead, short brown hair lightly waved and back from her face, straight nose, firm lips, and her hazel eyes wide behind those very large fashion spectacles that suit few women. They suited her. Difficult to accept she was forty-three.

'We could sit by the fire,' she drawled, walking across the room. She was the same height as me, lean-bodied, long-thighed, broad-shouldered; somewhat unexpectedly, she was not wearing a bra. As I sagged into the chair she indicated, I was aware that, like me, her hands were shaking.

She sat on the opposite side of the fire with her back to the windows, her face almost lost to me against the light. In her spectacles I saw only myself. I looked at her beautiful, long-fingered hands now clasped tensely in her lap. I wanted to reject all previous knowledge of her from those searingly precise medical reports, and all the rest: champion swimmer, and we were dealing with drownings; mentally unstable, and we suspected serial murder; extraordinarily calm in court despite hostile cross-examination, and we were looking for someone extraordinary. But all that blocked by alibis: alibis from her work, from Peacehavens, from country house parties and walking holidays with friends. But I had been staring too long. Her hands moved, smoothing her skirt.

'Kind of you to see me, Ms Grey. You understood my letter?'

'All too well!' This was said with such ferocity I jumped. But I was almost grateful to be shaken from my trancelike state, slammed back into another kind of reality. 'There is not much about my situation you are likely to see. Ever!' This sudden switch to rage reminded me I had no idea how to fetch a nurse. 'You understand I am a short-stay voluntary patient?'

'Er — yes, I do.'

'Only a private nursing home like this can cope with my needs. I come here when things get bad. Much of the time I can lead a normal life.' The ruefulness of voice, slight shrugging of shoulders, were as expressive as medical reports. Every day this superficially self-possessed woman had to struggle for possession of her own mind. And now she was back here again because she had been losing the struggle.

'I'm sorry you've had to come back, Ms Grey.'

'Thank you, Mr Snell. But I've learned to love this place as much as my home, not only because of what it is but also because of what it does. It is a place of renewal as well as retreat.' She looked down at her feet, then directly into my face. 'I expect to be here every year at about this time or later. February to May is the suicide season, you know.' She spoke so calmly that, had it been anyone other than her, I might have believed

I misheard. We were silent together for some time.

'I've come to see if my department can help you.' The words were dragged out of me. 'We are now empowered to help out financially and in other ways.' Never had the script so much sounded like claptrap.

'I understand what you are trying to say. But I have a good job with a publisher, work I can do here as easily as anywhere else. I have helpful colleagues and friends — and this place whenever I need it.'

'Work does not disqualify you from help from us or your attacker.'

'My attacker?' She began rubbing her hands on the arms of her chair. Her body started rocking gently from side to side.

'Why shouldn't he be made to assist you?'

'Do you really think? Doesn't matter. Waste of time.' She crouched lower in her armchair as if preparing to spring at me. 'He's dead. He died several years ago in an accident.'

'I didn't realize you knew that. I'm sure you don't want to talk about it.' Bumbling Mr Snell! Would she pick up his mistake?

'Mr Snell, I don't *care*. I knew him, of course, before the attack. He was a local boy, John Downley; same tennis club as myself. Always very quiet, withdrawn. Lived alone with mother. That we knew each other and he was the retiring one was used against me in court.' She sighed. 'It was in the local paper — that he died, I mean. He was . . . was drowned. In a lake in a park near his home, near my former home. I was staying here when it happened but a friend sent me a copy of the local paper. It made no real difference.'

'You thought he'd already paid his debt?'

'Paid?' Her voice crackled like footsteps on broken crockery. 'Men never pay enough. And they'd *love* to do it again. Always on the lookout for their next victim. A few months in prison doesn't change an animal except to make it more animal. I want them to die, Mr Snell; just want them *all* to die.' So did I but I had to keep the interview moving.

'No, Ms Grey — '

'No? You're either stupid or a fraud, Mr Snell. And what did you mean just now: 'You didn't realize I knew about his death?' How could you imply he might pay some kind of compensation if you knew he was dead?' She sprang to her feet, began pacing up and down. Feline. I looked for a bell push. There wasn't one. She stood over me, eyes glittering. 'What do you really want, Mr Snell? Am I just another cog in a piece of research; your PhD? Or are you some kind of sex freak?'

'Not at all. I meant from his estate. I — '

'Let's try you out.' With a cold carefulness that further alarmed me, she took off her glasses and put them on the shelf over the gas fire. Then she burst into frenzied action: ripping down the zip of her dress, she stepped out of it naked except for a black thong. The string of pearls snapped, flew in every direction, rolling, bouncing. Then, eyes unfocused, she was in my lap, wriggling herself against me. Spittle ran down her chin.

'Come on,' she hissed. 'Tell me what you really want or I'll start screaming rape, you seedy little man!'

'But I'm a respectable man. And you're the one undressed.'

'Blame the woman again, will you? Not your fault. You were led on. Poor innocent! As my judge you'll give a stupid short sentence. What's the verdict when I scream?' Every sentence was accompanied by a savage bouncing action against my groin.

'They won't want to believe you this time, either.' I delivered the blow, sick with self-disgust.

Her breath hissed between clenched teeth. Then, very slowly, she slithered off my lap and onto the floor, round breasts brushing along my thighs, down my legs. She huddled at my feet, clutched my ankles. She neither sobbed nor cried out, but huge tears ran down her face, fell into the crevices of her folded body. I leaned forward, held out both hands. She made no attempt to stand but took my hands childlike against her wet cheeks. So we sat silent together before the fire.

Much later, when her breathing had quietened, the room was possessed by the soft hissing of the gas fire, the buffeting of the wind against the windows. Her scent, her nakedness, began to fill all the space of the room. 'You are sad for me?' she asked at last. 'You understand?'

'Yes — but I don't understand very much — being a man.'

'To let me sit here like this — no fuss. You didn't take off my dress?'

'No, you did.'

'And my pearls?'

'You were in a . . . rage. You broke them.'

'They're not real.' Then: 'Please shut your eyes.' Nervously I did so, felt her move away, heard the dress rustle. 'You can look now.' She was standing in front of me, dressed except for her shoes and the pearls. 'I don't know what to say, Mr Snell. I am not even sure what happened.'

'Then say nothing about that. Tell me instead of your life here.'

She sat down again in the chair opposite

me, breathing slowly and deeply. After a long pause she began to talk, to turn those police files I had pawed and pored over into heartrending reality.

Thirty minutes later I went shakily downstairs, leaving her crouched over the spilt pearls. I met Mrs Athelsteyn-Platt in the hall.

'I hope your visit went well, Mr Snell. I was beginning to wonder.'

'No, no. Everything was all right. I may call again in a few days. I'll telephone first. Thank you for your help.'

I walked quickly away along the drive, gulping at the clear air like a nearly drowned man, while the wind moaned in the planes above me. Now on my right, the valleyside south-facing slope seemed almost as unappealing as the waste on my left. A few perfectly aligned cabbages were insufficient to offset the shabby neglectedness of many other plots where shambles of weeds were interrupted only by the chilled greyness of former bonfire sites. From up there Mr Johnson had propelled inaudible words after me, sent them grinding down the slope as remorselessly as the glacier that had once scoured it. He was a friend to Madelaine. What I was to her I could not begin to fathom.

6

I knew them well enough, the victims of crime, but their deepest feelings were only half-revealed to me. I came closest to understanding their sorrows when all their privacy was stripped away by our investigations, but that process also caused them to rebuff me. They smothered grief with a strangulated politeness; offered tea but guarded their raving hurt. Despite that I have heard, like a passionate whisper in a darkened room, the one agonized feeling they will rarely admit. It is not the desire for justice, that abstract our wretched judiciary can never deliver. No, the feeling concealed from me, except in their deepest distress, was lust for revenge. That this lust was never slaked left lives poisoned long after the criminal had served his derisory sentence. But just as the victims have kept their secret, their truth unacceptable in our mealy-mouthed society, so have I. And I have done so out of a self-serving, career-protecting cowardice.

The first time I had been forced to face this was with a forensic medic when working on a particularly brutal murder. Both of us, nauseated and enraged, were leaning against a large oak tree close to where the ravaged corpse of the child had been found. He suddenly burst out: 'After this the only thing that will *really* enable the parents to live again is execution of the animal who did it.' Shamefacedly, he had lapsed into silence — but not before we had nodded at each other. Something we have chosen to name civilization denied the power of our most primitive feelings, and therefore their consolations. We parted, ashamed of something other than the words he had spoken. Had he lied? Had I colluded with a lie? And were we any more guilty than the close relative of a murdered loved one who publicly proclaimed they *forgave* the slaughterer of their love? What lay unspoken in their heart when sleepless in their cold double bed, or standing bereft at owl time beside the empty cot?

Now I had to face all this yet again and much more cuttingly than in the role of the meek Arthur Snell. I was about to take on the mantle of the worst of criminals: the unrepentant and probably insatiable rapist. And what would happen to me inside all of that, to both my compassionate and raging selves? I was talking to my fear-cramped self because there is no one else willing or daring enough to hear me. There were enough people around who *might* hear me, here in SIU's mobile command centre: officers coming and going, others watching their screens.

Now sitting beside Frimmer in front of the TV monitors, I believed I knew exactly where I was: inside the head of the octopus that was SIU, a fantasy denied neither by the rectangular shape of the dark-blue, unmarked truck nor by the outlines of the blue-tinged, flickering screens in front of us, the eyes of the octopus steadily watching. The timeless, unwavering stare of the hunter. A slight movement within the head, response to a gentle buffeting of the truck by an April breeze, simulated a trembling adjustment, confirmation to the simple brain of tentacles slightly repositioned.

Frimmer rolled his chair back from the banked screens, muttered at Jim Douglas, who promptly pressed a floor button with his right foot. The rear doors of the truck flicked open, temporarily blinding me with daylight that blurred the outlines of the two men entering. The doors shut and the liquifying blue light repossessed sight, but it was several seconds before my eyes read the presence of Paul Henderson and David Thomas.

'Your back-up.' Frimmer's curt explanation cut across our greetings.

'I'm to get back-up after all, am I, sir?'

'Remote,' said Henderson, almost apologetically. 'You can't expect close cover on this one.' We all knew what he was saying: that their main function was to report back on exactly who knocked me over, to make my death a usefulness for SIU.

'Well, hello to you two. No idea you were involved,' I said edgily, tugging at my beard; worn only because that had become Corelli's choice. 'Are the other three survivors from our course involved in this?'

'No!' said Thomas with such abruptness I knew there was something else I hadn't been told. I was aware of Thomas's rapid eye-flicker across the blue distance to Frimmer; that Frimmer's face darkened as he nodded his head downward below the fan of light from the monitors. 'Pearson's dead.' Thomas dropped the words; stones sinking into the depths.

'Chasing rapists, for Christ's sake?'

'No, Jack,' said Thomas. 'On a drugs bust in New York. Shot down in an alley but not before he nailed his two attackers. City cops found the three of them lying together. In touching distance, so they said.'

Yet again a sense of a dislocation, that while at the centre of things and believing I knew what was happening, I remained ignorant of the scope of SIU operations. And no one ever again to be offended by Pearson's eating habits. How often we deflect shock by recalling the inconsequential.

'I'm sorry,' I said lamely, pulling at my damned beard again.

'Yes, well,' said Thomas, equally uncomfortable. We both knew I was to be put at risk within minutes. 'Everything cleared for you, Jack, so we hear. The other likely next victims of our killers are now in protective custody; all very proper — consultations with their solicitors, etc.'

'And Corelli soon to be the same,' I said, almost envious.

'You look quite like him,' said Henderson, wanting to be clear of the maudlin.

'Is that meant as a compliment?' I demanded.

'It'd fuckin' better be,' said Frimmer. 'After all the trouble we've taken. Now watch the action. Corelli's due out in less than five minutes.'

Seated at the bench that ran the length of the truck, we watched the blue-tinged screens interpret the daylight world outside. On the opposite side of the road to where we were parked, the prison wall ran the length of the short street, its blankness punctuated only by one door, the 'back door' of the prison. No encounters with the media here. To our left a white van stood at the opposite curb and seventy metres away from our control truck, its shadow slanting diagonally up the prison wall. Otherwise the street was deserted. A red light penetrated the bench in front of Frimmer, then a voice distorted as if through water.

'He's coming out. Go!' said Frimmer into his mike. Then, to the rest of us: 'Watch this team working. They're good.'

At the far end of the street to our right a couple with their dog on a lead. The man bending down, letting the dog go free. The woman laughing, tilting her golden head at the dulled sky.

Then Corelli, *my* likeness, was in the prison doorway, standing indecisively. The accompanying warder gesticulated past the white van towards the shopping centre bus stops and a safe anonymity. The door closed on the warder. Into unfamiliar loneliness Corelli took a few tentative steps. Dead man walking. No one in the blue dark doubted that.

From behind Corelli the couple with the dog closed rapidly, following him towards the white van. At about the same moment the end screens of our banked monitors showed large vehicles had blocked both ends of the street. I doubt Corelli noticed, had time to notice. The dog was at his heels, chasing a small yellow ball his master had tossed for him; the beautiful woman laughed with her companion. Corelli, hugging his small parcel of possessions, neither hand free, was ineffectually trying to avoid tripping over the dog. Master and mistress both said something, perhaps calmingly, to Corelli. The side doors of the white van slid open and Corelli, couple and dog were gulped in. The van pulled slowly away from the curb leaving a bright yellow ball in the gutter.

'Neat,' said Frimmer, uncharacteristically smiling, revealing teeth like Stonehenge. 'She's a good girl, that one, DC Green. Hoping to get her on our full-time strength one day. You ready, Bull?' Damn fool question. Of course not. 'Thought you'd like some good news before you depart this life for another.' Was his sadism really unconscious?

'Ready as I'll ever be, sir.'

'I'll let Henderson tell you, seeing as he's been supervising some aspects of the work.'

'Yes, sir. Right, Jack.' In the half-light I could have sworn he licked his lips. 'In the three hundred old rape cases we've looked — '

'How many? Are you telling me SIU's ploughed through *that* many?'

'Told you you were a small cog in a big

machine, didn't I, Bull? Not that you're ever unobserved by us.' Frimmer was obviously having a good time. 'I even know that when you moved from Mrs Giles's you couldn't find time to say goodbye to your friend Jayne. I know everything about you, Bull.' The sense of betrayal his remarks might have triggered in me was blocked by a vindictive satisfaction that he was wrong.

Oh, no, you don't, I thought. You self-satisfied bastard! You don't know that two days before I moved out from Mrs Giles's place I took a walk in Highgate Woods and retrieved a loaded Webley. And you'll never ever know how much I've grieved for Molly Poling. And you'll never understand — because I don't — just how that news of Molly affected my meeting with Madelaine Grey.

'So did those three hundred reviews justify the effort?'

'Yes, Jack,' said Henderson quickly, before Frimmer could intervene again. 'We've got four convicted rapists lined up for new trials involving other rapes. We've got a rapist confessed to a murder for which the local Force had never even found the body. On top of that we've now got several ongoing new cases not previously reported. That we were ready to reopen tired old cases has loosened some women's tongues.

'And there's news on your little list as well; the eleven so-called marginal cases you were given to review. We've got a murder confession from Brigadier French and his man Samuel Atkins. But don't get too excited, Jack. They've only confessed to the one: Isobel French's rapist, Treyford, the guy who fell off a roof, landed face down but had a nasty bruise on the back of his head. And it don't look like either'll go down for murder. Manslaughter's favourite. 'The boss made me do it.' 'My man's not very bright. Don't know what gave him the idea.' Usual defensive guff. And the Brigadier can afford a top brief.'

'Never mind that,' said Frimmer, with familiar irritability. 'SIU's already back in the good books of several forces. And if this Corelli thing works out — '

'And what about the other one, the other case I wanted moved from cold to hot?' I could feel my mouth struggling with the words.

'Madelaine Grey?' said Frimmer. 'Well, we took your report on board, but the fact another barmy resident has wire cutters on his allotment didn't take us all that far. OK, so you found the wire fence had been cut when you drove round the estate, but no link with your suspect. Forensic got nothing off the wire or the ground nearby. And, whether you like it or not, the fact Madelaine Grey *always* seems to have an alibi for any case we might link her to won't cut the mustard with CPS.'

'You don't go for the fact that all the circumstances in which she's alibied are similar? And the similarity is that the situations are *never* watertight?'

'It's not a question of what I might fucking go for, and certainly not what *you* go for, Bull. We need evidence and you haven't found any. No one goes down in an English court on the basis of a copper's intuition.'

'But you accept that the inmates of Peacehavens are not as tightly supervised as the trustees believe? All patients register in writing when they arrive, also when they leave. But even if the book was checked every day, as the staff claim, there's not necessarily a physical check on bodies present in the buildings. Patients can slope off undetected for days at a time; especially as the whole system is corrupted by patients frequently being sent elsewhere for medical tests and checks. And that on her walking holidays and house parties with friends the arrangements are so laid-back her alibis mean nothing. The girls chose to go off on their own quite often, they didn't all do the same walks, etc.'

'Forget it, Bull. You've got enough to deal

94

with now. She's not on the hot list. End of story.'

'And her bigoted Christian family, shamed when she insisted on the prosecution, abandoned her. Is that motivation?'

Frimmer shook his head irritably, not bothering to speak.

I stared at the man. Why was I persisting when I knew he was right? And the much bigger question: why persist when I *wanted* him to be right, and Madelaine to be untroubled? Perhaps it was only a matter of transference of my anxiety? I was on the point of becoming the most available and enticing target for a killer or killers.

'You ready now, Jack, or should I say Jake? Your chance to be the big cog in SIU — for a short time anyway. At least, that's what we're hoping, your poor bloody minders.' Thomas's words cut the silence, suggested a different kind of irritability. Envy? I wondered if he had found out I had been paid in the acting rank of Inspector since the beginning of January. Like a price on my head.

'Yes,' I said. Somebody murmured 'Good Luck', but it wasn't Frimmer. He sat on his swivel chair, back to the screens, and stared at me. Then he spoke as if the words were ulcerating his mouth.

'Right, Bull. Remember you're not *just* a

pretty face. If you do survive this one we'll still want you on our books.'

I stepped down from the truck carrying a parcel similar to that of Corelli's. As I walked towards the shopping centre my breathing was as deep as a diver surfacing from the depths of some tremendous plunge. Knowing I was being watched on those octopal screens kept me in role, denying myself the pure pleasure of either a liberating skipping step or, even more satisfying, of booting that yellow ball along the gutter. Even though my role condemned me to be someone else, a condemnation more overpowering than in the case of Arthur Snell, I felt the surging thrust of a liberation. Now I could pretend I was clear of all that past *stuff*: that arithmetic of sorrows.

And, in that moment, when I might have expected to feel most afraid, I did not. Despite all the insistences of becoming Corelli, somewhere within me was an unexplored space for me to refocus, to be free. Tethered goat I might be but I was also a hunter. Suddenly, I felt distinctly bullish again; liked the feeling, liked the pun.

And yes, part of my skippiness *was* due to Frimmer's final remark, but much more to my acknowledgement I was once again the independent and unswervingly hard man that was me, and me at my best. And if that caused psychologists to point to a similarity with our killer I dealt with that easily enough: the worst *that* might mean was that we were equally matched.

And my namesake? I know that a gorged and glutted octopus hides pieces of its victim's flesh under nearby rocks for later consumption. The law is clear about police and victim rights of arrest and detention. If he is to be 'disappeared' for several weeks there can be only one outcome: no later resurrection. I will not see Corelli again.

Now I am Corelli.

PART THREE

Man's oldest image of fate is the image of a woman

Liz Greene

The Astrology of Fate
Published by George Allen and Unwin

★   ★   ★

The awkward fact remains, for men and women, that each was once dependent on woman, and somehow a hatred of this has to be transferred into a kind of gratitude if full maturity of the personality is to be reached.

Donald Winnicott

Home Is Where We Start From
Published by Penguin

7

Billy Mundam is a fair man: ask him. Gives another man a break; buffs up his reputation by taking in ex-cons. Used to dealing with scum, but something about the man standing at the other side of the paper-strewn desk disturbs. It is not the ex-con haircut nor the matted beard, so suppose it is the name: Corelli. He feels imposed upon: an ex-con is one thing, a wop ex-con something else.

'Pity your hair's so short.' Corelli nods; knows this is not the real issue. 'I mean — ' says Mundam, resentful also of muzzlement by laws he despises. (All that shit about racism when we're just telling the truth.) ' — I mean — if I give you a job my customers'll guess you've been inside.' Corelli says nothing. They both know his hair is regrowing even as Mundam complains. Further irritated by the man's silence, Mundam strokes his vast moustache, sits up straighter in his leather chair, sucks in his bulging belly. He wonders what was Corelli's crime. Rehab did not disclose. He suspects something sneaky feeble: stealing old ladies' handbags? Not a Billy Mundam offence. As a mature man, another favourite self-description, he always beats the system in bigger ways than *that*; never caught despite the dodgy moments. And another thing: *he* has never rolled over a woman, except when selling cars, but that's business, and once off his forecourt they're not his responsibility. He sees himself as an old-fashioned gent around ladies; no contradiction that he obtains satisfactions only in the local whorehouse where he believes himself to be favourite. He thinks that a different girl each time reflects his popularity not their collective repugnance.

'I sometimes wonder why I bother,' he says.

'Because you are a good man,' says Corelli.

Mundam is confused. Others have measured his worth as sharp, keen or astute. (Astute is his favourite.) 'Good' is surprising. At the back of his brain stirs the possibility this wop is taking the piss but the evidence is against: the man's shabbiness, subservient manner, dependence on his, Billy's, goodwill. Another's dependence *always* reassures. (How slickly he sells cars to pig-ignorant motorists dependent on his expertise.) The two men stare at each other, Corelli the first to drop his gaze.

Corelli doesn't need to look at the man any more, has recognized him: the ridiculous 1960s-style moustache, essential for fondling when a new thought strikes the brain, the beer gut edging over the straining waistband like a sack of hops about to burst. Large soft body, small hard mind. A diktat in that mind: raped women were asking for it, begging even. Corelli suppresses a shudder at the image of that grossly fat, moustached face between a woman's legs. A relief to reflect on the years of dodgy car dealing that have led to the big time for Billy Mundam: the chain of garages and car showrooms, the lifestyle that lacks any sense of style. Aware of Mundam's discomfiture, he looks away from the china-blue eyes bulging in the fat face; again looks down at his own feet, hides his lust for the man's suffering.

'Well — look here, I mean. Got the business to think of.' Mundam strokes his moustache. He believes he has a business-man's gift for finding solutions: passing the buck is favourite. 'Well, seeing as I've had a letter from rehab, and that the new probation officer, Mr Thomas, looked in to mention you, it seems you're worth a chance. Whitsun soon: business picking up. Tell you what. Give you a trial here in this garage where I can keep an eye on you.' He strokes the moustache. 'Go find Ted Croucher, my manager here. He'll set you up polishing cars round the back. But you keep off my forecourt with that haircut. Got it?'

Corelli sidles slow along the forecourt, celebrating a fool feeding his own destruction. Every word from out of that fat face polishes the sharp spike of malice Corelli is honing; and he is precise in his reckoning. No insult missed, not a word discounted. Corelli has serious business here but it will not prevent the crucifixion of Billy Mundam.

Corelli stands in front of Ted Croucher while the man enjoys insulting him, unwittingly lining himself up for his share of approaching disaster. Amused that swarthy and black-haired Croucher is more Italian in appearance than himself, Corelli does not bother to protest about the man's wordy insults. He is even more amused that Thomas is supposed to be his probation officer. He doubts the ninety days of training they shared has prepared Thomas for his job any more than he has been prepared for his own. While Croucher works himself into a lather, Corelli reflects that everyone's a user of someone for something, watches Croucher's lips becoming wet with spittle. He fantasizes the split mouth spluttering its own blood and the broken too-white teeth. He has not previously contributed to the breaking of false teeth.

The other staff accept Corelli good-naturedly enough. They've seen it all before with ex-cons: easy come, easy go. No threat to their status. They can wait to see how Croucher makes Corelli jump. No one is sufficiently interested to notice that whatever job he happens to be doing, Corelli is always on the forecourt at exactly two o'clock every afternoon.

Pay day is Thursday for any casuals or temps. Mundam enjoys reminding employees he is the proprietor by unnecessarily supervising payments in the manager's office. Croucher handles the pay packets.

'Corelli's next,' says Croucher.

'Right,' says Mundam, 'Let's see how it goes with the wop.'

The man stands hesitant in the doorway. He knows trouble.

'Come in then,' says Mundam, moustache straight and level, blue eyes shining malice. 'Sign here for your money. Bet you're ready for it.'

But Corelli doesn't sign. He inspects his pay packet. Looks from Mundam to Croucher and back again.

'What's the matter, wop?' demands Croucher, his scowl dragging his greased widow's peak almost to the bridge of his knifelike nose.

'Pay packet has been opened. Money is wrong. Twenty pounds short compared with what Mr Mundam agreed me.'

'Some of your cars not clean enough. *And*

errors at the pumps. Accounts make up the wages but I deduct what's lost,' says Croucher.

Corelli ignores him; stares at Mundam until the man begins to feel irritated. And there is something wrong somewhere. This wop needs breaking in a lot more. Another word with Ted later.

'You're not suggesting some sort of fiddle, are you?' says Mundam. 'Not you in your position: just out.'

'Just want my right money,' says Corelli, sullenly.

Croucher steps round the desk, grabs Corelli by the shoulder. 'Watcha mean, right money? This *is* your right money, fella. Don't start a grouse or you're out on your ear, and no reference either. Then you'll be up shit creek without a paddle. What'll you do then, smart arse wop?'

'Even in the prisons no one laid hands on me,' says Corelli, softly, looking directly into Croucher's face. Croucher lifts his hand off Corelli's shoulder. Unfortunately, Mundam laughs.

'You've been told, Ted, told by a little wop! My top manager just got told!' He has no idea of the agonies that will result from this foolishness. And he is too eager to twist another knife. 'You, Corelli, shut the fuck up or you're out. Just remember where you've come from and who took you on. Sign for the money and piss off!' Corelli sighs and signs, then pockets the money. He knows he has to serve his time here like a prison stretch.

On the forecourt and in the workshop is disappointment. There has been no explosion. But, for the moment, the other staff leave Corelli alone; they are aware of the man's fitness, have heard rumours of his jogging the streets after work. They will wait for a lead from the manager. Croucher has Friday off; Corelli has Saturday and Sunday. On Monday Croucher tightens the screws.

He orders Corelli to clean his new Jaguar for him, then complains loudly about the result. Corelli stares at him across the gleaming bonnet but says nothing. This infuriates Croucher more than words: dumb insolence. He orders Corelli to do the whole job again. They both know there will be no tip. Corelli's compliance encourages Croucher to criticize everything he gets the man to do, to refer loudly to 'that convict wop'. By Wednesday the atmosphere is so poisonous that one of the older staff protests to Croucher who scowlingly moderates his language. He knows, as does everybody else, that tomorrow is pay-day two for Corelli, and that there will be more unexplained deductions. But Thursday brings more than pay for Corelli.

'Mr Thomas, your probation officer, is in my office,' says Croucher, sulky that the pay confrontation will be delayed. Corelli walks past the man without speaking; both know the significance of that.

'Good morning, Corelli. Have a seat.' Mr Thomas is finding it hard to keep a straight face, but for Corelli this is easy. 'Checked the room, Jake. It's clean. Tape recorder in the desk drawer but switched off. No need to take a walk. Any news?'

'No.' Corelli is curt.

'What helps, Jack?'

'Fucking not calling me Jack.'

'Er — sorry — Jake.' Thomas is suddenly wary, recalling reputations, incidents on the course. Not even poor old Pearson could match *this* man.

'How long've I got to hang around here? Stone settled his list?'

'At long last, boyo: fourteen dead rapists. But still no clear lead to a killer or killers.' Silently, Corelli acknowledges his own vulnerability might be greater than Billy Mundam's; to kill fourteen successfully must make a fifteenth almost a triviality. 'Anything I can do?' asks Thomas, not liking the silence, fluffing his untidy red hair with his right

108

hand. Corelli says nothing about his runner being a red-headed Welshman. Not the time to antagonize. But he has to express some of his frustration.

'You know why we're doing all this: this elaborate set-up?'

'To catch a serial killer or killers,' says Thomas, simply.

'No. Because we *can't* catch them. All this fucking — fucking *stuff* is because we've failed to catch him or her or them.'

'Not really our bag, though, is it? SIU's trying to plug other people's gaps. Not our fault. We don't even know for sure who we're after. Team of two or three men still favourite with Stone. But then you reckon something else.'

'Yeah. Always have. Our killer's so *fastidious*. Take Stone's final list, OK? Fourteen suspicious deaths of discharged rapists and GBHs on women. Not one knifing or coshing: no bloodshed, for fuck's sake. OK so someone knows about DNA, but all these deaths so neat and clean. Fastidious *is* the word. Not sure this is how a man would do it: all these revenges and nobody slashed or had their brains on their face?'

'You don't rate the ice-cold control freak?'

'Could be *part* of it. But listen! If *you* were so enraged, so mad you were willing to kill at least fourteen times, don't tell me you wouldn't want to smash in a face, cave in a skull or slash a windpipe.'

'Suppose not,' says Thomas, feeling too overwhelmed to argue.

'Right then. Now something you can do: get these keys duplicated.' He pushes wax impressions and print-outs across the desk.

'All these? Soon found your way around.'

'Yes,' impatiently. 'Mundam's nifty sports number, Croucher's Jag and a getaway car for me.'

'Things in mind?'

'For when Frimmer presses the bloody button. Don't worry, I can wait. All I've got for him *now* is that Croucher's Jag is new but the wheels aren't. Spotted that when cleaning the bastard's car. Check around: easier to take the tyres off somewhere quieter before emptying them.'

'Drugs as well, Jake?'

'You don't think Frimmer chose this garage for me by sticking a pin in a list, do you? For all you and I know there could even be a link with the case Pearson was on. Now, got anything else for me?'

Thomas is relieved he has not. As he takes up his briefcase, makes for the door, he says goodbye in a voice he has not heard before. No reply: but he knows he is watched all the way. Walking to his car he cannot stop wiping his forehead; feels himself impaled on something monstrous. He clings almost prayerfully to the consolation: 'At least the bastard's on my side!'

8

Corelli had hoped to dream of Jayne, her supple body willingly spread-eagled on the great bed in her flat; the lightness and simplicities of shared lust. Instead he is visited by Isobel French.

Together, he and the sad bloated woman wander through a house of many small seedy rooms, the walls lined with photographs of the other ten victims he had interviewed. In every room Isobel complains that her photograph is not included, that he is not paying attention to her pain, now swollen with grief at the loss of her father, taken because he avenged her. Desperate to silence her, he pulls her to him, puts a hand over her mouth. Then he feels himself smothering in the layers of defensive fat she has accumulated. Disgusted, he pushes her away. Gasping for breath, he breaks out of the dream.

He looks at his watch: only midnight. The bulk of the night lies ahead with the distortions of his rambling mind set against a discordant, muted chorus of familiar sounds: black groans of sleepers whose daily struggles infect their dreams, the too-easily identified noises from the lavatories, the stairs creaking under the surreptitiously returning drunks, the snuffling growl of the landlord's German Shepherd, a dog loathsome for its bad temper as much as for its smell, and the landlord as obnoxious as his dog. And always a background of the blended stenches of damp laundry, uncleaned lavatories, unacknowledged vomit stains, carpets impregnated with grime and dog hairs; all of these intensified by the Whitsun warmth and by the large number of long-broken sash cords that keep so many windows jammed shut.

One help for Corelli is that he has been strong enough to force open his window, and then prop it with a wooden batten from the festering back yard. That is one amelioration; the other is that no meals are provided so the occupants are spared the odours of mouldering meats and overcooked cabbage.

But there is another more insidious stench ground into his skin and irremovable. Living with it he knows it well enough: the corrupting effect of being a police officer. And it is all-pervading in the force, uniformed or plain clothes; the poison of it wrecking marriages, breaking those apparently well-ordered homes to which his colleagues returned drained and contaminated. Inescapable. For tonight, more certainly than usual, he is sure of his decision not to marry.

His hating, hateful mind throws up the wild thought, perhaps rooted in the dream, that being married to his career has led him into some kind of crazy, multiple love affair with suffering women. Not the kind of 'love story' to appeal to a timorous publisher seeking the cosy safe-sell saga. No. What he is caught up in, or more accurately dropped into, is some terrible Grecian mythic trap: his own fate inseparable from that of these women. He is in every sense displaced.

Fading on the exterior front wall of the house are stripes on the brickwork that form a pale shadow of the word 'Hotel'; the sign itself long gone. Now the building is a rooming house for men; not surprising that the alloyage of smells is aggressively male. This is the world awaiting so many discharged rapists. No wonder they respond to inflated job offers from complete strangers, and go unsuspecting to their deaths.

But Corelli knows, from that far distant life as police officer working in London, that this is not the base of the pyramid. The men he lodges with are clinging to the edge of a precipice overlooking a lower circle of hell: men's hostels, dosshouses, soup queues, park benches, the gutter. Every man here has some money, and most of them have jobs, but none

114

of them will work his way out of this lifestyle. For most of these wage slaves this is as good as it gets, will *ever* get. Corelli wonders how many of this multicultural herd yearn for their impoverished homelands where poverty is not disgraceful, not a prop for a vicious capitalism. Do any of them long for the greens of Ireland, the blues of the Mediterranean, the Adriatic? Is England better than their homelands; really better?

'Tush,' mutters Corelli, echoing the late Mr Burton, Director of a Children's Home, who dismissed every complaint and protest with that one word. He remembers when he had threatened to run away: Mr Burton had stared at him, then, 'Tush'. And when he was brought back by the police, all that Mr Burton had said was, 'Tush', and then, 'Bend over'. Corelli supposes that when he escaped the fourth time and the police decided not to return him yet again, Mr Burton had privately acknowledged that with 'Tush'. Corelli wishes that within his own present-day secret life he could as easily dismiss whatever distresses him.

Irritated by his half-formed thoughts, he gets out of bed, pulls back the threadbare curtains and stares across the rooftops of the sleeping town. Out there the majority forever seek the great delusion: the trouble-free life.

He almost wishes he could be one of them despite the trumpet call of his wrecked childhood to live this, his inescapable life.

But despite the confusions of his rambling mind, he knows the core of his depression for what it is: the acute frustration of physical inaction. In more than half a year only that training course had kept his body on full alert; that and perhaps being with Jayne. For all the rest he has been clumping about in the depths of other people's misery. To pursue and arrest someone would revitalize his congealing blood; to beat someone would restore full circulation. Like the killers he stalks, he aches for action to validate his sense of self. How accurately the profilers had pointed to that similarity.

At times he very much wishes someone dead — even bloody Frimmer; sometimes *especially* bloody Frimmer. He knows under-cover life is smothering something in him, choking his initiative, reducing him to the small cog Frimmer has named him. But whether his thoughts hang on the rooftop view of the town, or on the sad lives of his fellow lodgers, or on the frustrations of belonging to SIU, he knows he is struggling with an avoidance: think about anyone other than of Madelaine Grey!

He is consumed by her, like a small fish

gulped down whole by a larger one. But he still cannot name the nature of that connection. Not even her nakedness with him had been erotic: too much pain with it. *Now* he can acknowledge how ungrounded he was when they met, how vulnerable because of the news of Molly's suicide. But he has found no explanation for that powerful and consuming experience of *collision* with Madelaine. But perhaps he knows absolutely nothing of women other than their anatomy.

Feeling almost as he did on hearing of Molly's death, he returns to his bed, reflects morosely on the grey chasm of the weekend that lies in front of him. His chief refuge, the public library, closes early on Saturday; all day Sunday. The workmen's cafe where he eats will be closed Sunday, leaving him with the choice of not eating at all or going to the local pub for lunch, where his shabby clothes invite whispered comment. (He gives no consideration to the awful idea of bringing food back *here*.) At least in the pub no one has cause to remark on his regrown hair and neatly trimmed beard.

On Monday he endures the rising hostility of some of the younger staff made bold by his meek acceptance of a second wage cut last Thursday. (He never bothered to point out to Croucher that all forecourt petrol sales are self-service, that payments are made in the office and electronically recorded; that he polishes cars better than any other staff.) His midmorning tea has lavatory paper in it; his white coat soaked in petrol; his wash leather stained with engine oil — and he has to pay Croucher a ridiculous price for a replacement. But no one has the courage to touch him — yet.

At 2 p.m. he drifts on to the forecourt. Seconds later, Henderson drives a dark blue Ford to the pumps, ignores Corelli, tops up his tank then drives the car over to the air pump. Then he looks directly at Corelli, signals his own inability to check tyre pressures correctly. Without haste, Corelli walks over and offers help.

'This Wednesday!' says Henderson, his horsey face alive with excitement. Corelli expels a long, slow sigh echoed by the air going into the front offside tyre.

When they are both attending to the rear nearside and the car screens them from observation, Henderson slips a package of car keys to Corelli.

'As requested, Jake,' he says. 'Frimmer's got the media lined up, even national TV. Every media agency gets a photo of the real Corelli first post Wednesday. Frimmer claims we're fully backed right up to Downing

118

Street; specially now Stone's researches have set up more than a dozen new trials — and mostly with guilty pleas. But *you* are still the biggy, Jake. Just now you have Frimmer over a barrel and the bastard knows it! So get greedy if that suits. Doubt you'll ever get the chance again!' Both men smile and shuffle to the front nearside wheel.

'Right,' says Corelli, feeling lighter than the air in the hose. 'Wednesday. There'll be a 999 call from here at the end of the lunchbreak, say between 13.30 and 14.00. Got it?' Henderson nods, replacing the dust cap on the wheel. They move to the rear offside. 'You see that second-hand black Volkswagen inside the pound? I'll be driving south in it. I need a road block behind me that stops all traffic including local police. I want to drive to Frimmer's command truck knowing that absolutely nobody is trailing me.'

'Right. Er — yes,' says Henderson, standing straight as Croucher approaches. 'Thank you very much for your help.'

'No trouble, sir. Have a nice afternoon.'

Without leaving a tip, Henderson walks away to pay for his petrol, unaware that for completely different reasons both Corelli and Croucher are amused by his meanness. For Corelli the first priority is not to reveal his elation. The second is to keep wound up tight his intention to exact the fullest revenge. He already knows how much he will be helped in that by the experiences of carrying out tasks for the last time: he might even get a good night's sleep in his miserable room on Tuesday. He is unsurprised how much that particular 'last time' matters to him. It is not only the killer who is fastidious.

Early morning Wednesday. For the last time Corelli dresses in his grimy room, pockets what he needs, wraps his few other possessions in his pyjamas and leaves the bundle outside the nearest bedroom door; useful for someone. Silently down stairs that have defeated drunks, but he wouldn't mind disturbing that dog and giving it a good kicking: a silly flurry of excitement. Then out of the front door, feeling himself expanding, stretching in the certainty he will never re-enter; unsurprised the day promises to be fine.

At the cafe he celebrates by ordering double eggs and bacon and extra fried bread. As working men's cafes go, the place is not that awful, but again he is buoyed up by knowing this is another 'last'. Then the early bus to work. He arrives before anyone else and with about two hours to spare. Everything so carefully planned and so often daydreamed begins to click smoothly into place.

Escape route first. The great padlock on the gates of the used car lot succumbs to his 'penknife' with an ease that would shock Billy Mundam. Bigger shocks are planned for him. The duplicate keys for the Volkswagen allow him to move it and repark conveniently for the exit. A neat disablement of the engine guarantees it will neither be sold nor moved this morning, but he can reactivate it in seconds. He puts his jacket with its heavy weighted pockets into the boot, slams it locked shut, relocks the gates of the enclosure behind him. He walks across the deserted forecourt, round the back of the workshops, crosses some waste ground and climbs through a broken fence into the local park.

He had intended to lie on a bench and doze but, realizing there is no one else in the park so early, he jumps the barrier round the children's play area and, like the child he never was, tries every slide, swing, rope and wheel strong enough to hold him. His excitement is within him, but his questing, raging mind he banishes outside the barrier where it slumps, silent, resentful and forlorn, on the nearest park bench.

9

Having repossessed his mind, Corelli walks slow and arrives late on the garage forecourt. He has followed the more circuitous route through the local shopping centre, and at the newsagent's took his first deliberate step towards chaos. He bought a box of matches. He also allowed himself a moment of enjoyment inspecting the newspaper racks. Tomorrow they will be full of *him*. Croucher shouts at him while Corelli is still thirty metres away. Closing the gap, Corelli lets spite slide past, feels the malicious words ruffling his shoulders as he walks through them. Croucher detects nothing of his fate in the sweet smile Corelli offers.

Corelli polishes cars, more careful than usual in avoiding fingerprints on his gleaming work, hugging to himself the reason for that extra carefulness. He feels within his body a slowly intensifying vibration; familiar confirmation he is moving closer to violent action. No one bothers him until Mundam arrives at the morning tea break. Lateness is owner's privilege but nobody else's. Informed by Croucher, Mundam walks over to Corelli, bawls him out for lateness, threatens dismissal. Mundam intends Corelli will go Thursday after getting a last plundered wage packet. Corelli knows he leaves today, and that Mundam will play a passive role in sadistic ceremonies of dismissal.

It is not long before a ferocious shouting match develops between Mundam and Croucher in the latter's office; the volume so great it can be heard in the workshop even above the sounds of machinery in use. Corelli stays straight-faced despite knowing that the cause of the row is the anonymous note he has sent to Mundam. The accusation that his manager, Croucher, is using this garage for shifting drugs will certainly have frightened the man, but Corelli suspects that much of the fury in the row arises from the fact Mundam has not been cut in on the deal. Lunchtime the row is still rumbling and the workshop staff are glad to accept Corelli's offer to 'mind the shop' while they all go to the cafe. Now Corelli knows his moment, believes he has been waiting for it less than a month. Later, he wonders if he had been waiting for half a year.

He walks to the locker area in the workshop, helps himself to a pair of latex gloves. Using the keys cut for him by SIU, he quietly drives Mundam's red sports car into the workshop, enjoys the change in the tyre whisper as the wheels pass over the threshold. There is the same pleasure in moving Croucher's Jaguar. He slides shut the great doors, enclosing himself with the two cars. Every action savoured: he so much looks forward both to destruction and discovery. Inside the workshop area he manoeuvres Mundam's car so it is aligned off-centre with the inspection pit. Then he lowers the inspection lift that is next to the pit, drags clear the car that was on it, and drives the Jaguar on in its place. He watches the Jaguar as it is carried to the maximum height the lift can achieve. Then he swivels it through ninety degrees. He allows a moment of enjoyment: the sports car facing the inspection pit, Jaguar overhanging it.

Corelli leans into the sports car and, with a baulk of timber, puts the car into a fast revving forward lurch. Deliberately mis-aligned with the pit, the car plunges down and sideways, crunching into it, twisting half over towards its right side. The protesting metals, scraped paints and crunching glass fill the workshop with a kind of shrieking bellow followed by the gentler sounds of dripping liquids.

The next task is more difficult: to drop Croucher's Jaguar off the lift and on top of

Mundam's already damaged car. But Corelli has worked out, repeatedly daydreamed, how to achieve this second stage of the catastrophe; even how to ensure the underside of the car does not too heavily foul the edge of the lift and so prevent its fall. It happens as planned although Corelli only just jumps clear in time. The vehicle drops nose first on to the wreck in the pit. The cacophony is deafening: smashing glass, crunching metal, the twisting frameworks of both cars, the wrenching of hinges. Corelli's symphony of sounds climaxes in the violent explosive bursting of a tyre. Afterwards, like applause, there is muted tinkling of fractured glass, drippings of petrol, oils and water. Croucher's car remains vertical on its nose in the pit, the car completely distorted by the force of the impact. The neat touch of leaving all the doors open before dropping the car has intensified the damage. Almost deafened by his successes, Corelli pushes the customer's car that had been on the ramp across the mouth of the pit. It will form a temporary firebreak. Then he slides open one of the large doors. Outside, the hum of traffic; inside, the drip-dripping of wreck and ruin. There is not long to wait. Mundam has sent Croucher to investigate. Corelli, smiling, steps aside, waves Croucher into the workshop.

Soft laughter from Corelli impels the man into futile action. Stuttering incoherently, he lurches at Corelli. Corelli brushes aside futility, chops Croucher across the throat with the edge of one hand that is like a steel bar, smashes his other hand flat against his sternum — a blow that almost stops Croucher's heart. From the ground, Croucher looks up at his assailant but not really seeing, the life remnant within utterly absorbed in trying to continue breathing. More than anything in his collapsing world, he wants to stay on the ground but the sound of Mundam's voice coming closer spurs him into more futility. Almost affectionately, Corelli helps him to stand. Then looses ferocity again. For the first time both men experience the smashing of false teeth; additionally, for Croucher, the breaking of his jaw. As he falls there is just enough time for Corelli to snap his victim's left arm. With Mundam's shadow spreading across his broken face, Croucher slides groaning into unconsciousness.

Corelli allows Mundam a moment for seeing and comprehending. Then he swings his locked, clenched fists from somewhere behind his right hip in a scything arc that slices into the fat of Mundam's belly. He feels he is cutting the man in half, his fists sinking out of sight; is only half aware that the cruel blow is matched by the hissed explanation, 'That's for Molly!' The only reply an agonized expulsion of air. A wrenching swing on the falling man's right arm dislocates his shoulder before his knees strike the concrete. He kneels at Corelli's feet, holds his ruptured gut with his only functioning arm. Corelli leans forward, reaches for the man's wallet. Mundam, mistaking the gesture, sobs for mercy. Corelli extracts money, replaces the wallet.

'See, Billy. I take what you take out of two weeks' wages plus this week up to today. You see?' He slaps the man across the face with the money. Then he grasps him by his wobbling chin, stares down into his face. 'You see? No theft. OK?' If Mundam could have nodded he would. He can only offer fat tears coursing his cheeks. Corelli brings his fist down on the crown of the man's head, bestowing unconsciousness. 'For all those raped women!' he shouts, oblivious of madness.

He switches his raging energy to the fire extinguishers by the doors, hurls them into the wreckage, savours more responses from the wrecks. Then he removes his white coat, the one that had been soaked in petrol by someone as expression of contempt for him. Enjoying the symbolism, he drags it across the mix of fuel and lubricants in the pit, lays it like a fuse; strips off the latex gloves, adds them to the pile. One match ignites the coat, gives him time to retreat, hide behind another car.

The explosion is everything he had ever wished. Trapped within the pit the flaming mass is forced up, and surrounds the Jaguar in a mockery of auto da fé. The force of the fire punches a hole through the lofty roof of the workshop. The red paint of Mundam's car is instantly absorbed in the multiple reds of the inferno. Torched tyres and smouldering oils begin to belch out the thickest of black smoke. Corelli spins on his toes, regards his two victims. Which one to drag out first to safety?

Shuffling feet in the doorway; then stillness. Some of the mechanics returned from lunch stand paralysed before Corelli's holocaust. Mundam sighs like a baby in sleep; begins to vomit. Somebody shouts a query about what happened. Corelli smiles at the men in the doorway, walks towards them. 'They fight,' he says, waving a hand over his victims as if anointing. Even if there was time, no one will question this. After their earlier ferocious row, the immediate assumption is that the two men had fought each other. Panic smothers any query as to why they are both unconscious. 'Call emergency services!' shouts Corelli, above the sounds of the fire, of the glass panels shattering in the roof. By the time Corelli is driving the Volkswagen from the pound, the two bodies have been dragged clear and shaky voices are gusting into mobiles. Emergency services will need few instructions about location; the pillar of fire and its black oily smoke will guide them from the far limits of the county.

Corelli drives south knowing that behind him, but out of range of his rear-view mirror, road blocks are swinging into position. In the designated street, and on the agreed spot, he sees the dark blue truck parked. He brakes sharply, pulls in behind it. He hardly has time to free himself from the seat belt before Henderson is out of the truck and waiting to drive the Volkswagen. His job is to dump the stolen car in Browcaister without being intercepted by local police. He is not pleased to delay for the time it takes Corelli to get his weighted jacket out of the car boot. As Henderson drives away the back doors of the truck reopen to admit Corelli.

In the familiar blue marine space he is unnerved by an experience bizarre even for that crazed day: a splattering noise which, for a moment, he fails to recognize as applause. That and smiling faces, Frimmer's handshake and greeting, combine to affect him as strongly as the workshop chaos. By the time he can comprehend the warmth of his reception the truck is moving smoothly away from the kerb. He cannot see clearly, blinks his eyes furiously. He is rescued by Frimmer, who puts a hand on his shoulder and leads him along the length of the truck to a tiny room screened off from the rest of the interior. Frimmer closes the door, pushes him into one of the two folding chairs. He produces a hip flask and slumps into the chair opposite Corelli.

'You're off duty!' Embarrassed, Frimmer speaks as if they are on a parade square. 'Drink this!' Corelli is too distressed to refuse the brandy, a drink he doesn't care for, but the resultant coughing fit is a good cover for embarrassment. 'First reports indicate a job well done. Corelli's mug'll be all over national front pages tomorrow, and stolen car reported in Browcaister. Reckon that'll spring the trap, Bully boy.'

'I can be Bull again, can I?'

'Sort of,' says Frimmer, further discomfited. 'Appreciate the severe stress you've been under recently.'

'I'm just er — beginning to, sir.' The half-truth floats between them.

'OK. But you've just got an indication of what the team thinks.'

'Christ!' says Bull, beginning to shake

130

again. These layers of approval seem grotesque. He is also unnerved by physical closeness with Frimmer, their knees touching.

'More brandy,' says Frimmer. 'Look,' he says. 'To be precise, it's not so much about being Bull as getting you out of circulation for a few days. Got the loan of a safe house from M15. Henderson'll drive you there once he's dumped the car you used. I want to avoid the idiot public rushing at us with identifications. Be plenty of false sightings. Think of it as a week's leave plus the chance to reread Stone's 'hot list' cases.'

'And I'm supposed to forget all those poor cows I interviewed, am I?'

'Look here.' Frimmer pauses. 'There's just one other thing.' He pauses again. Having no idea what the man is trying to say, Bull can offer no help. 'You need to check out a tendency you have ' — a weakness, Bull. Beware compassion. It's a bit like an octopus: sneaks up on you, grabs, sucks bits of flesh, undermines.'

Bull is astounded that Frimmer, Director of SIU, is saying this to him *and* while they are sitting in the blue truck. Then he is no longer shaking but steel-hard. He feels the weight of the gun inside the bundled coat he holds on his lap. He has the means and the motive, and sitting here, knee to knee, the opportunity. Then he is undermined by his sense of humour. 'How far can coincidence go? Ha! As far as me bearing some resemblance to Corelli.' As if unnerved by Bull's silence, Frimmer plunges into further details.

'All the stuff you might need is in the safe house, and you're booked into a hotel in Browcaister for subsequent weeks.'

'You still think this trap'll work, sir?'

'I'll look fucking silly if it don't. Stone's OK. *He's* protected by how many prosecutions we're getting from his researches. But at the moment not many people know about you. I'll not be able to hide you when the accounts get made up, and especially if there's no result to justify the expense you are. Don't see you slipping through the net under 'sundries'.'

Bull is too drained to say it but as a potential fifteenth victim, the killer might well regard him as no more than sundries.

10

Diary for the week at The House

Thursday 10.00. Not sure why I've decided to write this. Therapeutic? Perhaps reminding me I still exist as Jack Bull.

Arrived here Wednesday 15.30. Henderson drove so smoothly I slept most of the way. So no precise idea where I am! Not that I'm going to be allowed out. This place is a *fortress*. H. parked outside tall wrought-iron gates at lodge. No one in sight. Then orders given via gate intercom. H. to drive away at once; me to wait. H. pissed off I think. Wheelspin as he drove away. As dust settled gates opened and I entered. Gates shut. I was trapped between two identical sets of gates. Reminded me of game park entries designed to control wild animals. Guessed I was being scanned. Worried about reaction to the Webley but then thought they might expect that; no reason to question. They didn't. Olive-green Land Rover rolled into view from behind lodge. At same time inner gates opened. Driver got out, walked round vehicle to greet me. Has a limp. Dressed entirely in black. Slight bulge of shoulder holster under jacket. He stopped about two metres from me. I kept my hand well clear of my jacket pocket! 'I'm Tom. Welcome to The House. Get in.' No handshake. A neat, stocky, dark-haired man. Air of self-containment. Guessed he was ex-SAS.

Wondered what he made of seedy me: bruised knuckles, bloody shirt; smelling of brandy, fire, burning oils and rubber.

At front steps of house Tom introduced me to Dennis. Perhaps same background as Tom but wearing white housecoat with high-buttoned neck, incongruous over bulge of holster. Showed me to first-floor room — lovely views of grounds. Clothes laid out: everything slightly worn. Assumed they're for 'post-bonfire' Corelli. And a shabby leather suitcase with initials JC!! A slow hot bath.

Dennis served a good tea in the small dining-room. New world of polished furniture, flowers in vases, views across lawns in late-afternoon light. Bitter contrast with previous slum living. Strong desire to go out and walk. Dennis insisted showing me the house first. Introduced me to colleagues Philip and Jimmy: early forties, clones of Tom. So looks like team of four plus domestics. There's an outdoor heated swimming pool, a small gym and a library. On long centre table in library: fourteen red box files — already knew the grief in them. Insisted on my walk. Dennis said dinner at 20.00. Also stressed that for security reasons guests never allowed outside the house after dark.

House is lovely Queen Anne. Anything that might spoil symmetry is at rear: stables, pool, etc. On each side, well clear of house, two mature Lebanon cedars. In front lawn, about twenty-five metres from house, two matching island flowerbeds, both without trees. Nothing blocks field of fire. Only other trees are two groups, one at each of the Victorian Gothic lodge houses. Grounds not that large: say ten hectares. Bounded by high Cotswold stone walls with curved capstones. Stumps of large trees near walls. No tree allowed to overhang. Other evidences of security — but need to look hard; wires, scanners, etc., around. Knew I was observed but not bothered. Lovely dusk following the fine clear day. Doubted Mundam and Croucher were enjoying the evening in their hospital beds!

Back to small sitting-room for TV news. And there I was! Wanted for questioning. Big fire at garage. Two men hurt, workshop destroyed, a dozen cars lost despite efforts of staff and firemen. Fame at last! Excellent dinner kept laughter at bay. Waited on by Dennis.

Couldn't sleep so went for midnight swim — fool that I was. But the experience! Need to write as I felt. Somehow that matters. I floated naked, starfish spread, face down, mouth and ears under water, eyes wide open; felt the warm water of the pool riffling against back and buttocks; moonlight filtering into the water around me; caressed by light as I held my breath. A moment I *really* needed; a moment poor Abercrombie never knew in icy winter water. (*Poor* Abercombie?)

Raised my head to breathe in the moon-marked night air, water-blocked ears allowing part-penetration of unexpected sounds. Heard Dennis's piping voice: 'Sir, sir! I told you the rules.'

Turned on to my back. Absolute calmness in me. Face up to the stars; crystal brilliance not even the moon could mask. Another shrillness from Dennis. (He wore high-collar clothes buttoned up, but when he had bent down to pick up my dirty shoes I had seen the top edge of a terrible scar across his throat.) 'Being Abercrombie,' I said, sliding the words across the water. Rolled over on to my face, swam slowly across the pool. Then underwater lights were switched on. I felt my nakedness threatened, wanted, impossibly, to cup my genitals and swim at the same time. And I felt the ironic parallel: those eleven sorrow-filled interviews exposing, threatening my manhood.

'Swim to the steps at the shallow end — sir!' The furious command from Tom. Gently breast-stroking, I could see Dennis and also Tom, who stood further back from the pool with hands on hips. Beyond them both, just outside the reach of the pool lights, I saw several more other moonflecked dark figures. So much for assumption about staff of four guards. Out of my depth in several senses.

Climbing the steps, embraced with a giant bath towel by scowling Dennis. Sensed sudden movement from Tom. Turned quickly, saw ending of his gesture to men behind him to move away. Dennis was inclined to tut-tut at me but I excused my irritating behaviour by saying I never sleep well on my first night in a strange bed.

At breakfast the air of 'gentility' was recaptured. Dennis served me excellent food and coffee. Tom drove the motor mower past the windows: I suspect that is his main task, and his cover as well. Other guards out of sight. But Dennis keeps his mobile as close as his gun. After breakfast, Dennis, slyly grinning, said: 'Papers in the library, sir.'

Newspapers laid out on side table. I'm in every one! Nationals full of the story with photos of the wreckage and Corelli mugshot. Local papers: no photo of me but emphasize opinion Corelli is still in the Midlands. I see the point of Frimmer's tactical decision to hold me here a week.

Thursday 19.00. After gym session, I worked on the red boxes for an hour. (None relates to anyone I interviewed from the cold list.) Stone's analyses very persuasive: familiar summary notes in every box, but big problem remains. For these fourteen most 'suspicious' accidental deaths of rapists, there are no totally convincing links to either the rape victims or their families as killers. Not only is Family A not tied in to murder of Rapist A, they are not tied in to murders of *any* of Rapists B to N either. One family, including victim's twin brothers and her husband, made a lot of noise in court after the verdict, and had the 'manpower' but no reliable link there either. Every case has motive, intentions and, in a few cases, suggestion of opportunity, but nothing sufficient to take to CPS. Lack of *alibis* not that relevant when looking at deaths spread over ten years. How many people, including me, can produce an alibi for (say) 27th February seven years ago? But Stone *has* turned up something needing explanation. Proposing a mass murderer is to postulate a person or persons of obsessive determination (madness?), and with the combination of cunning and luck that seems to favour some serial killers.

Later. Another session in the gym and then a swim helped me clear that weight of 'stuff'. Then I rechecked my Corelli wardrobe and documents with which I would re-enter the world. Looked out, saw a familiar black car blocked at the outer gates. Tom in the Land Rover picking up the visitor. Me maliciously enjoying Frimmer being treated no differently from myself — and seeing him with a briefcase!

In the library: Frimmer explosive. 'Congratulations on making spectacular headlines! But what's this with two injured men?'

'They got in the way.'

'Got in the way! Christ! One's got a fractured skull and had to have his spleen removed. The other's got — well, you fucking know what he's got.'

'No teeth!'

That brought him back to the boil! Said one interesting thing but obvious enough: 'You've always gotta press the boundaries, haven't you?' I threw him by agreeing and suggesting that was one of the reasons I'd got on to his course. 'Like the midnight swim last night?' he yelled. That made me think. Was he here because reported event raised possibility I was barmy? That'd sink his ship: *only possible lookalike field man gone nuts*. No surprise he cross-questioned me on my health. He's only concerned for me because he doubts my ability to sustain the role. Then he said something that went way beyond all previous shit.

'Would you like Jayne to come and stay for the rest of the week?' I was literally struck dumb. My only thought *then* was that had we met in my room instead of the library my gun would've been within easy reach. Second time I've got to that point with him!! So strained the silence even he was forced to acknowledge grossness. 'Just a thought,' he said, his tombstone teeth chewing on the words.

But the creature was unstoppable. Through a haze of rage I heard the bastard procurer ask if I'd looked at the red boxes. Really enjoyed saying I had but so what? He was even less happy when I quoted Inspector Hinchcliffe re Abercrombie: 'Making cases we can't solve.' Maliciously twisted the screw with ideas that (a) maybe Atkins and French *are* our mass murderers, but now 'hiding behind' one manslaughter charge: serve a few years instead of life. By time of release SIU *would've folded!!* Or (b) the avenger(s) we sought had *no other direct connection whatsoever* with ANY of our listed rape cases. Frimmer couldn't cope with these hypotheses, so took refuge (that's the right word) in briefing me.

Our hunter-killer might get suspicious if Corelli made no attempt to disguise himself, so I'm to remove the beard but keep the heavy framed specs. I'm already booked into a small residential hotel. 'All documentation on that is in this file,' he said, taking it from his briefcase. 'Everything forward-dated for next Wednesday. Rest of the week here to learn it.'

Very glad to see the back of him. (My rage also to do with his original procurement of Jayne to waylay me in that gym.) After lunch I slept on my bed until Dennis woke me with offer to shave my beard. Did a good job with lather and open razor. Felt cleaner in several senses.

Friday to Sunday. Positive changes in me. Work in the gym, the pool, running the bounds of the grounds easing me clear of a lot of shit. Been reading novels from the library. Reread the Corelli file Frimmer left me. But it isn't just about *doing*. I live in the feeling of that midnight swim: but the free floating somehow linked with responsibility. Hard to find the words. My commitment rooted not just in distress of women but also in something now belonging to me. Somehow this case has become personal for me. SIU now merely the provider of 'tools' for the job.

Monday. Last night an awful dream. I am in the dock accused of a terrible but unspecified crime. The jury is the eleven rape and GBH victims I had checked out on Stone's 'cold' list plus Samuel Atkins. I feel angry Atkins is holding Madelaine's hand. The judge unknown to me but both hands are replaced by steel hooks. The foreman of the jury is Molly Poling. She steps out of the jury benches and pleads with me to confess my guilt and so save my life. The more she pleads the more I resist even though I have no defence. She becomes more desperate, tearing at her clothing, running her hands through her hair. I see her face turning waxen; life leaving it. I wake sweating; the sheet damp round my neck. Takes most of the day to work off the effects of the dream. But the memory is embedded in me, almost to the craziness of phoning Frimmer for extra confirmation Molly is *really* dead, that vivacious bright-eyed smile forever extinguished.

Tuesday. Want to get back into Corelli role now and END all this.

Wednesday (Written up at end of day in my room in Browcaister) Henderson drove me here, dropped me near station. Browcaister only a few miles from Mundam's wrecked garage but all its local papers were hit by a D notice forbidding the naming or photo of Corelli in their write-up of the mayhem at the garage. National daily papers stolen from my hotel porch before anyone could take them in. Don't want the locals identifying me. Not foolproof. Couldn't blank TV. But additional protection is that a week has passed with its fresh catalogues of national and local crimes and disasters. *And* I've lost my beard.

Last morning at The House had final workout in the gym, then slow, soothing swim. After lunch found Dennis has packed my shabby bag. I transferred concealed gun to new 'Corelli' jacket. Dennis said all red boxes in library will be sent on to SIU. Last look in mirror. I still don't look all *that* much like Corelli. But only a very few people, strangers to us both, need to be convinced I am their target.

11

The Larches, Belmont Avenue, Browcaister, boasts no such tree but offers a prim tidiness that appeals to Corelli. Waiting to die is to be his major preoccupation, and he prefers to do that where everything is in its place. He is admitted by Mrs Olive Gridley, the proprietor. She is not easily impressed by paying guests but there is something about this new one that discounts his shabbiness. He would like to believe the favourable first impression has something to do with the initials on his suitcase but is not yet ready to risk humour.

Following her up the stairs to the first floor allows him to assess her body: tall, slim, long-waisted, short-legged. She attacks the dark pink-carpeted stairs as if denying middle age, pushing herself upward rather than climbing. Perhaps she is uncomfortably aware of an inescapable rear-view inspection, wishes she had worn her best blue instead of grey skirt and green jumper. Corelli is surprised by his room. From plans of the building provided by Frimmer he knows it to be square; is not expecting half a pyramid under sloping eaves. The two outer walls are only four feet high before the sloping ceilings intervene. To reach the sink in the corner requires a crouching gait. Two tall windows let into the eaves provide relief, or will do once he can drag the net curtains aside. Everything in the room is white except for slate-grey curtains and the dark pink carpet. He begins to suspect a carpet job lot.

Mrs Gridley leaves him to unpack his case but invites him down to 'my quarters' for afternoon tea. She informs him there is a bathroom with shower next door but he already knows that; why else would Frimmer have manipulated him into a room where Corelli cannot keep watch over his potentially lethal electrical and water connections?

Face and hands washed, he leaves the room silently, easing the Yale lock shut behind him. A brief inspection of all the other doors on the first-floor landing confirms their vulner- ability. He is in a genteel and spacious house, new-pin clean, and the pink carpet is ubiquitous; cheap pictures on the walls, and somewhere downstairs will be a flight of plaster ducks. He steadies himself against the banister rail. The dominating colours of this sunlit house: white walls, white woodwork and dark pink carpet are suddenly stained by greys, blacks and blood-red. Something more than a cloud passing across the face of the summer sun. This respectable, prim, net-curtained house is to be a killing ground?

Mrs Gridley presides in her ground-floor private sitting-room. The trio of ducks fly diagonally down towards her fluorescent-lit cocktail cabinet. In this room the net curtaining is so heavy electric lights are always on. 'My quarters,' she says to anyone who queries. It is always a special occasion welcoming a new guest, particularly a man; not that she will ever voice this latter qualification. She has absorbed layers of respectability thicker even than her make-up.

Mrs Gridley has a harsh voice that ought to emerge out of a pink lipsticked mouth beneath a slightly moustached upper lip, beneath a slightly hooked nose between pale-blue eyes slightly too close together, beneath a broad forehead, under lightly permed brown hair, surmounted by a high-crowned hat with a huge and wicked brim. Only in the last particular does she disappoint, being addicted to brightly coloured headscarves vaguely piratical in effect. Corelli doubts anyone has ever dared to tell her that, and he isn't going to rock her boat. He doubts if the late Mr Gridley ever dared speak of that or indeed anything else relating to his wife's appearance. Black and white photographs, among his lady wife's treasured bric-a-brac, reveal him to have been a

146

slack-jawed, hand-clasped, nervous man shorter than his spouse. Corelli wonders if stature determined Mrs Gridley's preference for head-scarves; large, glamorous hats would have reduced the deceased to embarrassing midgethood.

'Jake is not Italian,' agrees Corelli. 'I am half-English, brought up here. That is why I have little accent.' He knows reassurances are welcome as additions to the references thoughtfully included with 'his' original letter and enclosed cheque. But he never doubts the chief recommendation is that his cheque was for three instead of the requested one month in advance. 'You have a very smart hotel here, Mrs Gridley, most delightful.'

'Much of *that* is thanks to *Bernard*,' she says simperingly, but Corelli does not rise to this. 'He is my *decorator*,' she explains grudgingly. 'I guarantee him at least two rooms to revamp every year and he keeps his charges a little lower in return for regular employment.'

'A good arrangement. Perhaps he also obtained for you the carpet?'

'How did you guess *that*?' Astonished, she pushes a plate of small cakes at him.

'You are a shrewd business lady, I can tell. Also you have good taste.' In two brief sentences he has combined her own favourite self-evaluations. The warmth of mutual

147

goodwill is beginning to push the ceiling higher from the floor. The ripe moment. 'Although I am here to start a new job in Browcaister I will not be taking the post full-time for a few days, and even when I do my hours will be irregular.'

'I will, of course, be *giving* you a *front* door key as well as your room key,' she says. 'Come and go as you please. But I do like to *bolt* the front door at night by eleven. And please, *please* do not lose your keys. I've had more than enough trouble with keys in this business.'

Hastily, he explains that his irregular hours will apply to the day as much as the evening, and that is why he has chosen her much recommended residential hotel rather than a guest house. 'Those places have such silly inconvenient regulations about coming and going.'

Mrs Gridley is not wishing to be seen as either silly or inconveniencing, but cannot quite control herself. She leans heavily across the table. 'You mean you may be *with* me during the day?'

Corelli agrees, explains he intends to deal with his paperwork in his room. He sits well back in his chair while she maintains her predatory crouch. She is a well-seasoned lady, despite cosmetic acids. He recalls the old advert about 'letting your armpits be charm pits'. She does not.

'You are not required to be *regular* in your place of *employment?*' She senses drama. He feels amused, as if being cross-questioned about the state of his bowels. What would she make of his true employment?

'No, I am a trouble-shooter, a loss-adjuster. I deal with emergencies.'

'How *interesting*. And will you be bringing family to Browcaister?'

'No. I am bachelor, and both parents dead. I am unattached.'

'*Unattached*? You may well find a bride here in Browcaister, Mr Corelli. Perhaps you prefer the *mature* type?'

'Indeed I do!' He will not disclose that excessive use of emphasis utterly disqualifies. Instead offers his best smile. This makes her 'all of a quiver and ups-a-daisy', as she later tells her friend Audrey, next door. Audrey's place is one of those guest houses with the silly regulations.

'My *late* husband,' she says, unaware that emphasis implies he has merely missed a train, 'left me nicely settled as you see. But one gets *lonely* at times, doesn't one?' He nods agreement above the jam tart he is destroying. 'I do so hope you like *your* room.'

'I do, thank you.'

'Mr Anderson left very suddenly. A *completely* unexpected promotion for him. *Fortunately*, your enquiry letter arrived at exactly the right time. Normally, I will consider only *personal* recommendations. I am *determined* that my hotel will never be at risk from workshy dodgers on benefit. That is why I always *insist* on *employer* references and *always* check them. I've heard too many sad stories of how *difficult* it is to get a scrounger out once he's inside a respectable residential hotel.'

'I understand,' says Corelli, soothingly; also understanding that Mr Anderson will never know his career has been redirected by a gentle wave from a SIU tentacle. 'I will enjoy that your hotel is so quiet.'

'So do I, Mr Corelli, so do I. But I *must* be honest and explain that at *this* moment in time all my *other* guests are out at work, and Margy, my cook, has not yet arrived to prepare this evening's dinner. Now to *business*, Mr Corelli. Thank you for the cheque with your letter: unexpected but *helpful*. It covers more than a month, of *course*. Now, meals are breakfast and dinner. No midday except Sunday when I offer a nice salad to anyone who *signs* the list for it. I also ask you to sign if you require Saturday and/or Sunday night dinner. Margy does *all* dinners

150

except weekends so I fill in there. Breakfast 7.30 to 8.30, even on Sundays. Dinner is always seven *prompt*. You will change your bed linen on Tuesdays putting your bottom sheet and *one* pillow case in the linen bag, which I leave on the *landing* Tuesday morning. Your top sheet then becomes *bottom*, and fresh linen will be placed on your bed by *me*, and I clean your room the *same* day. You are free to make your own arrangements about personal laundry but I *recommend* the same company as I use for bed clothes. I always *insist* that — '

As her voice hops and skips across the dusty arable of her trade, Corelli floats his mind away. Despite her various regulations life here will be a kind of heaven compared with the dump he was in before the sorting of Mundam and Croucher. Nor will she inhibit — but that must wait. That harsh, clanging voice has plunged into a questioning tone.

'No, I have no questions, Mrs Gridley. I will go to my room for a few minutes and then go into the town. Thank you for tea and cakes.'

Her practised winsome smile would have slipped had she followed him upstairs. After softly tapping on the doors he eases his way past the locks into each bedroom in turn. All are en suite: only his room is not. 'Lucky bloody Frimmer,' he thinks, acknowledging again the implied vulnerability of his situation. He checks through the personal possessions of each of his fellow-guests, and also the locations of every lighting and power point in each room. Initially, as at any murder scene, he knows people only through their possessions and locations.

Back in his own room he finishes unpacking and discovers his mobile phone, appropriately scarred but new to him. He recognizes the strangeness of his own reaction: despite a unique number that will bring immediate contact with Frimmer it represents a freedom rather than entrapment by SIU. He can telephone anybody at all. But so what? Who is anybody? And what would he say? The switch from exhilaration to depression is instant, leaving him momentarily gripped by a kind of black paralysis, like a caver who suddenly realizes he cannot crawl to the exit as rapidly as the flash flood overhauling him. The time it takes to hide his gun where Mrs Gridley will never find it is just long enough for him to re-establish equilibrium. Feelings akin to suffocation propel him from his room.

Anyone following him into town might have been puzzled by Corelli's behaviour; by his eccentric choice of route, his apparent self-satisfied inspection in shop windows. But no one follows — not now. Then he finds his way to the library without having to ask directions; the town map committed to memory. He applies for a reader's ticket. His address at The Larches plus a faked reference on behalf of J. Corelli, confirm his suitability. He chooses several books. After this purposeful activity he behaves like a clockwork toy in need of rewinding, stuttering through the town, not window gazing but corner loitering. At each corner where he stops, he leans against a wall and rifles through the pages of one of his library books. Either the man likes standing in the sun or he wants to be seen. Then his behaviour changes.

He visits the two largest stores in Browcaister but buys nothing; appears more interested in the people than the merchandise. He soon identifies the store detectives; to him they are as conspicuous as Mrs Gridley's formation of diving ducks — and about as lively. Then Corelli returns to the first store visited. This detective is just a little keener, fractionally more awake than his fellow worker along the street. Corelli watches him pounce on a tired, middle-aged housewife who has forgotten to pay for a pair of gloves, while two girls walk out of the store wearing stolen skirts under their school uniform topcoats.

Corelli walks back to The Larches, checks that if necessary he can enter the building without using Mrs Gridley's keys, climbs silently to his room to avoid another assault of verbal emphasis. He pulls back the net curtains, opens both windows and leaves his bedroom door open, allowing a through draft to disperse the heat that has built up under the sloping roof. Knowing temporary freedom from wariness, he takes off his shoes and jacket, stretches out on the bed. At the moment there is no one in the house who might wish him dead.

12

'I'll introduce you to my other guests, Mr Corelli,' says Mrs Gridley, from the bottom of the stairs where she has just caressed a small copper gong. Her confident smile reflects not only proprietorship in action but also that she is now wearing her best blue dress. She walks ahead of him into the dining-room; the length of the dress makes her legs seem even shorter but he won't tell.

'Good evening, *everyone*,' she says, too loudly for the size of the room. 'I am *pleased* to introduce you to our new *resident*, Mr Corelli. Ms Sykes — Mr Corelli. Mr Corelli — Ms Sykes.' He receives a shy almost furtive glance out of a fat face. No flabby hand is offered. He feels he already knows of her from her room: Bedroom 1 at the front of the house with the sad intimacies it has held secret until his arrival.

'Mr Hammond — Mr Corelli. Mr Corelli — Mr Hammond.' Mr Hammond of Bedroom 2 offers a podgy unsteady hand, welcomes Corelli as 'old boy'. 'Mr Robinson — Mr Corelli. Mr Corelli — Mr Robinson.' No words, only the limp hand tentatively offered. Already established as one of life's victims, it is inescapable that having Bedroom 3 next door to Corelli guarantees future misery.

Corelli makes his way to the unoccupied table numbered with a polished brass 4. It stands in the front window bay in clear view from the front garden and, more worryingly, from the street. Reminded of the open view across flowerbeds at The House and the tactical reason for that, he feels a chill at the back of his neck as he takes his seat. He is also somewhat disoriented by the room itself. Everything that can be fashioned from pine is; even the chimney breast is pine-clad.

His pine table faces the centre of the room like all the others, and bears a white rectangular cloth laid diagonally so that the pine corners remain exposed. His white napkin is in a pine ring; the cruet set is pine, as is the place mat. He touches the rosebud in the pottery vase to confirm it is real and not wood-carved. A second pleasant surprise is the wine list, which is short but includes reasonably priced old friends.

There is tomato soup, lamb chops with new potatoes and cabbage, apple pie and custard, coffee. There is no choice except with or without custard, but the food is excellent; nothing from a tin, freshly cooked and served hot. Mrs Gridley is a smoothly efficient waitress despite an inclination to chat. Corelli fantasizes about Margy, the cook who works in the deep recesses of The Larches beyond Mrs Gridley's 'den'. From SIU files he knows she is a young and slender single woman, generally too shy to emerge from behind the barricades of Mrs Gridley's quarters; but possibly the only person under this roof who does not defer to Mrs Gridley. Mr Hammond certainly defers, almost grovels when she places wine bottle and glass on his table; she refuses his offer to share in a manner reminiscent of the old Queen.

The four of them eating, Corelli watchful in his window seat. He sees the other three as the stuff of residential hotel life. Ms Sykes — Evelyn — is fortyish in years, hip and bust. (Sexy, too-tight underwear now abandoned in her right-hand top drawer; in the left are more comfortable garments, and her wardrobe hangs drab with grey and beige.) Now she dresses to conceal. Moon-faced, slow eating, her features pucker slightly over her book like a small child encountering multisyllable words; an impression she is never far from tears; probably known to colleagues at the library as 'Poor Evelyn'. Few friends. There are some letters in her drawer but they are mostly from hurt, bewildered and lonely

Mummy, with whom she spends only one weekend every two months. Now, Evelyn lives in the world of romantic novels. (Her cupboard is jammed with such books unofficially borrowed from her work.) Life was not always so. Her share of ordinary human passions may have been banal but the residual bitterness is sharp enough. (In her hollow-rattling jewel box are two engagement rings.) At this precise moment between apple pie with custard and the excellent coffee, she is not turning the pages of her book. She is reconstructing her life to accommodate this new man with his superb physique and Italian name. A new face promises not excitement but threat — until it can be seen to resemble or clearly contrast with other more familiar faces. But the bland unsalted porridge of her existence cannot easily absorb this stranger, foreign and darkly gypsy-like. She frowns. Gypsy is a category outside her experience and therefore unacceptable. Mr Corelli will remain merely a name until something in his behaviour can be recognized as familiar.

Albert Hammond is a fifty-year-old over-weight dinosaur who has waded from a swamp where education was minimal, wife-beating manly, and scattered bastards confirmed virility. The harsh light of today is blinding: rebellious women — worse still, clever women, contemptuous children, unsympathetic lawyers. (A drawer full of solicitors' letters all confirming hopelessness.) Court orders have emasculated him. He cannot afford a mortgage, and The Larches is only possible because much of the cost is defrayed as work expenses — but presumably not the wine. The sloping forehead and bald dome overlay a mind hopelessly bemused by his battle to exist in the new era. Much of his bemusement has to do with the veins broken in his nose, the unsteadiness of his stubby fingers. (In a bottom drawer the empty bottles lie waiting their turn to be smuggled away.) And he has lost the salesman's consolation of believing his own sales talk. He knows himself a hewer of wood in a plastic age.

Frederick Robinson is a highly qualified engineer. (A folder in his top drawer is crisp with degress and certificates.) His life, sixty aching years, is a wail of undeserved misfortune. Ignoring career prospects he had stayed in the same job while nursing his widowed, bullying mother. After her death it was discovered debts far exceeded assets. The family home had to go. (He also has a collection of solicitors' letters.) Frederick had moved to a bedsitter, saved hard, paid off the remaining debts. Then he became ill and lost his job. A pattern formed, locked round him: new job in the declining world of manufacturing, victim of the cruelty of last in first out, illness, fight back, new job, another redundancy. Redundancy payments always less than he had fantasized. (Carbon copies of all his querulous letters somehow more demeaning than Albert's collection of soft porn magazines.)

Now, reduced to a packer but having worked steadily for twenty months, he has discovered an eczema growing on his hands. His toilet bag is full of proprietary treatments. Because he works in a food factory he dare not go to a doctor. This latest threat and his history of decline, if not already known to Corelli, might be inferred from Frederick's appearance. He is tall, gangling, concave-chested, thin-limbed, slack-jawed; most distressing are the rheumy eyes with their permanent hint of tearfulness. The firm line of the hooked nose is dissipated by the jungley tufts in each nostril; the hairs, like all his hairs, white for thirty years. And with the fingers of one hand he picks at the flakes of skin between the fingers of the other. Frederick Robinson: victim. A new misfortune awaits for no other reason than being the occupant of Bedroom 3.

Corelli sees these three plus Mrs Gridley as his close companions during his final days.

(Only his killer might live closer in those catastrophic last moments.) None of them would have been his choice but the idea of their companionship as he moves towards death unexpectedly raises in him a feeling close to affection. Judged by the standards of his recent experiences, they are admirable people: fighters in their own limited way. They have kept themselves above and clear of the world he had inhabited in that sordid boarding house while working for Billy Mundam. They belong to a dwindling disadvantaged stratum of society still clinging to fading hopes of becoming established middle class. A policeman for ten years, he formulates such opinions without recourse to sentimentality. He smiles into the remnants of his apple pie and custard: he is only thirty, earns vastly more than any of his fellow residents, but is the one least likely to celebrate next Christmas.

Corelli becomes a genial companion, stalking like a smiling tiger. Mrs Gridley has a previous engagement, Ms Sykes and Mr Robinson decline for unspecified reasons, but Mr Hammond is delighted to be invited out for a drink. (What else is there for him to do when too tired to be excited by photographs of pubic hair?) By 10.30 p.m. in the Rose and Crown, Albert and Jake are chums. Corelli, quite enjoying Albert, is relieved Frederick Robinson will be the target.

Next evening, Corelli continues to charm. He asks how their day went, leads each of them into private exchanges in the hall or lounge or TV room. Ms Sykes, without understanding why, explains she is not to be found in the town centre library when Corelli visits because she works in a small branch out in the country. Mr Robinson suddenly discovers he has admitted to Wednesday afternoons off, and to his preference for Frederick rather than Fred. Albert Hammond foresees more jolly evenings ahead, and Mrs Gridley is quite 'topsy-turvy' having discovered roses from the new guest placed, so discreetly, on the table in her den. She decides she has *selected a gentleman* to live *with* her. She is charmed by the gentleman and the 'with'.

At the start of his first weekend at The Larches, he realizes he is the only resident who has signed for Saturday evening dinner. A quiet evening with his library books will be pleasant. He has not added Mrs Gridley into the equation. He arrives at the bottom of the stairs just as the gong shimmers with its final note. Mrs Gridley awaits; points out the oddity of them eating in separate rooms. He accepts her suggestion they dine together in her den, is pleasantly surprised by the outcome.

She, smelling sweetly of lavender-water, wearing a dress he has not seen before, serves a meal as good as Margy could have managed, and the bottle of wine is better than any on the dining-room wine list. He is secretly amused at the possibility he is ensnared by a different kind of stalker. As the wine flows they become united in the positive desire to charm the other. By the time he is ready to ask a favour of her she is bright red with generosity and good-heartedness, the best evening headscarf discarded, her perm shaken into unusual suppleness. His wish to put a car in her car park at the back of the house is received and agreed with an eroticism both beguiling and pathetic. (Even Frimmer, who has decided possession of a 'company' car now fits with the Corelli persona, without too much contradicting his former poverty, might have been surprised by the air of complicity that now links his man with the proprietor of The Larches.)

Mrs Gridley closes this delightful episode by producing an excellent brandy to accompany the coffee, and on departing, Corelli bows charmingly over her offered hand, brushes it so lightly with his lips. She reciprocates with the information that her first name is Olive. (Later he will be amused to discover the wine charged to *his* account.) He leaves for a late evening stroll while she sits befuddled beside the brandy bottle. They both know she has never had a guest like him, but only he has an intimation of how much grief might erupt from his residency.

Returning to the hotel, he pauses with his hand on the gate, stares at the solid frontage of the Edwardian villa on which Mrs Gridley will not permit any vulgar window card announcing the satisfying lack of vacancies. The street lighting, falling across the frontage at an angle, casts an odd pattern of shadows which create a misleading appearance of structural lopsidedness in the bay windows. He is beset by a sudden pang of melancholy as if the visual distortion mirrors an internal state. The pang, like an alarming glitch in his heart rhythm, jerks him back into homesickness, the desire to be once more surrounded by his possessions, particularly the books and pictures, and with that ever-interesting view across Hyde Park. Everyone at The Larches is hiding behind a ramshackle persona but himself most of all, as if he personifies the Gridley house but with all the windows clumsily boarded over, the doors padlocked by bailiffs and a roof sagging with its unsupported weight.

Sunday is another fine day and he drives his newly acquired car out into the countryside, almost indifferent to whether or not his actions might frustrate a stalker. In the evening the meal is served in the dining-room because Evelyn and Albert are both back from undisclosed travels. He knows the surveillance teams will inform him where they went but he presents an innocent interest in their weekend away. Evelyn has been to stay with Mummy, Albert to visit an 'old friend'. The latter clearly wishes to imply salaciousness but Corelli does not rise to that bait. Instead he enjoys the slight touch of irascibility expressed by Mrs Gridley: a shortness of manner accompanied by undue banging of plates and rattling of cutlery. He is content to speculate that her manner may reflect resentment that other guests have interposed between her and himself this evening. At the end of the meal he and Albert are left together, still sitting in the dining-room. For Albert this is the chance to express some hard conclusions about 'Shifty Sykes' and 'Gormless Gridley'. The astounding inappropriateness of his adjectives confirms what Corelli already suspects: the man has a very limited experience out of which to speak of women, not that this deters him from extrapolating his faulty perceptions on to the whole female population. Amused and irritated, Corelli bids him goodnight and retires to the more demanding company of a Graham Greene novel. Arrived in his room, he sits at the desk and reflects on the strangeness of his present lifestyle.

Strangeness takes possession of the new week, beginning on Monday morning as he walks briskly towards the gym where he intends to sign on. A young police constable, patrolling with that leisurely heaviness so soon acquired in the job, recognizes Corelli from the photograph he was shown a week ago. Remembering his instructions, he reaches for his mobile but allows Corelli to pass. Rounding the next corner, Corelli also uses his mobile, describes himself 'clocked' to the duty officer, Jim Douglas.

'Trouble ye not,' says Douglas. 'Mr Frimmer's sharp teeth are well known enough in Browcaister. Expect them to recheck in the next few minutes but there'll be no direct approach.' Douglas is right. A patrol car slides past at walking pace and Corelli is re-viewed. The episode leaves him irritated with himself; he would prefer his colleagues not to know of his nervy state. In the gym he is ferocious.

Enmeshed in his own secrets, his hyped-up state of mind is such he cannot permit anyone, not even Mrs Gridley, to have a secret of her own. On Wednesday afternoons she slips away from the hotel for the afternoon, and the timing of her departure coincides with Corelli's absence. He is in the library. Henderson confirms that the lady goes to bingo on that afternoon, and her secrecy about that is nothing more troubling than snobbery that she is addicted to 'a working-class activity'. Neither Henderson nor anyone else in SIU sees this information as particularly significant. For Corelli it is just as important as the fact, soon wheedled out of Mrs Gridley, that the spare downstairs bedroom is held in reserve either for any former guest passing through Browcaister, or for Margy if she feels too tired to drive herself home to her empty cottage after preparing the evening meal; or on a night when 'we put on a special event', as Mrs Gridley coyly remarks. That she is prepared to hold a room in reserve hints at the size of her inheritance from Mr Gridley.

By Thursday morning, the start of his second week in Browcaister, Corelli feels himself becoming familiar with the town as well as with The Larches. Lunchtime at The Eagle has become a pleasant ritual during which he has come to recognize another's ritualistic behaviour; the more so on Thursday when a sudden heavy shower drives him from the riverside garden and back into the bar. She is young, in her mid-twenties, and plies her trade with a smooth confidence that amuses him. It also suggests that she is picking up regular clients, and that the manager gets a bung. The daily procedure is unvaried: perched on a bar stool by noon, the polite acceptance of the first offer of a drink, a brief conversation and she and client depart. Neither the first or second of the lunchtime clients appears offended by the pace of her trade. Corelli calculates that she is certainly earning more than he is — even with his acting rank of DI. He is aware of the speculative way she lets her eyes slide over him, is amused at his own discomfort that today he is revealingly dressed in wet T-shirt and jeans. Perhaps that explains what follows.

Abandoning her usual pattern, she wanders across the bar and sits at his table. He allows the grin on his face to betray his perception of her. To his astonishment, she blushes slightly. Until now he has not encountered a modest tart. The stereotypical conversation lurches into motion: she is Una, he is Jake, and yes he will buy her a drink. It is sufficient for her to raise an eyebrow at the man behind the bar. The drink is brought and paid for; she sips, eyeing him over the rim of the glass.

He is aware that he is a much more attractive proposition than most of her sag-belly clients, but wonders if she has either sniffed out his occupation or has some other secret reason for her hesitation: perhaps the embarrassment of acknowledging to herself that he does not look like the kind of man who would ever need her services. She sits straight-backed in her chair, slender with a narrow face, long nose, grey eyes, blonde hair worn very short. She wears no jewellery but her pale green summer dress is expensive, as are her shoes and the small shoulder bag now cast casually on to the chair next to her. Apart from a light touch of lipstick she wears no make-up. Smitten by a sense of something like comradeship with a fellow actor, he is impelled into frankness.

'You are very attractive, Una, but I never pay.'

'Guess you don't need to.' She traces the edge of the table with her forefinger. Then. 'How about something a bit special? But I'd have to clear it with my partner first.'

In danger of becoming overwhelmed with information both specific and implied, he selects the obvious implication of, 'partner'.

'No, silly. I mean Kathy. We live together but we're not dykes. No, business partners. I work The Eagle and some other pubs; she covers the two hotels at the edge of town. You know?'

'I see — or think I do.' Corelli is suddenly overtaken, not so much by lust as by a kind of lassitude; a feeling of pleasurable irresponsibility. She can lead as she likes and he will follow. The titillation is not just sexual. There is a frisson of pleasure in reflecting on Frimmer's response when he finds out. (He wastes no thought on 'if he finds out'.) But as Corelli he is absolutely alibied: all he has to say is that he is in role. He enjoys the fantasy of Frimmer roaring uselessly down the telephone. Then both he and Una are aware of a heavyweight leaning against the bar and staring morosely in their direction. 'Business?' says Corelli.

''Fraid so. Will you be here tomorrow, Jake?'

'Yeah. But if it's fine I'll be in the garden.'

She takes up her bag but leaves the half-empty glass on the table. Her client is soon mollified, buys drinks and, a few minutes later, trots docile at her heels. Corelli is left to examine his feelings as he carves his way into the pub lunch. He enjoys an internal entertainment comparing Una with the lady inhabitants of The Larches. Yet again he is stretching between very different worlds; in this case the tension not that severe. So he wonders why he feels a kind of faint alarm; an alarm that seems to imply something greater than his habitual iconoclastic disposition to press against boundaries. What he might be about to dive into is not so very threatening. Is it?

PART FOUR

There are some characters in this world who are marked down for destruction, and to these no amount of rational argument can appeal.

Lawrence Durrell

Justine
Published by Faber and Faber

★ ★ ★

Fate is as liquid and elusive a word as love.

Liz Greene

The Astrology of Fate
Published by George Allen and Unwin

13

I had always been aware of the fall of the cards, of gravity tugging impartially at Queen of Spades, Ace of Hearts; cards fluttering like slow, sorrowful birds whose delayed migration presaged their deaths. As I watched the tumbling cards I fell into the same trap as every gambler, believing that watching guarantees control. Perhaps that was also Frimmer's mistake. And some cards bore strange symbols: a woodlouse struggling to surmount an obstacle, a bright yellow ball lying in a gutter.

I had not fully understood the power of those two particular images — toppling woodlouse and abandoned yellow ball — and might not live long enough to do so. But they stood sentinel in my memory stream signposting the route to my death, and confirming the deaths of others: Pearson, Molly Poling, Peter Abercrombie, possibly fourteen other rapists, and certainly that of the real Jake Corelli, supposedly protected in a safe house. The yellow ball signposted his fate as clearly as mine.

These memories and reflections were made

the more powerful by the light of my own fear which shone on them like a spotlight searching for the points of greatest pain. I attempted feeble reassurance by reiterating that I had not previously waited passively for an attempt on my life, and by a highly successful serial killer. As a detective I'd had my share of violent attacks, usually inflicted by persons far more frightened than me, but I had never been remotely passive in *those* situations. (The most frequent criticism levelled by senior officers had been that my responses were inappropriately forceful!)

The clearest indicator of my present condition was that my mind no longer drew any lasting benefit from my bodily states of high-level fitness and athletic sexual performance. That connection now resembled an electric cable through which virtually no current flowed despite my attempts to overwind the generative power of body. I suspected that one of my unconscious reasons for setting up a sexual alliance with Una and Kathy was the hope that demanding and enjoyable sex would distract or heal my mind. It did neither.

The Larches meanwhile was becoming a place in which I was skulking. Frimmer's increasingly querulous phone calls as to why I was spending so much time off the streets illuminated my behaviour without changing it. I did not deny the benefits of staying with Olive Gridley: her large breakfasts, Margy's splendid dinners, the quiet of my own room where I could read undisturbed, the casual friendliness of the other residents, and of Olive herself. Even Evelyn Sykes now talked with me over evening coffee or when we chose to watch the same TV programme. But within these contacts I had to check my fantasizing mind as it roamed through scenarios of my corpse discovered by Olive Gridley or one of her residents, or even that one of them might die with me.

I was also troubled by the fate prepared for Frederick Robinson. My formerly cavalier attitude to that had been undermined both by getting to know him, and by my fragmenting hold on my own role. I took this up with Frimmer, which further damaged our already dysfunctioning relationship. As our phone connection was made I heard the familiar soft click confirming Henderson or Thomas was also listening in. Instead of making me more circumspect, it fired up a bloody-minded recklessness. Frimmer was his usual unpleasant self.

'What happens to Robinson afterwards is no concern of yours!' I jerked my mobile further away from my ear.

'Sorry, sir. I think it is. I also think my concern is making me operationally less effective.' I knew *that* would get to the bugger.

'For fuck's sake, don't go sloppy compassionate on this! *And* you'll have enough to worry about the moment he leaves.'

'OK, sir. Hear this. I want the man to be found a better paid job, to get medical attention for his skin condition and to be moved to lodgings as good as and no more expensive than The Larches.'

'Going to do that anyway — so no sweat.' But I was unsurprised that Frimmer bit back the next day.

'I understand you've taken to visiting ladies of the night?' I swear I heard his crumbling teeth grind together.

'Yes, sir. But only during the day,' I said pertly. I pulled my mobile away from my ear while he did his roaring number. I was lying in the sun on the river bank and childishly 'aimed' my mobile at a group of ducks. I doubt they heard anything but I laughed aloud when they did a web-footed scuttle away from the bank. I wondered if Frimmer heard my laughter. Eventually, he quietened, perhaps because of lack of breath.

'Listen to me, sir. I chose them but all I'm doing is staying in role as Corelli. I'm confident that's what you want.' Frimmer's desperation was reflected in the feebleness of his reply.

'No way are they legitimate expenditure. If you need to use a couple of brasses, you fucking well pay.'

'Not to worry, sir. No payment is involved. It's called the pleasure principle.' I so much enjoyed switching off, enjoyed recalling previous comments he had chosen to make about my relationships with women. I wished that sense of enjoyment and of being in charge could have lasted for longer than it took me to finish my walk beside the eddying river. What Henderson and Thomas made of all this brouhaha I had no idea. There was no opportunity for a chat, their brief being to lie well back from me except when given a contrary order. I supposed that any sympathy they felt would be proportional to the level of stress they believed I was enduring. But maybe everything was much simpler for them: simpler not to care too much, not to think.

Back in my room I stared into my reflection in the mirror. It still didn't look that much like Jake Corelli but that didn't trouble me. (Even less did the dark reflection hint at any connection with that seedy, down-at-heel, long-haired blonded Arthur

Snell.) Much more troubling was that the reflection did not accurately mirror me, Acting Detective Inspector Jack Bull of the SIU, and an idiot part of me wanted to know where I had gone. The truth was my weird behaviour was troubling me as much as Frimmer. I felt a sharp pain in my right hand, looked down and saw that my hands were tightly locked together, the skin whitening in the knuckles, reddening in the fingers. I acknowledged one of the few certainties left to me about Jack Bull: he was not praying.

That afternoon was one spent with Una and Kathy, for what the three of us laughingly referred to as afternoon tea. I never knew what Una had said to persuade Kathy about those afternoons but the outcome was delight filled. Once they had gasped over my burn scars they had, in every sense, embraced me and my body; the scars always softly touched. We were an easy threesome together, able to speak our wants and our fantasies uninhibitedly and enjoying both our mutual and differing responses. Like so many men, I had dreamed of a threesome and now I had it with a slender, long-faced blonde, Una, and a buxom, well rounded redhead, Kathy. The latter's buxomness would become stoutness but that would happen long after I was gone from there.

Our athleticism I certainly enjoyed. One of their favourites was the three-decker sandwich with me as the top slice; mine was the see-saw in which they both rode me at the same time while facing and caressing each other. Just as delightful was a shared sense of playfulness which spilled out and beyond the confines of bed; a playfulness in which I almost felt myself to be me again. So we shared the shower, really did have afternoon tea.

I knew that if I ever tried 'explaining them', or indeed us, I'd get a very poor reception. What made my viewpoint even less acceptable to most people was that I saw myself as such a fortunate man. Once Kathy had met me and the three of us had shared two Tuesday afternoons, they then proposed we meet Thursday afternoons as well. I wasn't silly enough to discount the advantages I had: that, unlike most punters, I was a fit and skilled enthusiast who personified some kind of 'otherness' for them.

At first it was difficult for me to accept their complete lack of sentimentality in all this, so firmly rooted it prevented me from sliding down that road. And that was the nub. I wanted to be sentimental, to pretend something other than the earthy reality of our liaison. However much they cared for me, enjoyed me, I was kept firmly in my place as *they* defined it. It was confirmed by our shared unspoken assumption that safe sex was obligatory, by them never allowing me to overstay my welcome, and by me not attempting to. We accepted their working evenings could not be curtailed, just as we accepted no more than a brief glance between us if we passed in the street. And most strongly adhered to: I was *never* invited to spend any other time with them. Our relationship was summed up by the least articulate of the three of us: Una.

'You know, Jake, most of what we do together — what we do with you — neither of us does with our punters.' The shyness with which she spoke made the implied compliment that bit warmer. Was I right to transcribe her words to mean something about our mutual generosity? There was also the comical possibility I had had a more varied experience of sex than they. My one regret was that she and Kathy knew me only as Jake Corelli.

In contrast, the connections at The Larches were held rigidly in a kind of impoverished formality. Conversations there had the taint of failure rather than success: Evelyn's 'confession' that she was obliged to live at The Larches waiting for Mummy to die so she could inherit the family home — the bitterest note was her complaint about her family's longevity; Albert's depression centred on the arrival in the marketplace of cheaper but superior furnishing fabrics to those in his samples; Frederick's tired and tiring belief that all his 'bad luck' must mean he was overdue for a really big break. (My God — if only he had known!)

Bolstered by a combination of property rights and snobbery, Olive Gridley largely escaped the odour of negativity which tainted her guests, but I perceived her rigidly respectable life as a kind of capitulation when compared with that of Una and Kathy — the difference between a country cleric and missionaries to the Amazon Indians. I chuckled a good deal over that ridiculous analogy. A more interesting comparison might have been between having sex with Una and with Olive, but I was never sufficiently crazy to check that out.

One comparison available was that between our conversations. With Olive, superficial observance of all proprieties gave a kind of salaciousness to our talk: that 'nudge-nudge, wink-wink' so characteristic of middle England, compliments always tainted by flirtatious, feeble double entrendres. With Una and Kathy our sexual frankness and explicitness made all that redundant. Yet it was those triangular conversations that caused me the greater pain because it was there, where I most wished to be me, that I had to deny my own identity as carefully as I did at The Larches.

So, in living Jake Corelli's daily life, I oscillated between two worlds which were like two contrasting oceans, similar only in the salt of their common humanity. The sea creatures in the two could not have been more different: the exotic, sinuous, plunging, colourful life in the one, the grey-tinted, slow-swimming, sluggish, shallow water creatures in the other.

And Jack Bull? He was like some kind of narrow linking canal between them, alternating in direction of flow with every change in the tide: moon-dominated. That illusion of reciprocal balancing free flow helped him ignore the rigidity of the enclosing banks: duty on the right and madness on the left. Part of the problem was that he and Corelli, not always in unison, were forever eroding and abrading both banks, and that there was no respite for me, Jack Bull, to recollect and regather himself in all this. I was left with only the certainty that Jack Bull was failing to hold all the pieces together.

14

'Not sure I can go on with this, sir. I'm struggling to hold my act together.' I held my mobile steady with both hands but that did nothing to reduce the trembling in the rest of me.

'OK. Tomorrow, Tuesday p.m. Here's how you do it.'

'Not tomorrow afternoon. Got an appointment.'

'Those fucking women. Give 'em a miss. That's an order.'

'No chance. It has to be tomorrow morning early.' In the moment it took him to get furious with me, I had time to be amazed he had not questioned my first statement. Had the bastard been expecting me to fall apart? But I was too shaky and he too concerned for a row to develop further.

Tuesday 09.30. I sat in the tiny partitioned room in the blue truck. The foldaway desk flap under the frosted window was set up and carried a box of paper tissues and the doctor's black bag. And it was the inconveniently fat doctor who was most responsible for our crushed discomfort. Frimmer had to growl at me, of course, couldn't help himself, but my shaky state was obvious enough and he was also somewhat constrained by the doctor's presence. Frimmer and I knew which of us had most at risk in terms of career. I only had my life to lose, but if he could get me to lose it at the right time and place he would be in a clover field of praise and vastly increased financial backing; not to mention the Honours List where I would not even be named posthumously.

The doctor was a stout, balding man with dark, angry eyes, who wore his shiny pinstripe with all three buttons done up across his chest and belly as if that would protect him from infectious patients. I doubted he would catch anything from me. I was examined with a brusqueness that was almost offensive; a butcher checking out a slab of meat past its sell-by date.

'Put your shirt back on,' he said contemptuously, bundling his stethoscope back into his bulging bag. To Frimmer he said: 'Whatever this man's into get him out now — and I mean right now.' Tightly buttoned suit confronted a suit much slept in. There was a shocked pause which Frimmer and I both used to readjust our faces — but from very different expressions.

'No can do, Doc. Keeping him in the firing

line is getting more pressing, not less. After all this time.' Frimmer gnawed at a knuckle.

'He's right, Doc. That's the one option we don't have,' I said. In the past agreeing with Frimmer would have made me smile.

'What's the point of calling me in if neither of you will listen? I'll spell it out, gentlemen. Ready? Watch my lips. This man is so stressed he's a step away from requiring residential psychiatric care.' I didn't know what that did to Frimmer but it silenced me.

'Are you saying there's nothing you can do to keep him going, Doc?'

'No, I'm not saying *that*! I could prescribe a range of things, but not if I'm to consider the consequences. 'Keeping him in the firing line', as you put it, may well lead to complete collapse.'

'Right, sir,' I said to Frimmer. 'A few rest days back at The House?'

'Sorry, Jake — er, Jack. With the luck we've been having in the last nine months that'd be the crucial period when our killers planned to take you out. You didn't hear that last bit, Doc.'

'Course not. I can be as deaf as you two.' He fingered the buttons on his jacket as if doing so might release some strong internal pressure. 'But I hear he spent some time at The House. A rest, was it?'

'Not exactly,' I said, suddenly irritated, 'more a strategic withdrawal. I needed to be out of circulation for a short period.'

'Pity you didn't consult me about *that*. Suddenly taking the pressure off and then slamming it back on may partly explain your present parlous condition.' There was an uncomfortable pause while he stared angrily into the space between me and Frimmer. 'Right then. So what's it to be?'

Frimmer didn't answer him directly. 'You stay where you are,' he said to me. 'The doctor's coming outside so I can explain a thing or two to both him and Henderson at the same time.'

I might have protested but as they edged out of the tiny room, Mr Stone came in. He bade me good morning then stood looking down at me with his back against the wall, hand and steel hand hanging at his sides. The combination of his immaculate appearance and hawkish stare had the faintest suggestion of an undertaker about it. He was certainly measuring me for something. He crossed his arms so that the stainless-steel hand hook nestled almost out of sight behind the other elbow.

'Bull, there's an encouraging development from our reresearching old cases. We've turned up some telephone attempts by

188

someone to get information on prison discharge dates from prison officers, social workers, rehab, etc. But I hear you're finding this operation a bit much.'

'Just a bit. Doctor any good, sir?'

'Yes. Don't be deceived by his manner. *And* he's one of the SIU medics. Knows the score.'

'What if you chose the wrong man for this work, sir? I'm tough enough to be a tethered goat but not to cope with the women.'

Then Stone made a gesture that really broke me up. He pushed the box of paper tissues across the desk towards me *but he did that with his immaculate shining steel hand.* Why that upset me so much I didn't fully understand. Neither of us spoke again. When Frimmer and the doctor came back, Stone silently edged his way out.

The doctor stared at me. 'Seems you're caught up in a grim case.'

'Trouble is, Doc, distancing myself from these tragic women by labelling them 'cases' isn't working like it used to.'

'I'd've thought the main stress would arise from being hunted.'

'Not so.'

He avoided my eyes, then put two phials of pills on the desk. 'Now get this right, my lad. The green ones'll calm you without disabling.

If you had to you could still handle firearms. But these orange beasts — ' He rapped the second phial on the desk ' — they'll wipe you out. One before bed and don't expect to hear the dawn chorus. Set your alarm clock if you need breakfast otherwise you're on for an early lunch. You follow me?'

'Yes, Doc. I'll be safe enough. Got a wooden wedge for the door, and both windows have fitted locks.'

Something stronger than professional concern spread across his face, sliding down into the fat creases, rising up over the bulges. His eyes were suddenly even darker. 'Well, let's hope and pray you're not meant to die in a night-time fire. You'll be deaf to fire alarms, sirens and the crackling of flames.' He turned on Frimmer and barked at him. 'And my notes'll show I advised against this. Good day to both of you.' He closed his bag with a vicious snap, almost pushing his belly into Frimmer's as he squeezed out of the room. As the door slammed, Frimmer made an uncharacteristic gesture of helplessness, almost Yiddish.

'Er — well,' he said, as if lost for words, a condition so rare I wondered if he'd been sucking on one of my triangular orange sweeties. 'A good man, our doc.' Another awkward pause as if he had something else to say but our circumstances prevented him. Then, 'Right, Bull, I've called in the make-up man. Get you checked over before you leave us.' I would have preferred a different wording.

After the make-up expert had twittered around my hair and given me some more of the chemical for emphasizing the pouches under my eyes, I followed Henderson out of the blue truck and back to our cars. He was to lead me, the sick colleague, back to Browcaister just as he had led me to the SIU truck. We exited the truck to a murmured chorus of 'good luck' from men too embarrassed to look away from the TV monitors.

'Not a heartfelt farewell,' said Henderson, maliciously.

'Doubt they'll collect for a wreath either,' I said, walking across to my car, the medicine phials and makeup bottle clicking against each other in my pocket. Perhaps not *exactly* like a suicide bomber.

Four hours and one calming green pill later, I was lying with Una and Kathy in a threesome spoons; Una with her back into my lap and I with mine into Kathy's. It was one of those honey-drenched post-coital extended lovings when no one's arm or shoulder is uncomfortable, no one has a restless leg or suddenly needs the loo. One of us sighed with pleasure, and it passed through the three of us like another caress. A sort of kindness. The partly drawn curtains wafted slightly in the slow-stirring sun-baked air, carrying in fragments of sound from someone's TV: the steely pinging of rackets, the swelling murmur of the crowd. 'Today is Ladies' Day at Wimbledon,' someone said. 'Mixed doubles here,' I murmured. The faint chuckle from Una passed through her back and buttocks into my chest and lap, through to my spine and exited into the warm roundness that was all of Kathy. For the briefest moment I could delude myself I needed no medication; perhaps that I needed nothing.

A summer-drenched time later, the discreet summons of their blanket-wrapped alarm clock eased us apart, edged us towards showering, late afternoon tea and the affectionate farewells that bridged the days apart: each to our own separate sorrows of working and waiting. We coped with that by a kind of dismissive cheerfulness and never talking about it.

Back at the flat earth of The Larches, I went to my room, pushed the medicines to the back of the desk drawer, and lay on the bed with the curtains open. The next thing I knew was the dinner gong vibrating at what felt like the same frequency as my body. I drifted through the evening: the good meal, social chat, a trip to the pub with Albert. A part of my mind wanted to debate my condition as being either post-coital relaxation or the result of green pills. I dismissed that nonsense by speculating what the effects of the first orange 'bomb' might be. But Frimmer got to me again before I could find out.

'We could be nearly there, Jake. But there's chance to speed things up, get a bit more focus without arousing suspicion. We've talked often enough about the dangers of blowing the operation by putting you too obviously in the frame, but Stone's come up with a possibility we might risk using now time has passed.'

'Yes, sir?' The assumed meekness of my manner pushed me towards giggling. If Frimmer caught a whisper of my behaviour I assumed he must have attributed it to my medication, decided not to make it an issue. I wasn't the only one in SIU hanging on by his fingertips.

'You know there's an archaeological dig going on at the site of Browcaister's Roman fort?'

'Yes. It's just on the edge of town, overlooks the river.'

'Right. You be there Friday morning, 10.00 hours, dressed conspicuous for black and white photos. We've got to the stage where we do need your photo in the local press — and apparently accidentally. We've fitted it up that the cameraman will be ours. He'll be tracking you round the site. I can persuade two editors to use some of his work in articles about the dig in return for certain tip-offs — not about you, of course. So be smart, distinctive and your photographic best. Get into some shots with those spectacles, some without. You getting this?'

'Yes. So I'd better not take the Doc's orange pill Thursday evening.'

'Mebbe not,' he said gruffly. Then he wanted to recheck the whole thing but I cut him short by saying I didn't want to keep Frederick Robinson awake in the next room. That silenced him. We both knew how crucial Frederick was going to be.

I stripped off, sat on my bed and looked at the orange pill. Why trust that doctor? He had no knowledge of any allergy I might have; had not even asked. And wasn't there a touch of cruelty in his reference to me dying in a fire? When he examined me he must have guessed the origin of my body scars. But then why trust Frimmer either? Whatever the final outcome, he would have no problem replacing me from the next training group, could even select for unquestioning obedience: the area of my greatest failure. The words churning in my head began to stir up that familiar impatience with myself whenever I slid into introspection. With a gesture childishly defiant, I snatched up the pill and swallowed it without water.

There was no obvious immediate reaction so I began checking my wardrobe in case I needed to buy something for the Friday camera call, but the white cotton trousers were clean and so was the black and white striped T-shirt. As I swung shut the wardrobe door it was almost too heavy for me to move it. Then my body started to become too much for my legs. I just made it to the bed. Being a fine night I had intended to sleep under a single sheet. I was vaguely aware that had been a good decision because lifting a single sheet took all the strength out of every muscle in my very fit body. Then I was sliding down, being dragged down by something that reached up for me from a black, unfathomable depth. Like Peter Abercrombie. I had just enough time to wonder if it was death.

15

Trapped in deep water by entangling, down-tugging tentacles, my struggle to escape merely increased the pain in my straining lungs. In my ears a pulse throbbed like repeated heavy blows. I could feel strength draining from me. Despairingly, I rolled over on to my back. The sound of blows grew louder. I heard a name called, distorted and muffled by the water: 'Mr Corelli! Mr Corelli!' Perhaps because that hated name was not mine, I managed to wrench myself clear and struggle to the surface.

Someone was pounding on a door. An alarm clock was fracturing the edge of the day. With a huge effort I got free of the sheet that was round my neck and face, hit the alarm clock so hard it bounced off the bedside table and on to the floor. There was a pause in the pounding on my door but that name was called again, and by more than one person. I climbed out of bed, wrapped myself in the sheet, unlocked the door pulled it towards me. Frederick Robinson lowered his fist, gaping at me. Behind him, Olive Gridley gave thanks to a god.

'I — we — we were getting worried. Your alarm clock's been ringing for ages.' Frederick stared at me like an underfed goldfish. Behind him, flush-faced Olive wriggled her toes in the dark pink carpet.

'Jake,' she said. 'Er — Mr Corelli. Everyone *else is finishing* breakfast. I did *sound* the gong.'

'Yes,' I said, still struggling for air. 'Yes. Sorry. Suppose I slept deep. Didn't hear my alarm.' I felt I was projecting words along an abandoned, dried-up sewer. Frederick gave another open-mouthed gasp while Olive swayed behind him. Belatedly, I realized that my bedsheet was so soaked with sweat it had become transparent. 'Be down soon,' I said, shutting the door in their faces and falling backwards across the bed. Was this what an orange pill could do?

All I remembered about breakfast was that my fellow guests had left before I had finished eating, and that they had divided into two opposed camps. Evelyn and Albert attributed my condition to drinking, she acidly, he humorously; Olive and Frederick to the marginally less damaging perception of not knowing what to think. No one was likely to cite illness for a man who so often visited the gym and swimming pool. After breakfast I staggered round to the back of the house, sat in my car and phoned Frimmer.

'Ha!' he said, and then, 'Ho!' (We still had scores to settle; the other's reverses to enjoy.) 'Well, Jake, Doc said the stronger your reaction to that medication the more likely it's the right prescription.' We kicked that opinion around for a few sentences until I told him I believed I was incapable of driving. When I proposed staying on the green pills and only taking another orange 'bomb' on Friday night he immediately agreed. I rang off and sat in the car feeling something like disappointment because we hadn't had a row. My God, how strange is human nature, especially mine!

Olive Gridley's response was also uncharacteristic. When I walked back into the house she sidled up to me and put her arm through mine; first time she'd deliberately touched me. I wondered if she had been affected by the sight of my nakedness as viewed through a sweaty sheet. Then she proposed I join her that afternoon to watch Wimbledon tennis on TV in her sitting room. 'It's *Wednesday*,' she said, information I was pleased to receive. 'Mr Robinson's *half-day*.' I nodded. 'And I'm not *going* to bing — not going out.' This must have been Marconi's experience of that first life-changing blurred telegraphic message. 'Mr Robinson's bound to spend the afternoon in *the lounge* watching TV. You need to be *away* from such *people* and *I've got* the better TV set in *my room*.' My nods at both assertions she read as acceptance of offer.

I remembered little of the remainder of that morning other than sitting beside the river and staring at the slow-gliding water. It took a huge effort to turn the cogs in my head and identify two fears half-smothered by my drugged condition. First, that I might be impotent on Thursday afternoon. Second, that I would be unable to recognize I was being followed.

That afternoon I disgraced myself by falling asleep on Olive's settee as soon as she switched on the TV. Later, when she woke me for a splendid tea, her irritability at my loutish behaviour was clearly evident. Complimentary remarks offered on both the tea and her brand new colourful headscarf did not much modify the chill in the room. As to the tennis itself, I neither knew nor cared who had advanced towards the finals. The next afternoon I fell asleep in the arms of Una and Kathy but only after I had been satisfied one of my fears was unfounded. Nevertheless, Kathy jokingly commented on how deeply I had slept: 'No second helpings today, my dear.'

On Friday there was the photo session at the archaeological dig, but I coped with that well enough. Plenty of photos for Frimmer to slide under his greasy paws, for Mr Stone to prod delicately with his steel fingertips. And I was left free to deceive myself that being loved and sleeping deep were working their positive touches.

I took the second orange pill on Friday evening and my reaction was almost as severe as the first time. Mrs Gridley's reactions also remained severe. I was *not* invited to see the Wimbledon finals in *her* room, not after *falling asleep* in her company. She didn't say any of *that* but her pursed lips, bustling manner when serving my weekend meals in the otherwise empty dining-room, and refusal to indulge herself with normal chit-hat, conveyed her feelings clearly enough. If I wanted to watch the finals it would be alone (perhaps she hoped *lonely*) on the residents' TV.

Sunday morning, lying quiet in a riverside corner away from the tracks of weekenders enjoying sun and river, I wallowed in the disoriented state induced by that second orange 'bomb'. And as I did so a new and troubling identification of my condition struck me. Suddenly my inability to see anything clearly, to 'sort out' either myself or my circumstances, was hauntingly familiar.

'Your foster mum died earlier today.' 'No,

we haven't caught the man yet.' 'Aunt Corrie feels she's too old to give you a home.' 'All this running away is wasting police time, young man.' 'Tush. Bend over!' 'Can't do anything with him.' 'He's a waste of time and space here.' It was not only the sorrows but also the never being good enough to be wanted, the abandonments that had felt as if they were *my fault*. So I had become the silent watcher of a life I couldn't get my mind round as if then, as now at age thirty, I had been disabled by a drug.

But I had come through the awfulness of all that, hadn't I? By age ten I had acquired a capacity to endure and survive. Had I lost touch with that in the intervening years? Had I really allowed the weird and unique circumstances of this case to disable me when I had survived all that childhood, fought my way to recovery, and on the way served ten tumultuous but successful years as a police officer? I was almost pleased to hear my own sarcastic laughter. 'For God's sake, Jack!'

Harder to dismiss was the possibility my *current* failures had partially disabled me, not only in my role play as Jake Corelli, but more fundamentally in my suitability for this case as Acting Detective Inspector Jack Bull. Just how much did my so-called 'success with women' make me totally unsuitable to be allowed near anything to do with rape? What to make of my blurred distinctions between sex and love? Was athletic sex in a threesome with two tarts really about being loved and about loving? Worse still, had every relationship, however lovingly collusive, been an attack on members of the sex which had once repeatedly abandoned me? And how was it that despite so many contacts with women, I fatally misread Molly Poling? And I couldn't even *name* what happened between myself and Madelaine Grey. Whom of all of us were the mad persons?

Monday waking was misleadingly gentle. I anticipated the alarm by several minutes, was first resident down for breakfast and first to walk out into the soft rain-shower. I bought the local paper that produced its new edition at the start of the week. There were two pics from the dig and I was in both.

Then.

Sitting reading the paper over a pot of tea in one of the town centre cafés, waiting for the rain to drift away, for the blue to overlay Browcaister again, the first almost imperceptible tremor of approaching devastation nudged me. Sitting in the corner, it was easy enough for me to check out the other customers. None appeared to have any interest in me. But somebody was or had just been watching me. In that quiet moment everything so minutely prepared and set up by SIU came to the point of testing.

Now.

I paid for my tea, turned up my raincoat collar and stepped out into the passing rain. I turned left, rounded the next corner and picked up that signal again. At any other time I would have trusted it implicitly, but I was not yet convinced I was completely clear of the last orange pill. As I walked back to The Larches, my conviction strengthened that I was not only being followed but by somebody well practised. What I absolutely could not do was take any confirming action. Doubling back, faking a bus hop, leaving a shop by a rear emergency exit: none of those dodges were likely to be in the real Corelli's repertoire. And probably he wouldn't even have known he was being followed, particularly by the skilled operative who had homed in on me.

I walked round to the back of the house and got into my car. Took out my mobile phone. I was surprised how unexcited I was; hands and fingers steady, breath regular. In the moment before Frimmer picked up his phone I had time to visualize myself as someone who, having just finished climbing a craggy and difficult mountain track, now found himself facing a smooth and easy downward path to the next valley. That it could be the valley of death was a whisper brushed aside by Frimmer's abrasive voice cutting into my ear, and also by that familiar click confirming Henderson or Thomas was listening in.

'Morning, sir. Couple of questions first.' No more than a grunt from the great man. 'Any change in instructions to my back-up colleagues to stay well clear of me?'

'Absolutely none. Why?'

'Any possibility the local force is kicking against their briefing?'

'Not if they wanna keep their balls. What's this about?'

I grinned into my driving mirror. The rising note in his voice implied he already suspected *exactly* what it was about. But I wasn't going to leave him hanging. Everything to be played absolutely straight now.

'Maybe those photos taken at the dig have worked or the timing was coincidental.' Somewhere across the connections I could feel rather than hear the suspension of breathing. 'No visual contact so far but feels right.' Still silence but not of disbelief. We were reliving shared past experience. All my listeners knew well enough the validity of the feelings of being followed. We were also talking the possibility that the long, dispiriting months of work had suddenly come to fruition.

'We change nothing. Absolutely nothing. Got that?'

'Yes, sir. I'm due to drive out on another fake job this p.m. Chosen a small down-at-heel industrial estate so cover's good. And my tail won't risk coming into the estate — assuming they bother to track me by car. If they now know I live at The Larches they can always pick me up again from here.'

'Right. And you do nothing, absolutely nothing at all, to check out who they are.'

'Course not, sir. I'm Corelli, remember, not Jack Bull.'

'Yes, yes. We all stay exactly with the standing briefings. We're changing nothing. Got that? Back-up remains at a distance. Not quite time to oust Frederick Robinson. And no fucking stupid private initiatives to move things on. Let the killer dictate the pace. If we're dealing with a group then Corelli may not be tailed by their hitman but by a member of their team expert in that kind of surveillance: disgruntled ex-cop with saviour complex, for example. I'll get back to you later today.'

Any resentment I might have felt about his lack of good wishes was brushed aside by the revelation his mind was as much into fantasizing as was mine. 'Ex-cop with saviour complex!' I loved it. Loved it! Left me feeling quite a bit less weird. But neither of us could have suspected what would be the tragic outcome of changing nothing.

16

'Never thought I'd be back at The House.'
'Changing fortunes, sir,' said Dennis, vaguely.

We were standing in the library. The room was suffused with the soft light of the summer evening, turning the lovingly polished furniture to its deepest, most vibrant hues of brown, ochre and russet. The long centre table would have reflected back an unbroken plane of that vibrant hue which only solid mahogany can show, had the sheer surface not been dotted with place cards. The white cards, their own surfaces broken by black lettering, fractured the sheen of the table top by both their positioning and also by their clear mirror reflections in the gleaming surface of the wood. I knew most of the names. 'This for tomorrow?'

'Quite right, sir,' said Dennis. 'Meeting timed to start at 10.30 hours. You're the only delegate required to be here tonight. Guess this is the reason.' He walked to a sideboard and took out two sealed files: one thick, one thin. 'My orders are to get you to sign for both of these. The thick file, SIU/GOS 03, you return to me tomorrow not later than

08.30 hours. The thin file, SIU/GOS Summary 15 and dated today, you retain and bring to the meeting.'

'Yes,' I said, signing twice. 'This *is* the reason I'm here before the others. Couldn't risk having these papers sent to me in the field. By the way, I think I can place most of the other delegates but between J. Stone's and B. Frimmer's places there's a card with no name.'

'If *you're* not meant to know, sir, I'm sure *I'm* not.' The touch of petulance focused my mind on what it might be like to be Dennis: always kept on the edge of things, excluded from any active service other than the requirement to guard and care for a country house. He carried a gun but his hands were most often busied with crockery and furniture polish. 'And maybe you won't ever be told, sir. Best leave it.' Another pause, not looking at each other. 'OK, sir. Dinner in fifteen minutes.'

After the excellent dinner I put on my jacket and took a slow walk round the grounds. As I walked a connection formed between this evening and the first night of my previous visit. As the same stars began to pierce the clear and darkening sky, I felt something like ownership of a world far greater than the one in which I had been struggling. The darkness of waiting and doubting had been dispersed by the first signs of my enemy closing in on me. (It was now *that* personal!) And now I was walking the edge of a starlit night towards a meeting which Frimmer had assured me was to resolve the final details of my living or dying. It felt as if all sorrows, shabby disgusts and regrets of past years and months were sliding back into a shadowy and unreclaimable past.

Returned to my bedroom, I left the windows and curtains open, allowed in the scents from the flower beds, and the faint, acrid odour of the nearer cedar tree. I sat in the armchair and broke open the seal on the thick file SIU/GOS 03. It was a concise report of all the work done on this project by SIU in the last two years, including setting me up on the training course, then pitchforking me into the role of Jake Corelli. As for that poor sod, his detention in protective custody merited only a brief paragraph. New to me was an up-to-date summary (as of yesterday!) of all positive outcomes: even more old cases reopened as a result of victims being encouraged to come forward. It was also clear job changes had followed in at least two of the more laggard police forces.

There was also a summary of the fates

awaiting Billy Mundam and Ted Croucher. So far, the local force, spurred on by SIU, had brought more than a dozen charges against each of the two men, from offences relating to car dealings to the much more serious of drug trafficking. I allowed myself a gleefully malicious moment. No ambivalences about *their* fate. I was too tired to go deeper into SIU/GOS 03. Dennis had been clear enough that it was the slimmer file which would matter tomorrow so I switched to that.

It was the penultimate draft of the operational plan for successful closure of the case. Final draft would presumably result from tomorrow's meeting. The clear prose brought to mind yet again the movement of Stone's steel hand across a desk top, not that authorship mattered. No, what mattered and satisfied at the same time, was the sense of myself being safeguarded, that each step proposed carried an explicit concern for my welfare. I had long been aware of this attitude towards me in SIU, but in the grim waiting time that awareness had been eroded by my isolation and increasing depression. Now, literally in front of me, was reminder that I was not only part of a team, which until now had been kept largely in the background, I was a uniquely valued member of that team — and not only because of a superficial resemblance to Jake Corelli. It's one thing to be a tethered goat abandoned in a clearing, quite another when reminded of watchful protectors lurking close by in the jungle fringe.

I drew the curtains across the open windows, took another green pill, got ready for bed. As I slid into sleep I was aware of being held, as if in a hammock, by the operational plan to be discussed tomorrow. Aware also that the slimmer file excluded so much that was in the fatter, and that that was not entirely a reflection of the space available. Some of tomorrow's delegates were to be kept in ignorance of much of the background to the plan. For a brief moment I enjoyed the fantasy I knew everything.

Wednesday morning I woke to a clear, warm dawn, and was in the pool long before breakfast time. Then Dennis served a full English breakfast accompanied by fruit juice, coffee and toast. At 08.15 we signed in the file SIU/GOS 03. Dennis carefully resealed it in front of me. 'I'll give this to your Mr Frimmer. Now a word in your ear, sir. Two delegates are expected by 08.45. No idea why, of course, but thought — on a need-to-know basis — I should inform you. Clear someone wants the three of you to have time together before the meeting.'

'Names?'

'We have actually been told, sir. Unusual but we have. Yes. DC Susan Green and DC Ian Longhurst.'

'The goddess who dropped the golden apple in the gutter. Could be Longhurst was the man with the dog.'

'If you say so, sir.' Dennis blinked and edged away from me. But he was a damned sight less alarmed than Corelli had been by goddess, dog and dog handler. I wondered if Corelli had been allowed any time to feel that alarm, that intimation of death, before the needle went in.

At 08.45 Tom's Land-Rover swung to a halt at the front steps of The House. The two DCs got out and were welcomed by Dennis. I stepped back from the window. My supposition had been correct but I now observed them at a shorter distance. Astonished by nervousness, I walked back into the dining-room to await their arrival there for the coffee Dennis would offer.

She came in first, directly to me, held out her cool hand and grasped mine firmly. She had a voice like a soft bell. I could hear myself stuttering. I suppose I must have greeted lanky, long-faced DC Ian Longhurst as well, and also declined Dennis's offer of more coffee. In the time it took him to serve the other two, I managed to sit down and fake some kind of composure. I'm not the sort of man to be confused by a woman's beauty, not even Susan Green's, and I was aware that the ill-suppressed smirk on Longhurst's face was based on his misreading of my reaction. (Foolishly, I supposed he had become accustomed to her face. Perhaps that was *my* misinterpretation.)

She was a slender blonde about five feet eight inches tall. She had large, widely spaced green eyes, a broad forehead, straight nose and wide mouth. Her upper lip was long, the lower slightly thickened and curved; a mouth like a promise. Her firm chin rose out of a long, smooth and strong neck, and her blonde hair was cut shorter than collar length and slightly curled under at the ends. She was wearing a long-sleeved, cool shirtwaister vertically striped in cornflower blue and a soft pale green colour I couldn't name. Her bare legs extending towards my chair were lightly tanned and her feet were in flat-heeled sandals. All her limbs were graceful and her strong hands delicately formed.

Beauty — but that wasn't it! At least not in those first moments together. I was unmanned not, perhaps as Longhurst assumed, by her appearance but by something he could not have known. She was the fair sister to Molly's dark. It was the similarity of vibrancy in her that struck me; the fantasy that she and Molly would have been hugely drawn to each other. Two women making their way in a bruising world, but this one now facing me having had the firmer foothold. And yes, once again words failed me, and I had the uncomfortable feeling that might often be the case with Susan Green. And there was something else: I intuited this woman was going to teach me something, and that the lesson would not take place in a bedroom.

Their questioning about The House led me to mention the pool, and to Longhurst regretting he had no swimming trunks. I assured him Dennis would be able to find trunks and towel, but that if he couldn't I would loan mine — so long as he didn't mind them still being damp. I regretted I couldn't help her with that. She grinned at me, asked if we could walk the grounds together. (Why else had they been ordered to arrive so early?)

'Sorry, Sergeant. I guess that was a bit obvious,' she said as we walked down the front steps and out across the gravel drive to the lawn.

'That's OK,' I said. 'But call me Jack.'

'Right. Then in this circumstance I guess I'm not DC Green.'

'Susan?'

She hesitated, ran the tip of her tongue across her lower lip. 'Suzy. Now, Jack, I don't want to be contaminated by Mr Frimmer's manipulativeness — and certainly not with you. What's been set up here is the chance for you to talk with a woman, a new face on the block.' She gave an unexpectedly deep laugh that seemed to start in the root of her and then rise through the centre of her body into her open throat.

'What's funny, Suzy?'

'I suppose the opening remarks we've just shared could be interpreted as totally and utterly manipulative.'

'How about a deal? You and I distinguish between 'Frimmerspeak' on the one hand and what we want to say on the other?' I could feel the thickness swelling in my throat; the symptom which usually accompanied my first request to a woman that we go to bed together.

'Right. It seems you've had a pretty tough time, Jack. An action junkie required to wait around.'

'Guess you're right. But plenty of coppers work under cover.'

'True. But not many are waiting to be murdered. No wonder you gave Mundam and Croucher such a thumping.' (So right and so wrong. But it was neither time nor place to exhume old tales.) 'I wouldn't've wanted to be in your shoes in the last few months. I guess most of the team feel the same way, Jack.'

'Easy to lose touch with all that when you're out in the field alone waiting to be knocked over. But it's good to hear you say it. I got pretty depressed recently, but what always steers me away from too much self-pity is recalling my interviews with rape victims last winter.'

'Our Mr Snell?'

'Thank God I'm free of *that* role. But it's the sorrow I can't get free of, Suzy. Not good in a copper.'

'I doubt that, Jack. But what about your other role, as Corelli?'

'I'm coming to — it's coming to an end now.' We walked together in silence for some time. What I felt then, suddenly and unexpectedly, was a sense of *belonging*, not only in the team but specifically with her. She was the first to speak.

'There's a thing about all this I'd like you to know in addition to my admiration. You've seen clearer than most just how dreadfully hurt women can be by rape or GBH. And, like the rest of us, you know that the huge majority of rapes don't even get reported. But there's something else. Many rape victims do heal, and sometimes without any help from anyone else. Some victims don't even *tell* anyone else, never mind about telling us! I'm not just trying to sell a good story about my sex. This is also about wanting you not to be totally wrecked by your work.'

'Or by revelations about my own sex?'

'There is that.'

She slid the conversation away from our work and into private pleasures. I was content to follow, and amused to discover that physical fitness was passion for her as well. But much of our words were lost to me in the hazy pleasure of her company in that garden. I cannot recall how many times we strolled the grounds, only that we were standing together in shade under one of the cedars when the first of our newly arrived colleagues were driven past us by Tom. She stretched out her right hand to a sagging but stoutly propped lower branch, brushed the fronds caressingly to release the pungency of their scent.

'Tree of life,' I said foolishly. A sudden well-remembered warmth. In her I was meeting with a woman who might constellate old joys and pains. Not for her a temporary place in my life as passing fancy or just a sexual playmate; the power of her personhood would never permit that. The possibility of once more being committed in a loving relationship felt like an embrace reaching across the scented space under the cedar.

'Take care, Jack. And remember: we're all watching out for you.' Then, straight-backed, slender, gold-helmeted by the sun, she was walking away, leaving me sheltered within a great bubble of aromatic shade beneath the cedar tree.

But long before she reached the front steps of The House, the bubble holding me burst with a violence so great it felt as if the tree itself had fallen crushingly on to me. Somehow, wordlessly, Suzy had unlocked for me, beyond any doubting or questioning, the true naming of what had passed between me and Madelaine Grey.

17

The library, gloomy in morning shade, was made the gloomier by the heavy silence of the occupants and by their almost uniformly dark clothing. Suzy's summer dress and glowing hair seemed out of place; intrusions from a sunlit world where she and I had so recently walked together. I was almost the last to arrive; only Henderson's and Thomas's seats were unoccupied. My arrival was acknowledged by a slight inclination of Frimmer's head. Nobody spoke.

I had been placed at the bottom end of the table between Henderson on my left and Longhurst on my right, Suzy on the far side of Longhurst. I put my copy of the brief summary file on the table and sat down. Apart from the delegate place cards and each person's copy of the SIU/GOS Summary 15 file, the table was completely uncluttered: no water carafes and glasses, note pads and pens, no stack of reference files.

In the silence I looked at the three men grouped round the top end of the table. Mr B. Fimmer had to be wearing a new suit; impossible to believe the old one could have cleaned up that well. But beyond joking was the fact this occasion merited a new suit. There was nothing to be deduced from Mr J. Stone's familiar, immaculate appearance, not even from his decision to choose his Guards tie. He sat with both lower arms out of sight below the level of the table top. A hawk at rest but ever alert. Between them sat the man whose place card bore no name. He was losing his hair and didn't like that. He had moved his parting down low towards his left ear and dragged the wisps of longer hair from that side, across the bald dome, and down towards his right ear. Below this disfigurement was a face in which stress had tightened the corners of the mouth and eyes. Like a vertical slash across the pale face, a long and very narrow nose arced down from wire-framed glasses to his thin-lipped mouth. I supposed he might be a bureaucrat who would enjoy blocking the progress of meetings with issues of procedural correctness. Together the three men looked as trustworthy as a panel of Turner Prize judges. I sat happy with my prejudices as silence clotted the room.

Suddenly, we were disturbed by loud voices outside the door. Then Thomas and Henderson came in and were instantly intimidated into silence. Thomas sat on Suzy's right and offered me the feeblest of smiles. Henderson walked to the head of the table, gave Frimmer a large manila envelope, then walked down to the seat on my left between me and the only other stranger in the room, a very large man whose place card informed he was Detective Sergeant P. Whiddon. There was just enough time to read the compression of Whiddon's lips and the darkness of his complexion as indicators of rising anger before Frimmer spoke.

'Good morning,' he said, dragging a muted response from about half of us. 'Our purpose here is to resolve final issues for our operational plan now that DS Bull has reported he is being followed. The photographs in this envelope are inadequate confirmation of that. I'll pass them round.' As Frimmer took out the prints I was aware that DS Whiddon was looking even angrier. I was soon to find out why.

There were three photographs: distant views of groups of people in different parts of Browcaister town centre. In each a particular individual had been ringed in red ink. It was just possible to determine that it might be the same person and that it was an unidentifiable female. In the evidential sense, the photos were useless. I watched as they slid from person to person. The only one of us more than disappointed was DS Whiddon, who was now so angry he refused even to glance at the prints.

'Before I invite your comments,' said Frimmer, staring Whiddon into silence, 'I would like to introduce Sir John who is here representing the — er — Whitehall.' Sir John appeared to bow from the waist. 'DS Whiddon, head of surveillance, will now comment on this new situation.'

Aggressively, Whiddon pushed his large grey head forward over the table on to which he spread his hands, fingers splayed as if for balance. 'Thank you, sir.' He took a deep breath. 'First of all the very poor prints you have just seen do not reflect the usual quality of work produced by my section.' Frimmer half-raised his right hand in a placating gesture but that didn't cut the mustard with Whiddon. 'We are prevented from carrying out our remit by the instruction not to focus directly on DS Bull.' He turned and thrust his large jaw in my direction; an antagonism I didn't feel I deserved having never been consulted. 'I am well aware of the dangers of blowing this operation but if you want decent images the camera has to be pointed at the subject. If you want to know DS Bull's exact location at all times he has to be electronically tagged. If operational considerations make these impossible I can neither guarantee good pictures nor DS Bull's safety . . . sir.' Whiddon sat back, leaving two sets of smeared and damp palm prints on the gloss of the table top.

'None of this is disputed,' said Frimmer irritably. 'But our target or targets have repeatedly demonstrated a remarkable level of efficiency. SIU only got on to them in the first place because Mr Stone identified just *how* efficient they were. We dare not assume they are not surveillance literate. If they carry out just one sweep and pick up a response from Bull or identify a photographer, the operation collapses. Despite that risk I can inform this meeting of one specific order to DS Whiddon's team. It is to establish a stake-out in the front first-floor flat of 37, Belmont Avenue. The house is almost exactly opposite The Larches. We will have a continuous CCTV record of arrivals, departures and passers-by. Photo coverage is also established. Confirmation that contact has been made now tightens every aspect of our operation. The loss of an operative in the field is totally unacceptable.' I presumed he was thinking of me, but the quick glance passing triangular between me, Thomas and Henderson confirmed we were also thinking of Pearson dying in a New York alley. 'I will now review all aspects of this operation so we all know exactly what each of us is doing. You may make reference to the summary files while I am speaking but make no notes either on the file or elsewhere. The files will remain here when you leave.' Frimmer plunged into his review and spoke for about twenty minutes. It was a measure of how carefully we had all read the short summary file that there were very few questions. At the end of the discussion Frimmer deferred to Sir John.

'Thank you, Mr Frimmer. It is clear to me SIU has dug a deep pit for itself. At one level my remark is a compliment to all of you on the care with which you have set up this scenario; and especially so to DS Bull. But it could be said, *is* being said elsewhere, that you have all your eggs in one basket. This is not to detract from the several successes concomitant with that: a murder admitted, old rape cases reopened, victims in other previously unreported cases now coming forward. None of this is undervalued. But you have invested a huge effort in a hypothesis which has yet to be confirmed despite DS Bull's intuition and a handful of grainy photographs. And there is a more serious and longer lasting difficulty.' He steepled his fingers as if in prayer. The expression on Frimmer's face was that of a child whose favourite toy is just about to be stamped on by an irate parent.

'If you succeed in the field you may fail in the courts on the grounds that DS Bull has been used as an enticement and, worse still, as an *inducement* to commit murder. I don't have to tell anyone here what a competent barrister will make of that.'

'I suggest, Sir John,' said Frimmer, his breath rasping, 'that it is the long view that matters here. Apprehending anyone who attempts an assault on Bull will open up all those other cases so carefully researched by my colleague Mr Stone and his team.'

'With respect, Mr Frimmer, I fear that what you have just said may prove to be no more than a pious hope disappointed. No, let me finish. In the first place if someone makes an attempt on your man it may well be someone involved in a single specific rape revenge attack. They may have nothing whatsoever to do with any of the other revenge killings which Mr Stone has categorized as being linked. Secondly, you are operating on the basis of an assumption that if someone is arrested they will necessarily break down and confess. Yet your own records confirm that your serial murderer, if that is what he is, is not only extremely efficient but has committed more than a dozen murders without leaving sufficient evidence for you to act against him. Are we to be persuaded that such an individual, or indeed such a group, will break down and confess on DS Bull's grave?'

For Frimmer to be silent for so long was a measure of his rage rather than his inability to reply. It was fortunate for the continuing existence of SIU, and for its support from Whitehall, that Stone spoke next.

'If this aspect of SIU's operations succeeds, that is, DS Bull is attacked and we apprehend the assailant, then several things follow. Discovering the identity of our serial killer will facilitate use of all the circumstantial evidence we have. With no hook to hang it on all that is valueless at present. Secondly, the very limited DNA evidence we have will also come into play. And there is an even more persuasive factor. If what you refer to as our 'hypothesis' is sound then we are dealing with someone who, for at least ten years to our knowledge, has enjoyed continuing success in their gruesome mission. With every killing they have fed the sense of their own invulnerability, their belief they are untouchable and will continue to outwit the police. Psychologically speaking, discovery will devastate them — irrespective of whether they are sane or insane. Our profilers are absolutely united on this issue, even as they are divided on most others. We all know what happened to Shipman. Furthermore, our lawyers are confident that if the weight of evidence plus confessions proves persuasive enough we might well go to CPS without reference to an attempted assault on DS Bull.'

'What I am expressing here,' said Sir John irritably, 'is the wider view and I make no apology for so doing. This view has to be accepted now; afterwards — and that may well be after the death of a distinguished officer — will be too late. Your intentions are admirable but results will be judged absolutely and solely by due process of law.'

Another time and place I might have stayed silent and enjoyed the expression on Frimmer's face. The man was not only being lectured in front of his juniors, he was being told what he already knew. I got in first.

'Sir John, I wonder if I might clear up one issue here? None of us has any grounds for rejecting what you have just said, but I am aware that you have, for the second time, referred to the possibility of my death. That's not going to happen. I've been selected for my role on grounds broader than my superficial resemblance to a recently discharged rapist. I have also been given this job because of a proven reputation for looking after myself. I'm not bothered by the possibility that the successful outcome of our operation might have to exclude any reference to an attack on me. If we succeed that will entirely override any desire I might have for personal justice, personal revenge.'

'Thank you for saying that, Bull.' Frimmer was out of his starting blocks before Sir John even heard the pistol. 'All I want to add is that your safety and our collective success now depends even more on security. The whole team is here present except for DS Whiddon's team, and they can carry out their duties without knowing the precise justifications for their surveillance. All of you are now working only and entirely on this case. You will be directly informed of progress only by me, the sole exception being that Henderson and Thomas will continue to overhear all calls between myself and DS Bull. The summary file SIU/GOS Summary 15 is now redundant and you will leave your copies behind in this room. A replacement file will be created and constantly updated, but for security reasons hard copy will only be circulated on a justified need-to-know basis. This operation now has continuous first priority for both Mr Stone and myself. Are there any final questions?'

'No questions,' said Sir John smoothly. 'Merely observations. The negative implication of what I've heard and read is that after nine months' fieldwork you may not have a case.'

I was too angry to let that pass.

'Yes, sir. But I, and everyone else, absolutely reject any implication of failure or inefficiency.' Frimmer, startled, could only nod.

'I would not expect you to say anything else, Bull, and for the moment I am willing both to agree with you and convey that opinion to Whitehall. What I am less certain of is what to report about you. On the basis of what Mr Frimmer has selected to tell me it can only be laudable. A positive outcome will reflect positively on you.' He paused long enough for everyone to reflect on the implication of a negative outcome. 'But you can expect that scrutiny of your team's progress will now intensify sharply. That does not prevent me wishing all of you success, and expressing the hope it can be achieved without further loss of life.'

It was a good exit line. He shook hands with Frimmer, took up his briefcase and sidled from the room, avoiding eye contact with anyone until he reached the door. Then he turned, looked directly at me, made a funny sort of half-bow and left. I had no way of knowing if that personal acknowledgement influenced what happened next.

There being no further questions Frimmer closed the meeting. But instead of walking directly to the door everyone in the room, including Frimmer, came to me, shook my hand and wished me well. I was so affected by this I was reduced to a stuttering idiot in all my replies except that to Suzy. 'Thank you for what you've done for me today,' I said. She nodded her head.

'We're all backing you, Jack,' she said, her mouth slanting into that now-familiar grin. Then she was edged aside by Mr Stone.

'Stay behind,' he said softly, after wishing me well.

When they had all left the room I sat down again, aware of a slight trembling behind my knees. What moved me most about the team's response was its obvious spontaneity. It didn't matter whether or not it had been triggered by Sir John's acknowledgement of me. 'Christ!' I said to the closed door. 'That's better than any pill of any colour. No more of those.' Then the door was reopened by Mr Stone.

'Come on, Bull. A short walk in the grounds.'

Outside, Tom was just driving away from

the steps with the last of the delegates. In the far distance, another Land-Rover, perhaps driven by Dennis, was approaching the lodge. All my guardians withdrawing into the jungle, leaving me again isolated in the clearing. I felt a pang of loneliness despite having Stone next to me.

'It's hot,' he said, taking off his jacket, looping it on to his index finger and swinging it over his shoulder. 'Let's walk on the grass,' indicating the same direction in which I had set off with Suzy.

'I think I talked too much at the meeting, sir.'

'No, you didn't. And it was particularly effective because it came from you and not me or Mr Frimmer.'

'Mr B. Frimmer?'

'Bertrand — but never let on I told you! He hates the name; Bertie even more. Now, about you, Jack. Are you well again?' I nodded. 'Still on medication?' I shook my head, but I wasn't prepared to say I'd only just taken that decision. 'Guess you feel even better at the prospect of action — at long last.' We walked the next few paces in silence. 'You were aware we chose not to raise certain issues in front of Sir John. For reasons of operational efficiency we are sometimes obliged to act in ways which might cause alarm in Whitehall. Better they don't know about that, or at least not until the operation has successfully concluded. So we haven't specified what may happen to the real Corelli. Left Sir John with the untroubling assumption Corelli is due for release soon. Nor did we refer, either in the meeting or in the summary file, to gratifying progress in bringing charges against Mundam and Croucher. I doubt he could have comprehended the level of violence before they were arrested. But it now seems that incident was successful as confirmation of Corelli's release and location. Dumping your car in Browcaister plus the photo shoot at the archaeological site finally pinned you down — as it were! Well, I guess we'd better turn back. Don't want your landlady asking awkward questions about the length of your company's AGM. And I'm needed back at HQ.'

We turned on our track at the corner of the grounds, began our diagonal return across the lawn. With his good hand Stone took his jacket on to his other shoulder so it did not hang between us. He allowed the steel hand to hang slack in that space. I edged slightly away but only to allow space for it. I wondered how much of a dragging weight that was on his stump. For all I knew, it was lighter than the forearm he had lost.

'I choose not to wear a glove. Hampers me,' he said.

'Er — yes — sir.' Stammering fool that I was.

'The other matter, Jack, which we kept from Sir John — and always will — is what is about to happen to Frederick Robinson. You've been fully briefed on this for some time. 'About to happen' means next Wednesday on his half-day off from work. We now need the man's room. Not raising this in front of Sir John is not just because it's illegal but also because it might be seen by him as a piece of kite-flying. He and his masters wouldn't approve either of these possibilities. Not that I'm ecstatic.

'However, the probability our murderer gets up close and personal with the intended victim can't be discounted, and especially not in the light of the causes of death we've listed: so many of them having a domestic setting. The fact Abercrombie, the most recent probable victim, was prepared to make the miserable journey he did, also implies at least one personal and persuasive meeting with his murderer. So we make a room available at The Larches in the hope it will draw them close. Very convenient for one of them to be in the room next to Corelli.'

'Yes, sir. Very tempting. And I can be a

persuasive help to Mrs Gridley when it comes to advertising the room.'

'And if all this comes to nothing, your Mrs Gridley will soon find a new resident of her own choice.'

'No doubt, sir. But she's not *my* Mrs Gridley, in any sense.'

'Glad to know that. But I understand there are other attachments in Browcaister that need to be kept clear of The Larches and, ideally, clear of yourself.'

'No problems there, sir, especially as my instructions are to maintain a Corelli-type lifestyle.' He gave me a sharp look, aware of several interpretations of my words. He decided to let it go. Neither of us knew then that he had just made himself an accomplice to murder.

'Watch yourself, Jack. Our killer or killers don't know they're at risk, and by now could be in a state of mind of not caring anyway. We talk glibly about you being the fifteenth victim, but for all we *really* know you could be the fiftieth.'

Back at the steps, we shared another of those awkward handshakes, and then Tom drove him away to where his car was parked beyond the lodge gates. I watched as Mr Stone was driven away from me, wondering yet again how he stomached working for a yob like our Bertie. Then I went up to my room to collect my overnight bag. I stood at the window and took a last look out at the cedar tree where I had stood in shade with Suzy. Something definitive had happened in that shadow and it was not going to let me rest.

18

In the week leading to that next Wednesday, when Frederick Robinson's life would be brutally manipulated, other manipulations continued to distort my own life, a life now living me instead of me living it.

The affirming pleasures of Thursday and Tuesday afternoons with Una and Kathy were now tarnished by the possibility I was being stalked, something that as Corelli I could not confirm. No precise confirmations were offered by DS Whiddon and that unsettled me further. Was it possible my so reliable intuition had failed me? Or was it simpler — that having discovered my lodgings the killers knew where they could pick up my trail whenever it suited them?

Nor could I deny my disgust at what I was about to do to Frederick Robinson. And I was not consoled by the fantasy that violent upheaval might lead to improvements in his circumstances. There were professional justifications, of course, that we needed to force both his departure and the timing of it. There are justifications for everything.

These concerns bit hard on the bone

because they fed a continuing doubt. Had my time as Arthur Snell, valuable in its experience of playing a role, and of 'getting inside' the sorrowful experiences of so many women and their relatives, damaged my capacity for ruthlessness? Was there more truth in Frimmer's acerbic comments on compassion than I wanted to admit? Like Frimmer, I took refuge in a feeble mantra of my own: time will tell! I was soon to discover exactly what time would tell.

The experience of life living me was heightened that weekend by the coincidence of everyone being at The Larches for Saturday evening dinner. That in itself was unusual, even more so that the four of us shared Albert's wine; even Evelyn was persuaded to take a glass. Conviviality spilled over into the TV room where we sat together and watched a particularly silly movie. The noise of our laughter drew Mrs Gridley out of her den and persuaded her to join us. We all joked together that we had never done that before. I was the only member of the jolly group who knew it was a farewell party for Robinson.

He was delighted that we both had the next Wednesday afternoon free. And, yes, he would like to meet in the town centre and combine our two shopping trips, especially as

I would give him and his shopping a lift back to The Larches in my car. We arranged to meet outside one of Browcaister's two department stores, the one with the keener store detective. Repugnance at what I was about to orchestrate stopped me suggesting we might have a pub lunch together before shopping.

Once inside the store it was easy enough to persuade him we should go our separate ways because we had different requirements, and that we meet outside the exit at an agreed time. As our tracks crossed in the store he obviously enjoyed the companionship implicit in that. But he was unaware of Henderson sidling past him, nor did he see my meeting with the store detective: the accusation, the slyly pointing finger. When Frederick stepped out of the store a stranger, face distorted with suppressed excitement, came up to him.

Later, over dinner at The Larches, I made sure Corelli was seen to be relaxed, and was sympathetic when Mrs Gridley announced Mr Robinson was unwell and could not come down to dinner. As soon as the meal was over I went upstairs and knocked on his door. There was no reply. My crazy mind pitchforked me into the scenario of Robinson having topped himself. (That would really have buggered our plans!) I knocked again and much louder. To my relief he opened the door. He was ashen faced; mumbled that he wished to be left alone. I barged straight in and asked what had happened to him, said I had come home alone because he didn't turn up at the meeting point as agreed. He slumped on to the bed. Struggling for breath between sobs, he poured out his shameful story. A pair of socks in his pocket and he had never even seen them before. How was that possible? And when the store detective insisted on checking his bag, there were items not registered on the till receipt: two tins of fruit.

'What would I want with those when I have evening meals here?'

'Not any more you don't, Frederick. Best thing to do is move out now. Get a new address. Avoid a scandal, prevent this getting back to your place of work, avoid spoiling your references.'

'But where to? Where can I go?'

(To Frederick's amazement, Corelli knows exactly where, and can arrange everything by the morning. Even more helpfully, a green sleeping pill is produced.)

Thursday morning after breakfast I drove him across town to a temporarily hired guest house run by a delightful young woman: Ms Susan Green. He was soon basking in an atmosphere of positive concern. I suspected caring from other people was a new experience for him, even though it was only a comfort of strangers. Over coffee I explained that his offence made it impossible for me to get him work in my line of business. However, I did have some useful contacts but he would have to act quickly and be willing to move away from Browcaister. He was so relieved to be helped by me and Ms Green that our presumption of guilt was unchallenged.

'Save your thanks,' I said, 'until we're sure things've worked out right. I'll see what might be done about your shoplifting in view of the fact it's your first offence. Now ring this number today, say my name, Jake Corelli, and that I want help for you to find a new job, new place to stay. As soon as you're set up, phone me at The Larches and confirm both your new address and job.' As he groped through renewed tears at the piece of paper bearing Frimmer's office number, I had the discomforting impression he was close to kissing my hands. I justified my hurried departure by the need to get to my own job. Ms Green saw me to the front door.

'Bastard!' she said, not entirely friendly.

'It's this case, Suzy, for God's sake! This case! You'll move out of here as soon as? I'm concerned for your safety as well.'

'Mind on the case, Jack — er Jake. Not that I'm convinced you know what the case is. Christ! What you're seeing played in this one is the fate of women.'

'You mean rape is inescapable?'

'Yes and no. Fate is what we don't deal with within ourselves and then it hits us from outside. As long as women pretend the problem will go away when *men* change, the longer we'll suffer this fate. I don't believe rape will ever stop completely. Not even the death penalty for rape will achieve that; more likely turn rapists into murderers. At some mythic, primitive level it is built into the human psyche. And I know that in some circles I could be burnt as a witch for saying that. No, what women can do is to be ferociously against rape not only by persuading, educating — or whatever it takes with men, but also changing their own behaviour. At least fifty percent of rapes have a collusive element.'

'You mean they're asking for it?' I could hear my voice getting shrill; a peculiar echo of Albert, of what he and others like him represented.

'No, I don't mean *that*. Women are not *consciously* asking for it, for Christ's sake! But the woman who walks her dog alone after dark every night on a London common needs to be more conscious of her own behaviour. Ditto any woman going on a blind date.'

'But a woman should be able to walk her dog — '

'Jack! Should is shite! That sort of 'should' is a woman acting the spoilt princess. Let's get real. It's not about 'should'. In the real world if you keep asking for trouble you eventually get it. What we call fate is actually failure to deal with reality. Only last week, on my old patch, a woman was raped going home from the station down a long, unlit alley. What she said was: 'But I go that way every night.' As if that was some kind of defence against rape. That also illustrates the arrogance of my sex. 'How dare men!' instead of 'What can we women change?' I say we can fight!

'Only ten per cent of women who are raped or violently assaulted have the courage to fight in the courts. And by Christ it *is* a fight in our lousy society! Hardly surprising ninety per cent don't. But what is vital is to turn that round so that at least ninety per cent of women *do* fight.'

'But how? What's the encouragement, Suzy? The women I interviewed had all fought their cases. But that brought them neither peace of mind nor closure. And the one I most admired, who I thought really had got clear, topped herself. Christ knows what it's like for all the others. Makes me want to see our killer as hero.'

'Or heroine, Jake. It might help if there was a set term for rape no idiot judge could vary. But what matters more is that women need to be so much more radical and courageous than we are.' Then her knuckles whitened on the door edge. 'I just want my sex to *fight*. The alternative is too horrible: to live out our lives in terror and die in shame, shame we didn't stand up for ourselves and so not for our other abused sisters.' With an impatient gesture she began to shut the door in my face.

'This case . . . ' I said to the closing door, 'has made me a stranger to myself.' But the slamming door was more definitive than my groping for words. I turned away feeling yet again the bitterness of my isolation. Everything was just bloody useless words. I felt a kind of listless almost impersonal gratitude I was going to escape to an afternoon with my two girls.

The closed door did not isolate me from my concern for Frederick Robinson. That was why I had insisted he contact me as soon as he was resettled and why I had said so in front of Suzy. Frimmer would anticipate me doing exactly that. I doubted I would ever have an exchange with my boss which was not a power issue. Not wanting to consider how much I might be like him, I decided to get myself a sandwich and sit by the river. When I had time to kill that was my favourite place to do it. Time to kill! How could I have ever known.

As always, I arrived at Una and Kathy's exactly on time. I walked up the short path in their sheltered, high-hedged front garden, was amused to see the front door was ajar: now their habitual welcoming gesture. I called 'Hello' pushed against the door. It gave for about six inches and then there was a resistance. I pushed harder, called again, suddenly possessed by a huge anxiety. I recognized the smell. I forced the door wider open and looked round the edge of it.

The door was jammed against Kathy's head. While I had been sitting in the sun by the river, a first slashing cut had severed her throat, almost separated head from body. As she had fallen back, her dressing gown spreading open, a second, unhindered slashing blow had ripped into her naked body just above her blonded pubic hair and disembowelled her. Bouncing off the wall under the savagery of the attack she had fallen, twisted: a gutted corpse. Kathy's viscera, the yards of them, had spilled out of her and were now settling greasily against the skirting boards on each side of the little hall. Mangled colours of horror. And the carpet beyond my toes was blackening with all her blood. In death her compact plump neatness was becoming a stinking, spreading mass.

If she had managed to utter any sound before that first slashing blow severed her throat then Una — I made to step forward but there was no room past Kathy. And there was no need. As I looked up the stairs I could see, extending into view beyond the newel post, a blood-trickled white arm with its limp hand palm up, fingers still slightly curled. And the deep red stair carpet was turning darker; a blackness creeping so slowly down the stairs, down towards what had been Kathy.

I could hear a voice whispering, urging, ordering me to get out. But even as I began to respond, to turn away from horror, to put one foot across the step and on to the path, I was acknowledging the absence of bloody footprints on both step and path: the possibility the killer was still in the house upstairs waiting for me. But as I walked away from Una and Kathy, wiping my shoes off on their tiny front lawn, careful even though I knew I had not stepped in blood, I realized the killer had also left the scene. The odd position of Kathy's head against the door was horrible confirmation. In getting out the killer must not only have trodden in Kathy but also stooped to drag her slit body bag closer to the door, twisted the almost severed head at some impossible angle so that it fell against the door, holding it almost shut. The killer had not wanted the bodies seen by a passer-by, nor had she wanted me warned off by finding the door jammed tight shut. I had found the bodies exactly the way she had planned.

She. And her only fastidiousness this time was her decision to wear protective footwear. I never doubted it was she and that I had led her there. And all the background whispers from others about changing nothing, using my role to justify changing nothing, could not subdue the shrieking in my head that I had led her there.

I will never be able to say by what route, or in what time, I returned to the river and slumped on to the grass. But along the way I realized another vileness lay within that detritus of slaughter. The killer left no bloody footprints outside the door because she had arrived at their house literally dressed to kill. She had stood in the hallway, next to Kathy's disintegrating body, coolly changing or unwrapping her footwear. (Even my punctuality had aided her.) Other blood splashes could be hidden under a long coat, perhaps in the same way a wet suit had been hidden when leaving a park on a wet January night. Then she had only (only!) to push Kathy's near-severed head tighter against the door as she edged out of the house. Then a short walk down the path, across the pavement to a car.

For the first time I had seen the murderous hatred of our killer turned against women. She had killed her own, believing their chosen lifestyle fed the lust of the rapist Jake Corelli, and by extension, all rapists and all men. That exactly the opposite might be the case was not going to be debated in her maddened mind, not in the face of the blind mad fury unleashed by my self-indulgence. I was aware of other things not debatable. No ex-rapist could take the risk of reporting he had found two dead tarts. No undercover cop could admit to any part of it.

The bitterest irony was that SIU would not want our target to be charged with butchering two women because that would be a distraction. A distraction! I could hardly bear to allow the word space inside my head. Our aim was to solve many murders and collect all the kudos for doing so. In that context the fate of two tarts, and the resolution of their deaths, were marginal! And when Suzy had suggested 'heroine' for our killer I had not disputed; wanted to believe. Now, endlessly repeating in my mind, one phrase: 'A woman going out dressed to kill.' And that somehow *still* less terrible than 'a man going out to rape'.

I have never felt so small, so *seedy*.

Later that afternoon, by the river, I was aware of ambulances and police cars carving through Browcaister. I had no idea what their call-out was; most likely an afternoon rush-hour traffic accident. But the familiar sounds were enough to force me to my feet, to push me back to The Larches. In the hallway I looked into the mirror and saw a screaming face I dared not show to Olive Gridley or any fellow resident. I walked quickly to my room and locked myself in. The bed was disgustingly inviting but there were other more imperative tasks.

I dragged my desk to one side, carefully pulled up the carpet edge and lifted a floorboard. For Jack Bull, if not for Jake Corelli, I drew out the wrapped and taped bundle. I put it on the bed, then replaced the floorboard, carpet and desk.

I sat on the end of my bed and unwrapped the pistol. As I stripped it down, reassembled and reloaded it, I knew I was now jeopardizing everything for a second time. But it seemed so trivial a wickedness compared with what I had caused to be unleashed elsewhere. Elsewhere. I couldn't bear even to think their names. Even more appallingly in that moment, I recalled that one of my motivations for getting involved with them had been nothing more than an infantile desire to irritate Frimmer.

19

Handling the gun could have turned a key, locking a huge door on all emotional connections with the past; the touch of machined steel in my hands ejecting me from my former role of passively waiting target and into that of vengeful hunter. The truth was other. I handled the gun like a forlorn child clinging to the only toy allowed it. If I had any dignity left it resided in the fact I never seriously considered turning it on myself.

Only a few months ago I had confessed to a half-heartedness in the case, almost wishing the deaths of more rapists! Now that old stale posturing was cut away as swiftly and efficiently as Kathy's throat. Even my sorrow at Molly's death now reduced to the level of some kind of sycophantic murmur.

The bodies were not discovered until the next morning by a shocked and vomiting postman who had somehow managed to operate his mobile. I blocked all feelings about Kathy and Una lying untended in their deaths through the night, even though the only residual kindness possible would have been to tidy them away in body bags. Even in that practicality I had failed them. Frimmer was on to the tragedy within an hour of their discovery.

'These two butchered brasses: they yours?'

'Mine?' Our idiot questions gave me time to acknowledge Henderson and Thomas were listening, tapes were running. 'No, sir. Nothing to do with me!' But the lie was only a delaying of truths. My fingerprints would be found everywhere, including on the headboard of Una's kingsize bed. All that would be for Frimmer to resolve with the local force, assuming he still believed it realistic to defend Jake Corelli.

The next significant message was a phone call from Frederick Robinson two days after the girls died. The agency I had persuaded him to telephone (Frimmer) had set him up in a pleasant lodging house in Birmingham, and with a better paid job in the stock room of an engineering works. The final touch was that being no longer employed in a food store he could at last own up to and get treatment for his eczema. It was a struggle for me to concentrate on what he had to say, to be pleased for him; not because of any mean-spiritedness on my part but because I had already filed him away. Not only the two deaths but also two new strands of information coming in reduced both him and his good fortune to trivia.

Strand One. A hundred miles away in an old quarry was discovered a completely burnt-out car. Probably a can of petrol on every seat. The car stolen a week ago when Kathy, Una and I — No, delete that! A second set of tyre tracks confirmed that the driver of the burnt car had been ferried away by an accomplice. It was a *team*! Which of them would be directed to knock me over?

Strand Two. At The Larches, Olive Gridley, petulant at Frederick's sudden departure, exclaiming that she hated to advertise, never wished to attract undesirables. Christ, I thought. She's got me and Albert and can still say *that*. What'll she say when the shit really hits the fan? But I soothed, pretended existence of a business associate in property who owed me a favour, would do the advert, the screening, make a shortlist, and all at no expense. 'Ring this number. Ask to speak to a Mr Stone.'

Meanwhile, there was news from forensic that, despite the huge temperatures generated in the burning car wreck, they had identified that a quantity of plastic had been burnt which was foreign to the interior plastic fittings of the car. My suggestion that they might have found a remnant of protective clothing was not dismissed. But my query about evidence of any shoe or boot remnants, which often survive very high temperatures, was met with a curt denial. More significantly there were no traces of footprints around the wreck. Part of the explanation for that lay in the spread of the sheet of blazing petrol, but there were also indications the area may have been swept over with a coarse broom before the fire. If colleagues in forensic felt a degree of irritation at the lack of evidence, I felt something close to satisfaction. Such careful covering of tracks fitted the profile of our rapist killers who had successfully committed so many murders and left so little evidence to betray themselves.

At The Larches these two strands were now being tightly woven by Mr Stone, who telephoned Mrs Gridley almost every day to report progress. She was consoled by frequency of contact, but even more so by knowing it was all free. Mr Stone's company was obliging me as part of their efforts to persuade me not to declare them bankrupt. To be brought back into favour so quickly by Mrs Gridley might once have caused me a frisson of amusement; but not now, two deaths on. She was not a complete fool and must have identified a coolness in my manner without suspecting the cause. How could she ever guess that any woman associating with me might become a killer's target?

Meanwhile, forensic had found no trace of any weapon in the incinerated car. Nevertheless, that knife with what was believed to be its razor-sharp eight-inch curved blade was around somewhere. If it had been dumped on the journey from Browcaister to the fire site that meant a hundred miles of country to be searched. And there was no nonsense about locks or catches from bags or cases surviving the heat. We were dealing with people who didn't make those kinds of errors. What we needed was some kind of breakthrough, a piece of luck; something that rarely comes when you need it. What SIU got instead was yet another re-examination of the files to see if any link, however tenuous, existed between all those previous coldly planned and executed killings of men and the frenzied butchery of two women.

Frimmer never even bothered to confront me over my connection with Kathy and Una. Instead, he made exactly the same assumption as had I: that their deaths were directly linked to the case through me in my role as Jake Corelli. At first, I was shocked that this assumption was never discussed with me. But later, when less traumatized, I came to see that discussion would only generate more bad feeling between us without progressing the case.

Any hope of finding useful evidence at the scene of crime itself had soon been abandoned. Only the smudged bloodstained footprints on the stair carpet and the trace of glove prints on the stair rail confirmed the presence of the killer. I had said nothing when Frimmer told me about that. But when the phone was down his unfortunate choice of wording had ricocheted around in the carapace of my skull like a bullet fired into my brain. Confirmed? Were the ghastly remains of two butchered women somehow inadequate as confirmation of their killer's presence?

While luck did not favour SIU on the street, inside Olive Gridley's front door something happened which initially none of us even thought to name as luck. Perhaps that was partly because the originator of the event was Evelyn Sykes of all people.

'You know, Mr Corelli,' said Mrs Gridley in a warmly confiding way that made me think of cocoa at bedtime, 'our Evelyn has had a little *chat* with me about our search for a new *guest*.' Maybe something like consternation flitted across my face. (Was bloody Sykes proposing to bring a library colleague here? Never her mother!) 'No, no, not interfering, you understand, just whispering a preference.'

'For what?' I demanded edgily.

'It really is all *right*,' she said, brushing her hand along my clenched forearm. 'No, she's seen the adverts put in the local press by Mr Stone, and she just wanted me, us, to know she would *prefer* our new guest to be a *woman*. Balance things up a bit. I suppose she felt *outnumbered* by Albert, Frederick and then yourself moving in. I know she doesn't much care for Albert — not *her* sort at all. And of course she's *recognized* that you — well, that, well, you and I have — that *we* understand the ways of the world, don't we? I wanted to let you know this because *your* Mr Stone told me *yesterday* he is getting more *responses* from *men* than from women. Would it be *very* difficult to ask him to shortlist an *equal* number of men *and* women for me to choose from?'

'I suppose not,' I said stiffly, somehow thrown off balance by an issue that did not appear to carry much significance despite my own secret belief that at least one of the killing team was a woman. But perhaps my reaction was something about everybody now having more positive input into the case than myself — even Evelyn Sykes, for Christ's sake! That I even considered so nonsensical a view of things might partly explain what I did next. I dared not attribute any of my actions to grief.

The evening after that conversation with Olive Gridley, what I did was go out alone on what was frankly a pub crawl. I couldn't have stomached another evening either skulking in my room or drinking with Albert, so I slipped away from The Larches immediately after dinner without saying anything to anybody. Nor did I clear that with Frimmer, assuming that DS Whiddon's camera record would be sufficient notification. Avoiding both the pub where I first met Una and the one to which Albert most often made tracks, I went first to The Goat. A couple of drinks did nothing for me so I decided to move across the town centre to The Vine. And that was when I knew I was being followed. (I was equally sure I hadn't been picked up outside The Larches.) All I could do was stay absolutely in the role: Corelli drinking, and not risking checking for a tail or telephoning for back-up.

Now *there* was a downright daft dilemma: Corelli might continue drinking heavily but Acting Detective Inspector Bull needed his wits unimpaired. Fortunately, I got a corner seat in the main bar of The Vine close to the landlord's collection of potted plants. I could be seen through the windows when going to the bar and reordering. But by the time the hot summer night had settled forebodingly on Browcaister, Corelli had sobered and the potted plants were in a bad way. Time to move out.

I walked first into the maze of narrow streets of that part of the town but heard nothing behind me other than the tracery of distant thunder carving through the humid darkness. The storm was moving away from Browcaister, but as the night quietened I heard no sound of my tail. I left the old town behind me and began the slow, gentle climb up towards Castle Square. The name was a complete misnomer; there had never been a castle on this site. The steeply sloping square was Victorian and edged by large town houses of the late 1870s. They reminded me of similar houses in the street where Abercrombie had stood at the end of his final journey on a rainy January night.

Entering the square I heard, echoing back off the brick-faced houses, two quite different sets of footsteps. It was an effort to stay with the knowledge that beer-swilling Corelli wouldn't notice and, even if he did, would almost certainly not be bothered. I stepped off the kerb on to the wide expanse of tarmac, bent down and pretended to adjust a loosened lace in my trainers. The stepfalls behind me continued for a few paces and then stopped.

I never heard the car whispering down the

slope. The driver must have been relying on the gradient for impetus: the lights and engine off, clutch fully depressed. I only became aware of the car bearing down on me a fraction of a second before the driver switched on the engine and released the clutch. With a kind of uncouth lurching roar, the car was at me as I twisted back and sideways on to the pavement. I might still have been hit had it not been that the car struck the high kerb so obliquely it was deflected away from me instead of mounting the pavement. Then it was gone. Fading with the sound of its engine were footsteps behind me but now running away.

Sweating with more than the heat of the night and the sharp pain from a twisted ankle, I switched on my mobile. I gave my location and confessed to injury resulting from an attempted hit and run. Within two minutes Henderson brought his car to a stop beside me. Thomas leaned through the open window of the front passenger seat.

'Greetings, Sarge. Can see you're OK. But neither of us would 'ave expected to view you in this condition, boyo. Covered in dirt and filth you are. You got the car number?'

'No. Too quick and no lights. Didn't get sight of the driver either.'

'Possibly the drink talking, Tommo,' said

Henderson, getting out of the car and walking round the bonnet to me. He peered down at me, standing dishevelled in the gutter. You are a *dirty* little sergeant. Just as well I'm not allowed to give you a lift in my nice car.'

'Cut the crap! Get on to bloody Frimmer, root him out of his armchair. This is new. Attempting a messy and unreliable hit and run. Someone's rattled. *And* I was being tailed at the same time. Maybe further confirmation we're dealing with a team. My tail didn't need to pick me up at The Larches either.'

'No one else you've upset recently, like, and you're not telling?' asked Thomas. Then he jerked his head back into the car. Even in the weak sodium glow of the street lights he had made out the expression on my face. My anger was not only a response to his flippancy but also to implications of off-duty gossip about me.

'Well, OK, then? You can make it back?' asked Henderson. I nodded. He walked round to the driver's side of the car, climbed in and drove away, leaving me testing out my twisted ankle against the life-saving kerb. I chose not to imagine their raucous laughter as they drove away.

At The Larches they were all in their rooms. I moved as quietly as possible, not wanting anyone to see the state I was in. But once out of my damaged clothes I risked a late-evening bath to soak my twisted ankle and the several bruises on my body and arms. Body soothed but mind furiously ferreting into implications of the event, it occurred to me that the clumsy assault on me felt more a part of the vicious murders of Kathy and Una than of the relatively sophisticated and fastidious killings which Stone had been tracking for so long. Was our target cracking up under the accumulating stress? And there was something about the *timing* of these events. Ideas I had but we don't get convictions with ideas. And was it only coincidence I had a particular dream that night?

I am climbing a perilous staircase on the outside of a steep tower. I dare not look down into the sodium lamplit glow far below me. There is a reason why I must climb quickly but I do not know what that is. I feel a terrible sense of anxiety, a responsibility to avert some ghastly outcome. As I near the top of the staircase I see above me the head and shoulders of a woman looking down at me over the upper edge of the tower, her face unrecognizable in the pale light from the streets far below. I can tell from her contorted face and rapid arm movements she is urging me to hurry. But I hear no sound. When I am only a few treads below the top of the stairs the woman leans out too far and, with her face torn by a soundless scream, falls past me, her loose clothing dragging against me as she plunges into the town below. I cling tightly to the staircase. I could not have saved her.

I woke sweating, muscles knotted with tension, my chest heaving as if I had been holding my breath for a long time. In the dissolving blackness of the dream I threw the damp sheet off my body, heard myself cursing. I didn't need Suzy Green to tell me dreams of falling can be about failing.

20

'Come to my sitting-room after dinner,' murmured Mrs Gridley, placing a generous serving of roast beef in front of me. She took care to speak to me with her back turned to the rest of the room, and especially to Albert who had more than once muttered grumpy accusations of her favouritism towards me. I already knew why I was invited, having been tipped off by Stone that she had received the four applications for Robinson's room. But I had got more than just *that* information.

'No need to take up your landlady's request of yesterday, Jake. I mean her request about women applicants. Everything fell into place without that. You'll see what's happened now she's got the selected applications edited by me. And maybe congratulations to you are in order.' Laughing, he had put the phone down before I could question him. Not that I needed to. His final remark told me exactly what had happened.

Frimmer expressed himself differently and characteristically.

'At long, long last we have go. This time you play everything by the fuckin' book. No

263

deviations or variations of your own just because we were wrong and you were right all along. Try and forget for once that you're a smart-arse. Cool professionalism is what I want from you — if you can still remember what that is.'

In Mrs Gridley's den she offered a sheaf of papers.

'The *best* applications,' she said, seductively. 'From your Mr Stone.'

'I am most flattered, Mrs Gridley. But is it correct for me to see the details of a potential fellow guest?' (She could have had no idea how eager I was to see them!) 'I can respect a confidence, of course.'

'I know *that*, my dear. Wouldn't show you otherwise. But I value *your* opinion even though the choice is *clear* enough. See what I mean?'

How right she was! Stone had done a superb editing job which I suspected slightly diminished the attractiveness of three applicants while enhancing that of the fourth: a woman calling herself Mary Hutchinson. The information she had given, however carefully selected, did not disguise parallels with the contents of one set of SIU files.

I was in a state which must have rivalled the delirium of the fastest hound as it sank its teeth into the living flesh of a cornered fox.

But while months of anguish and frustration fell into place around me, I had to talk with a woman who could speak only trivialities. It required a huge effort of concentration to attend to what Mrs Gridley was saying.

'I'm very grateful for what your business *associate*, Mr Stone, has done. And grateful to *yourself* that it has cost me *nothing*. And I *will* carry out his request that all these documents be returned *directly* to him. He enclosed a stamped addressed envelope for that purpose.'

'Very important,' I said. 'The applicants have their own copies, and these must go back into his business files for future times.' There was no possibility I could allow Mary Hutchinson to see how her application had been subtly enhanced. 'Only one of these is worth interviewing?'

'Oh, yes, Jake. In fact she's so *suitable*, her references so clear, I'm *tempted* to skip the interview stage *altogether*.'

'Better not that you do that,' I said, looking serious while subduing the internal shouting English voice that agreed with her. 'Just in case there is something about her that you too much dislike. You are a businesswoman but it is into your home that you are inviting her.' Then the killer blow: 'You would not wish for a woman version of Albert?'

'Dear me, rather *not*. Poor man — but one's enough, thank you *very* much. Now there's just one *other* problem, Jake.'

'There is?'

'I did *wonder* if *you* might prefer to *move* into the vacant room? It is en suite and yours is not.'

'Thoughtful lady! But no, I am quite happy where I am. That room is home to me now.' Fortunately she didn't argue the point.

By the time the coffee pot was empty the four applications were in the stamped addressed envelope and I had helped Mrs Gridley jot down a few questions to ask. She was impatient for the interview to be held and would tell Mr Stone so tomorrow morning. In my incandescent state I left that detail to her, not least because I kept slipping in and out of my 'Italianate' English. Relieved that her full income was so soon to be reestablished, she proposed a celebratory brandy.

'I, *suppose* you *wouldn't* be willing to interview *with* me, would you?' she asked, leaning into me. Production of a half-full brandy bottle had led to her moving next to me on the settee.

'Not right, Olive,' I said, holding out my emptied glass. 'I am just one of your most happy guests. You are captain of your own fine ship. No crew member should interfere with your decision.'

Later, I staggered to my room leaving her somewhat downcast with the empty brandy bottle. However, I had agreed to be about the house on Wednesday morning at the time she had proposed for the interview. I had no doubt Stone would concur with that timing as readily as Mary Hutchinson. Until then I had to live with a turbulent mixture of emotions: relief, anxieties, satisfactions, terrors and self-doubts. Having wavered before, would I do so again at the crunch-point? And could SIU handle this extraordinary climax, so unlike anything they had dealt with in the past? Ridiculously, I almost envied the simplicity of Olive Gridley's viewpoint on it all. But then I decided not to think about her. What was to be visited on her and her quietly smug house could only be catastrophic.

After breakfast on that Wednesday morning I went up to my room and lay on the bed. I stared up at the ceiling aware of the slight trembling sensation in every fibre of my body. It reminded me of how I had felt after climbing out of that children's play area in the park before returning to Billy Mundam's garage for the last time. On that occasion I had the role of aggressor, but this time my aggression had to wait on that of another person.

This led me to think of Pearson: shot down in a New York alley while on an unrelated case. He must have had doubts rather similar to mine because both his attackers had died with him. That implied he had been already keyed for action as he entered the alley and walked towards his supposed informants. And perhaps there was another parallel between his fate and mine. The three bodies had been found lying within touching distance of each other. In a few minutes' time I would be within touching distance of my would-be killer. And shortly after that we would be living together under the same roof, eating in the same room, sharing coffee in the guest sitting-room, perhaps even watching TV together. And every night we would ascend the same stairs to sleep together, separated only by the party wall between our rooms.

But Pearson had died unsupported in another country. Not for him the instant telephone links with Stone, Frimmer and the blue control truck. Nor had he enjoyed the intimacy of almost instant back-up from Henderson and Thomas, the knowledge that DS Whiddon and his team were directly accessible across the road from The Larches. Undercover though I was as Jake Corelli I was also close-watched.

How I was to die was as unknown to me as

Pearson's death might have been to him, although in his case being gunned down was in tune with attempts to infiltrate drug crime in New York. But for me there was not only the complicating history of several previous different deaths — the falls, drownings, electrocutions and the rest — there was now a new uncertainty. An attempted hit-and-run fitted with no previous pattern of murders. Did that mean I might now be vulnerable to other crude assaults, and if so what did it tell me about the attackers? However much I might speculate on the change of tactics, I had now to accept I might be as much under threat out on the streets as in The Larches. Now there was no safe place.

There was another and somewhat ironic link between Pearson's death and mine. That he had died first massively increased the pressure on SIU to keep me alive. Two men from the same training group dying under-cover within a few months of each other would require very persuasive explanations in Whitehall. The continuing survival of Henderson, Thomas, Tenby and Jakowski might be offered in mitigation, but only four survivors from an original intake of twenty-four was a discouraging statistic in any recruitment drive. Worse still, the fatalities would be the two top men from that course.

The front doorbell rang, the sound not that loud through my closed door but it almost lifted me off the bed. I swung my feet to the floor and stood. A sharp, cramping pain hit my gut and just for a moment I was unsteady on my feet. I walked to the door and quietly pulled it ajar. I heard Mrs Gridley walk the length of the hall and open the front door. There was a muffled burst of conversation before the front door was closed. Then, without speaking, the two women walked along the hall to Mrs Gridley's sitting room.

I think the next fifteen minutes were among the longest in my adult life. (Childhood had been a rosary of long, nerve-racking waits in hospital wards or outside the closed doors of children's homes.) Then the two women emerged and came up the stairs. The applicant was to be shown her room in the confident belief she would find it suitable. I shut my door, leaned against it. As they walked past to the room next to mine, the room Frederick Robinson had once thought of as home, I recognized the voices of both women. As soon as they were inside, their voices now reaching me muffled through the party wall, I slipped out on to the landing and drifted silently down the stairs. Not long ago I had discovered two other women on a staircase. I could at least choose my ground for this first meeting with two women at The Larches.

Their voices, cooing like a pair of contented doves, became louder as they emerged on to the landing, turned the corner at the head of the stairs and began to step down towards where I had positioned myself near the foot of the stairs. Elegantly stepping downward, Mary Hutchinson was leading. From behind her Mrs Gridley, wearing her best blue and a matching headscarf, spoke an introduction she never knew was unnecessary. Then she was fading into the pink stair carpet, receding from me at the speed of light into a distant universe beyond the shadow of the other woman. Time stopped.

Ms Mary Hutchinson placed her right hand very briefly in mine, just long enough for me to know she was trembling the most. Her stare was one of confirmation: Jake Corelli was the man she had so thoroughly researched, had stalked through the streets of Browcaister but had never before met face to face. No one could have looked less like Arthur Snell than did Jake Corelli.

'Good morning,' I said, through tensely distorted throat.

She did not speak. Then her expression changed. It was momentary, like the flicker movement of a camera shutter across a lens.

She looked at me with exactly the same expression as she had when I entered her room at Peacehavens. And it betrayed Madelaine Grey. It was a look I had learned to name, having stood with Suzy Green under that cedar tree. It was a look of unutterable hatred, hatred of an intensity far beyond anything in my experience. And it confirmed the imminence of my death: the only event which could ever erase that lethal gaze. Another flicker in her face and she was her public self again: Ms Hutchinson, a professional woman seeking temporary accommodation as a base from which to work in local libraries. But she still couldn't speak to me.

Dressed for her role in black suit and white sweater, she was a kind of perverse representation of Molly Poling but one which replicated nothing of that courageous lost lady. Instead, in that charged moment, Madelaine was the grossest parody of recovering rape victim: the successful killer of men and slaughterer of young prostitutes. At that instant of our second collision, of confirmation of both our fates, I could think only that the one miniscule advantage left me was that I had seen her naked. Incredibly, that was the *only* thing I could retrieve in that moment. Everything else I knew of her — her rape, her medical reports, everything unearthed by SIU

— was momentarily lost to me, as if I now existed in a world only Jake Corelli would appreciate. Then my left sleeve brushed against Mrs Gridley's dinner gong.

The soft susurrus of the gong restarted the world's clocks, propelled us into the future where we must pretend to be ourselves again. The sound released us both and returned Mrs Gridley to her rightful place in our time-warped cosmos. She was delighted by Mary Hutchinson's enthusiasm for the room and for moving in immediately. What I desperately needed was time to enjoy knowing my target had taken the bait. I suspected that might be paralleled by her satisfaction at caging me.

21

In the temporary safety of my own room, Yale lock on, wooden wedge tight under the door, I pretended certainties. And that pretence was not indulged by colleagues, least of all by Frimmer.

'Yes, I *know*, Jake. Madelaine Grey. But that won't get us far, will it? Remember what Sir John said at our meeting at The House? We *have* to come to court watertight. Not that much joy for us in her decision to share a guest house with you, even under a false name. What'll a lawyer do with that, for fuck's sake? Might as well say she was there to be with bloody Albert whatshisname!'

'But, sir, it's a huge step forward in — '

'No, it's not, Jake. It gives a new direction and I'm not denying *that*. But a giant first step for mankind it ain't. OK? So now we can reassess the very limited circumstantial we've got plus the even more limited forensic. But what SIU wants is something more definitive.'

'Where's that leave me, sir?'

'Exactly where you've been for some time — but a fuckin' sight more careful crossing roads. But I've made changes. DC Suzy Green is applying for a vacancy as chambermaid cum general dogsbody at Peacehavens. With her bright little eyes she'll be checking out all kinds of dusty corners, especially on those days Ms Grey is with you at The Larches. We'll let you know anything helpful to you at your end. And I've made more staff available for rereading all the files yet again — but this time with Grey as sole focus of attention. If that new emphasis changes anything you'll also hear of that instantly if not sooner. Meantime Grey continues with her publishing job but from two centres.'

'Yes, sir. That fits with what she told Mrs Gridley. Also the justification for working in her room some days. But she intimated she'll be at local libraries, including the uni, a lot of the time. Has come up here to be near some key sources.'

'So how's it feel to be a key source, Jake?'

Mr Stone was less abrasive. But his matter-of-fact attitude was equally unconsoling. (Unconsoling? What did I expect them to say?)

'The business at last, Jake. I suspect you may be relieved as well as pleased. You wanted Madelaine Grey shifted to the hot list months ago. What a good thing she only ever met you as Arthur Snell.'

'Yes, sir. But I still wonder if Frederick Robinson and Bertie bloody Frimmer will be the only winners in this tragic-comedy of losers.'

'I understand how you feel — insofar as anybody else *can* understand what it's like to be in that particular hot seat. For that reason I'll let your impertinence pass. I thought you might like to know for background that Grey worked her references by using two of the women she holidays with. The story seems to have been that she only expected to be in digs for a very short time so decided not to trouble her boss. Seems her chums enjoyed making up the brilliant references she requested. A key phrase here is 'a very short time'. That could mean she's planning to use a tried and tested routine to knock you over. So one of many things my enlarged team of readers is tracking is whether we have a record of a death in circumstances similar to your own in The Larches. We're also researching any clues as to how she plans to get out and away as an innocent, uninvolved party.'

'Right, sir.'

'I don't know about 'right', Jake. Is there anything else we can do this end apart from the paper chase?'

'Nothing comes to mind now, sir. But I'll

let you know if it does. The one card we have is she doesn't know she's planning to knock over a police officer — and he's on to her.'

It may have been my dissatisfaction with these conversations which led me to check out the situation with Henderson and Thomas. Their enjoyment of my kerbside discomfiture may also have been a factor.

'You've been brought up to date by Frimmer and Stone. We need to be clear what all that means to us three in the field.'

'Could be we're nearly home and dry,' said Thomas.

'No we're not, for Christ's sake! And don't let Frimmer hear you say that. There's a long way to go to my funeral — I hope. In the meantime, you two stay even further back. One: because this lady is no fool. Remember all those accident verdicts? Two: if she does have a team you have to be clear of me *and* watch your own backs as well.'

I could almost feel their raised excitement level oozing through my mobile. What I needed were clear, cool responses free of any desire to demonstrate initiative. That was a reflection of lack of confidence not in them but in myself. If I was to have any hope of managing the last stage of the operation I needed all my colleagues to sit tight inside their specified action boundaries. A single unexpected distraction and I might be dead.

My internal dialogue was a kind of balancing act, but not between doubts and fears as in the past. Now I was examining Madelaine's options and mine, and the more I did that the more confident I became. I outclassed her and, just as important, she had no idea that was so. On top of that the whole strength of SIU was bent to the task of checking every one of the killings that might be down to her. All that patient research by Stone was beginning to be fleshed out — and with her flesh!

The most interesting thing about talking with Madelaine Grey was that it didn't happen. But she didn't merely deliver the social brush-off as she did with Albert. She expressed her distaste for me through her body language as well. When we passed in the hall she flattened herself against the wall, avoided looking at me and stayed absolutely rigid until I had passed her. On several occasions I gestured to her to pass through a doorway ahead of me but she always refused, offering no more than a determined shake of her head. All this was in contrast to her almost effusive responses to Evelyn Sykes and Olive Gridley. She even spent time with Evelyn, in Evelyn's room, going through her wardrobe and advising on what should be thrown out and what retained. 'Girls together!' snarled Albert who had already classified Madelaine as 'a stuck-up bitch'.

At breakfast and dinner I determinedly sought her gaze and when she felt unable to avoid my eyes she returned me a flat and unresponsive stare. Even when I quite deliberately spoke to her in ways that made a reply unavoidable, her curt responses were pared to the bone. That I disgusted her I never doubted but I also wondered if close proximity to her intended victim was disturbing her deeply. How much easier had it been to drown Abercrombie when he never knew she was anywhere near him? And it was likely they had met only once before and then very briefly. I certainly came to doubt that she had ever 'hooked' any of her victims with sex. Perhaps the traps had been baited only with money or job offers. But for Corelli she had no such snare because I had got a job before she could get me. Maybe her behaviour also reflected that after a sequence of killings spread over at least ten years something within her had become derailed, unhinged by the terrible pressures of what it was she had been doing. And for the first time I acknowledged that she had been a successful killer for longer than I had been a police officer.

In an odd way we came closest to 'conversation' when we were in our respective bedrooms. So I was never sorry to set my book aside and indulge in a kind of mental frottage from her life sighs and murmurs through our dividing wall. I could hear when she flushed the lavatory, took a shower, got into bed, turned lights off and on, opened and closed drawers and doors, dropped something. But if she prayed I never heard.

No doubt she was aware of me also despite my bathroom being a separate room. For me there was a kind of relaxed temporary intimacy in this sharing of sounds, though I never doubted she would have denied all awareness of them had I spoken. I also found my own response interesting in a situation I might have enjoyed for its eroticism. Not so. I was attuning to her as a hunter listens to his approaching prey. Our pseudo-sharing reminded me it was another sentient being I aimed to defeat, and defeat meant a fate for her similar to that of Myra Hindley. If Madelaine and I were ever to share an erotic moment it would be only in the passion of dying.

But dying requires a place and possibly a brief moment of ruthless physical intimacy: the violent fatal push in the back, the blow struck out of dark water, the smothering weight at the moment of drowning. Or the more remote caress of having touched the same electrical circuits or appliances. Where would she elect that moment for us? For me?

My room, being in the eaves of the house, had no attic above it. And the only rooms next to mine were her room and my bathroom. She would not strike from her room; not if her 'innocence' was to be protected. So perhaps the bathroom. But there was another route beneath me via Mrs Gridley's spare guest room; rarely used and then usually by Margy when she chose not to go back home after her evening work. Might I be vulnerable from below, the ceiling of the empty guest room separated from my bedroom floor by a few easily bridged centimetres, a gap with its own electrical circuits? That idea was enough to make me lift my bare feet off the carpet and on to the bed! Was it merely coincidence that I should have had these thoughts on a Tuesday evening, the day Mrs Gridley cleaned the bedrooms, and left our dark pink carpets temporarily marked with the tracks of her cleaner?

But before that particular association of ideas could work in me I was suddenly struck by the odd connection my mind had made between Madelaine Grey and Myra Hindley.

281

If that idea was pushed a bit maybe we had two powerful female characters both with weaker male accomplices. And if that idea was allowed to run who was Madelaine's? Then I knew.

Frimmer was not immediately impressed. 'Don't seem like a 'team', Jake. A barmy woman and an elderly gent probably equally barmy.'

'Maybe not, sir. But until that car was burnt out you were willing to run with the theory of one woman operating alone. And what struck me about Mr Johnson was his deep devotion to Madelaine. Could be his only commitment has been covering her tracks at Peacehavens and, on a few occasions, driving a car — including driving at me. But that could fit with something else: the issue of timing we've all been reflecting on, especially me. Something like this, sir.

'Johnson suspects what she's up to, maybe links her absences to stuff in the newspapers, but can't and doesn't want to prove it. Contributes covering up for her, maybe even cutting through the outer fence for her at Peacehavens. Then suddenly, he is confronted with the horrifying double murder of two tarts. Maybe he met Madelaine at the quarry, perhaps saw how blood-soaked she was before she changed, understood the reason for torching the other car, perhaps saw the weapon before she tossed it out of his car. Reality bites. Suddenly, the comfort of 'accidental deaths' has gone. He works out why she is at The Larches and guesses she is now risking more than she has ever done before. So what does he do? He makes a clumsy attempt to kill me in the hope of saving her. All supposition, sir, but it fits the timing and sequence of events.

'And there's another thing. Absence of evidence in the torched car. No remnants of bags, cases, shoes, etc. Any personal stuff that might have survived the heat.'

'So what?'

'Check out the bonfire sites on the allotments at Peacehavens. Look for one recently used, and perhaps even repeatedly used. Could be a way of making sure of destruction, couldn't it? And on their own doorstep.'

'I'll get back to you. Meantime watch your back!' snarled Frimmer.

22

As usual Frimmer's directions had been knife sharp. 'Melton Mowbray to Kirby Bellars. Take Main Street which is a residential street and cul-de-sac. At the far end is a church on the right. In front of it a turning circle. The Command Truck will be parked there. Beyond is open country so no chance you'll over-run. Be there 10.00 hours, tomorrow. You will be followed by Henderson and Thomas at a distance of four hundred metres. As they enter Main Street behind you it will be blocked off.'

I turned into Main Street at 09.55. Henderson and Thomas were too far back to observe me but I knew they wouldn't overshoot the junction. And none of us would make the turn without being clocked by the drivers of two unmarked parked cars, and of the dilapidated open-topped truck waiting to break down across the entrance to Main Street. I drove through a pleasant modern housing estate, then past some older more extensive properties standing in large gardens. The road began to resemble a lane, and I could see open country ahead.

The dark blue Command Truck was parked outside the church and on the same side of the gravelled turning area. It stood facing along Main Street towards the village centre. Manoeuvring it in that narrow turning area must have taken some skill. In that lovely spot overlooking open country under morning sun it was an obscenity.

As I approached I had to acknowledge mixed feelings of excitement and trepidation, a response intensified when I saw the roof dish of the truck emerging from its housing like a malevolent eye. Again that strange feeling that a high-tech vehicle had the characteristics of an animal. I parked next to it but without turning my car round. Then Henderson rolled slowly to a stop behind me and he and Thomas got out. There was scarcely time to offer good mornings before the rear doors of the truck were swinging open. 'Welcome to the aquarium!' I muttered.

We were greeted curtly by Frimmer, smiled at by Stone. DS Whiddon, not angry, just surly, dipped his forehead in our direction. Colleagues at the monitors risked a second to stare at us: the condemned man and two guards. In the nearest screen I could see the broken-down truck now blocked the end of Main Street. That reminded of the only time I had seen Corelli in the flesh. I could not repress a slight shiver.

Frimmer sat us at a narrow bench in the main operations room because we were too many to squeeze into his office space where I had been checked over by the SIU doctor. How many years ago was that?

'Right, Bull. Tell it all again. Timings — and those women,' growled Frimmer.

I hesitated. This was a moment akin to entering the confessional. I could hear only the faint electronic whisper from the screens and the harsh breathing that was Whiddon's. Then I heard the single deeply indrawn breath that was mine. 'What's been going on makes most sense if we focus on timings. Event one was the murder of Una and Kathy.'

The blank expressions on the faces of Whiddon, Henderson and Thomas prompted Frimmer to wave his hand at me. 'We've kept a low profile on that until now but it's time the whole team knew about them. So tell.' He was merciless. For me to have to tell was part of his retribution. Whiddon and Henderson heard me out in silence but Thomas could not repress a soft whistle of astonishment.

'We can't yet evidentially link their murders to Madelaine Grey but if they are then it's not a bizarre coincidence. The link is through me as Jake Corelli. I can't begin to tell you how that feels. So I won't. But what's clear is that when she destroyed her stolen car someone was waiting to drive her away.

'If we take the possibility she was following me the night of the hit and run, and so was *not* the driver of the car, we can read the sequence of events as follows.' As I repeated what I had suggested to Frimmer, I could tell very little from my colleagues' carefully blanked faces. I suspected that internally they were still trying to get their minds round the link between myself and Una and Kathy. But when I pointed the finger at Mr Johnson there was an immediate muttering of surprise. Frimmer cut in sharply.

'OK. Mad avenger with religious justifications or some such. Devoted acolyte. Fellow sufferer in same institution. Powerful unconscious sexual connections both ways. Father-daughter stuff. I'll not bore you with it all but our profilers go for it. Not a team in the sense we've been using the word but a crazy killer with an almost, almost harmless devotee convinced his role is to care for her. So Daddy attempts to knock over Jake Corelli to save her from herself. And before the rush to dismiss this idea I'll remind you we've all been willing to believe in the lone killer, and this don't stretch *that* idea beyond belief. And second, if anyone doesn't like it, then I advise him to reflect on some of the bizarre murder teams in the history of crime. No questions yet.

'Bull came up with a further suggestion. Absence of forensic evidence at the quarry maybe not entirely explained by heat of the fire. Some stuff including knife and footwear could have been put in a bin liner and taken elsewhere to be destroyed.' He nodded at me to continue.

'That was when I recalled the hillside allotments at Peacehavens where I met Johnson. He has a plot of his own. There are a lot of old bonfire sites up there.'

'Took it up at once,' interrupted Frimmer. 'Sent in a team supposedly from the local council environmental department concerned about pollution. So far, from a fresh bonfire site on an abandoned allotment next door but one to Johnson's, we've got fragments of shoe heel, woman's sweater, the bottom of a pair of slacks. No knife blade but I agree with Bull that was probably dumped elsewhere. And we daren't risk digging up the whole fucking hillside yet. Forensic are sure the same bonfire site has been used several times in the last few days. But Johnson, if it is him, hadn't succeeded in completely destroying the evidence before our people got there. Paraffin has been used to start and restart the fire and Mr Johnson keeps a small can of it in his allotment shed. Not that that in itself is anything other than circumstantial. Forensic promise to tell us rather more from the debris later. But the fact they've got some traces tells us something else as well. The fires were probably the work of an incompetent old man who didn't really understand the significance of what he was doing — in forensic terms, I mean. Now we've got DC Green in place in the house she's stepping up our efforts by sorting through everything around Johnson. If Bull is right the man is a weak link in just about every sense.'

'Big problem with this,' said Thomas, 'is it's all suppositions.'

'But there's something else, isn't there?' asked Henderson. 'If Grey has successfully murdered so many rapists over the years while acting alone surely she wouldn't now take Johnson on board: old, maybe a bit doddery, dubious mental health, *and* right in her face?'

'Good point, Paul,' I said. 'But I'm not sure it was like that; that he was 'taken on' in any clear way at all. I suspect they've never even talked openly about what she was up to. There's an analogy here that fits with what Mr Frimmer has just said. You all know the situation in which some old gent gets the hots for the nubile daughter of a neighbour. The old man behaves himself, doesn't even hint. You know the sort of thing: 'You make me wish I was young again, my dear.' No, there's none of that suggestive crap. But they both *know*, don't they? And maybe they both have harmless fantasies as well. But nothing is ever *said*, let alone done. I suspect this is how it might be with Grey and Johnson.

'He made it clear enough to me that he cared deeply for her. Probably quite unconscious around what Mr Frimmer has just expressed. And I can't imagine her saying to him, 'Like to help me with a few murders?' No, the background circumstances were probably never discussed. But I think he suspected, or perhaps confirmed from the newspapers, a connection between her absences from Peacehavens and the dates of various 'accidental deaths'. And that having already covered for her on some of those absences, felt himself already committed to her cause.'

'No one disputes that we can't go to court with this — at least not yet,' said Stone. 'But you can see where it might lead. If forensic declare those part-burned debris are related to our case, we have a link between times, place and persons. We'll know that within a few hours.'

'But sir,' bleated Thomas. 'If neither

forensic nor DC Green comes up with the goods, where does that leave SIU?'

'Staying on track at The Larches,' said Frimmer curtly. 'Bull?'

'Copies of the house plans, please sir?' With hand and hook Stone pushed them along the narrow bench. 'First-floor. You can see my room, Room 4, shaded pink — like Mrs Gridley's bloody carpets. Next door Room 3: Madelaine Grey's room, formerly Frederick Robinson's. My bathroom is that small one on the west side of Room 4, my room. But it's not completely exclusive to me. I've caught Albert throwing up in there rather than doing it in his own sink in his en suite bedroom. So don't regard my bathroom-loo as secure. In any case I'll bet that Ms Grey, like me, has got herself a set of keys made up.

'Irrespective of what's happening at Peace-havens, important though that might be, what is central to the case is that the woman has got into The Larches — with a little help from a certain Mr Stone. And so far no reason to doubt her intention. Our readers have found no parallels to this set-up in any of the other cases listed by Mr Stone. But so what?

'My guess is I'm to be electrocuted. And Wednesday is favourite being the day the house is empty all afternoon. The weekend is much more dodgy if only because Mrs Gridley comes and goes on no fixed pattern. But on Wednesdays we're all out at work, or pretending to be, Mrs Gridley is at bingo and pretending not to be, and Margy the cook doesn't come in much before five, roughly the time Gridley gets back from her bingo. How Grey'll set it up I'm not sure but if you look at the ground-floor plan you can see my room is directly above the spare room. That means there are electric leads immediately under my bed. There are bedside electric sockets in my room and, just the other side of the party wall are shaving and lighting points in my bathroom. All conveniently close to my bed.'

'Jesus!' whispered someone. I couldn't be sure if it was Whiddon or Henderson.

'How she'll exit afterwards I've no clear idea. But she's no fool and knows she could be traced through her application if through nothing else. Of course, she's no idea that was handled by SIU. But none of us can doubt her resourcefulness — not in the light of what we believe she's achieved. The bottom line *has* to be she's not in the house when I die. No idea how she'll set that up but I'm sure her set of keys includes those for the front door locks. I guess a lot depends on DS Whiddon's team and their record of her movements.'

'You can count on us for that,' exclaimed Whiddon. 'But a record of her departure might also be confirmation you're dead.'

'I'll take care of that,' I said, pretending confidence.

Later, when the blue truck and Henderson's car had both been driven away and out of Main Street, I remained behind looking out over the countryside beyond the turning space. My face felt hotter than could be explained by the sunlight. Had I spoken the truth when I said to DS Whiddon, 'I'll take care of that'? Or was that just another piece of foolish bravado — like taking up with Una and Kathy? I got into my car and drove back along Main Street towards The Larches and electrocution.

23

At breakfast the next Wednesday, Madelaine told Evelyn she would be out of the house all day, said she was going to Birmingham to work in the university library. I was aware she had pitched her voice slightly louder than was usual in the dining-room. And never before had she announced publicly her plans for a day. Evelyn shared my surprise but was obviously pleased. Perhaps she felt this communication was another indicator of their growing friendship. My deduction was more sinister.

Back in my room I stared at the dark pink carpet. Every Tuesday evening when I came in, its nap bore the smoothed tracks from Mrs Gridley's determined vacuuming; a week of scuff marks from my feet and hers eliminated. I got out the clothes brush my tailor had sold me and tentatively dragged it across the carpet. It left a satisfyingly clear smoothing which, in the angled daylight from my windows, appeared very slightly darker than the rest of the nap. On hands and knees, and starting in the corner furthest from the door, I smoothed the whole of the carpet.

Then I opened the door, looked out and listened. Everyone had left. So, while kneeling in the corridor, I smoothed out the last of my own Tuesday evening/Wednesday morning footmarks in my room before locking the door. I went down to my car, one pocket weighted with the brush, the other with my gun. I locked them in the boot and drove away from The Larches. I did not intend to return until the evening meal.

I got back from a pleasant day out during which nobody bothered to tail me. I spent the morning at the gym and the pool, the afternoon on a long walk beside the river, ending with a drink at a waterside pub. (Never The Eagle of course.) As I entered the house I could hear sounds of dinner being prepared, of water running, of the TV muttering in the lounge. I walked quickly to my room. With one giant stride, I stepped in and then pushed the door shut behind me. The angle of the light had changed since the morning but Madelaine's betraying footprints, so much smaller than Mrs Gridley's, were compressed into the nap of the carpet. Like some primitive hunter I tracked my quarry round the room. And like that hunter, felt the harsh clutch of an excitement.

She had not ventured to the far side of the room, either to the windows or the wash basin. But beside the bedside cabinet with its reading lamp there was a concentration of scuff marks in the carpet, some of which suggested she had knelt as well as stood. The lamp stood like a lighthouse that had failed all shipping. But when I so nervously flicked the plastic switch on the lead the bulb sneered in my face. I followed the lead down to the wall socket. Knowing my prey, I wasted no time bothering about fingerprint evidence. I took a small screwdriver from my mini-toolkit and opened up the socket. By a nasty little coincidence Mrs Gridley sounded the dinner gong just as the second screw came clear. The extent to which I jumped in fright undeceived me about my calmness.

Before I went down to dinner I ascertained that neither the plug nor socket had been interfered with. But the marks on the carpet had clearly betrayed Madelaine's interest. And she might well have betrayed herself in another way as well. After dinner I would scrape that area of carpet and send the fibres to forensic. Fibres and/or DNA might confirm she had knelt beside my bed: another minute link in the chain.

Madelaine played out her scenario very neatly. She came into The Larches while dinner was being served, muttered a flustered apology to Mrs Gridley, and in a louder tone informed Evelyn the train from Birmingham had been delayed by signalling problems. Albert glanced at me and then raised his eyes to the ceiling. The 'stuck-up cow' could do nothing right as far as he was concerned. I could admire her performance but knew that her previous earlier return and departure must have been captured by DS Whiddon's cameras. Once again not a *proof* of anything, but another tiny circumstantial brushstroke on the SIU canvas. She must have believed that when she sneaked back that afternoon the only risk to her lay in bumping into another resident or Mrs Gridley. She would have had plenty of excuses available to cover that mishap.

After the meal I returned to my room and double-checked *everything* irrespective of the direction of her tracks on my carpet. There were no signs she had opened the wardrobe, the little desk or my briefcase. I even checked the sash cords on the two windows. Nothing. But it was not a question of proof that caused me to strip my bed, but rather some kind of dark superstition about sliding my bare feet beneath the sheet. Absurd. What did I expect to find: Cleopatra's asp, perhaps? Despite the black humour implicit in my action, it was not something I intended to share with Henderson and Thomas.

Then for several minutes I stood absolutely still in the silence of the darkening evening, imagined myself Madelaine: standing in that room, staring, hating. But I *still* could not grasp the dark, plunging depth of a hatred first and wordlessly intimated to me under that cedar tree at The House. Nor could I anticipate what she might now be planning if she had decided the bedside socket was no use to her. Weirdly, it was in the next few moments I at last had that long-delayed and elusive lucky break.

I decided to check my hair colour before going out again, having long known how quickly my hair dye stabilized in fresh air. (How could I have ever explained dye stains on my pillow to Mrs Gridley?) I took my wash bag into the bathroom, where I lined up the hair dye and skin toner on the glass shelf above the sink. I also took out a new packet of paper tissues but accidentally dropped it on the floor. I bent down to pick it up. At that moment my face must have been about six inches from the bath side panel. I saw gleaming metal on a screw head in the painted panel.

I tottered across the bathroom, slumped on to the closed lid of the lavatory. I sat and stared at the bath. Mrs Gridley's friend, Bernard, had done a good job redecorating but, like most other decorators, had not bothered to remove the screws from the side panel of the bath before repainting it. God bless Bernard, wherever he was! I had seen bare metal exposed from under chipped paint.

It required a gut-wrenching determination to leave the panel alone, complete my make-up check, collect the bottles and used tissues, leave the bathroom, and then go out into Browcaister for a couple of drinks with Albert. When we returned at 11 p.m. he stretched my resolve a bit further by asking permission to rush into my bathroom for a pee. But how could I refuse when we both doubted his capacity, and that of his bladder, to get him the last few yards to his room?

When all the doors were shut except mine, when I could hear no whisper of sound from Madelaine, I went back to the bathroom with my little toolkit. I locked myself in and flushed the loo. The refilling cistern gave some slight background noise. Then I very carefully unscrewed the side panel of the bath. Being no longer locked up by dried paint, all the screws turned easily. Four of the six screw heads showed bare metal, but there were no flakes of dried white paint on the floor tiles. But then I would have expected Madelaine to remove any betraying paint chips.

The signature of my death was clear. The electric lead that led to the shaver light over the sink was buried behind the wall tiles. But where it passed underneath the bath behind the side panel it was exposed for several centimetres before it ran into a junction box. (Presumably another job botched by Bernard.) Where the lead passed close to one of the cast-iron legs of the bath, the protective cover had been deliberately frayed off. My pencil torch revealed the bare wires. And something more. Loosely wrapped round the lead was a black thread about half as thick as a shoelace. It passed from the frayed lead and down between the floorboards. A tug on the hidden end of the thread would pull the bare wire tight against the leg of the bath. I sat back on my heels and thought. What would it be like to be electrocuted and drowned simultaneously?

Some time later I was able to concentrate on the internal geography of the house. The point where that thread was most likely to emerge was in the corner of the spare room downstairs where there was a ceiling rose with pull-switch for the room's centre light. The end of the thread could be neatly concealed in the rose. But I would have to endure another wait before I could explore that room. And Madelaine? She would have to be in the house at the time I took my bath. How would she manage that and yet demonstrate the complete impossibility of her involvement?

As I replaced the side panel and collected my tools, my mind was fired up with the obviousness of the solution to Madelaine's problem. *She would no longer be living at The Larches when I died*. As I wiped the tiled floor with dampened tissues, taking up any telltale fragments of chipped paint, I was caught by several feelings: relief that I was *safe* as long as Madelaine lived 'with' me, irritation that I could not immediately go into the downstairs room and check my theory of how my electrocution was to be managed, and something akin to humour around conveying the news to Frimmer. But as the adrenalin rush subsided, the main feeling was one of satisfaction. Madelaine was now as much at my mercy as I was at hers. We were almost matched. Like marriage? 'Til death us do part?

Frimmer's reception of my news was puzzling. I thought at first it was related to my present inability to confirm where that black thread led. As soon as I had named my death I got the impression he began to think of something else while I was still talking with him. I deliberately stopped speaking in an effort to jar him back into attending, but all he could offer was to question the location of the shower in my bathroom. As I confirmed that it was over the bath, something he must have known from the maps we held, his attention appeared to wander again. But two days later when I was at last able to confirm that the black thread had been neatly tucked inside the corner ceiling rose in the room downstairs, he was his usual attentive and abrasive self.

'No relaxation because of what you've discovered. The whole team to remain on full alert. In the meantime, you keep well away from tall buildings and deep water, just in case. Even you could be wrong. And we don't want to be saying so over your coffin, do we?'

24

Imagining my own death had a calming effect on me not entirely due to my confidence I could prevent it. I was also affected by the move from speculations towards certainties, as if discovering Madelaine's intentions somehow confirmed mine. Our duel felt increasingly intimate and also more equal: no longer between tiger and tethered goat but between two matched beasts. And in the last ten years I had sunk my claws into more criminals than she had. But if my changed feelings brought me closer to her they even further separated me from colleagues. Contacts with them were now merely scene-setting on the stage where Madelaine and I would play out a drama of mutual destruction.

My peculiar blend of calmness and excitement I recognized as similar to that on the early morning before I went public as Corelli by assaulting Mundam and Croucher. As always with me, the prospect of imminent action swept aside anxiety and introspection. Now it was for others to agonize and dramatize. Mrs Gridley made the first contribution as I entered The Larches just before dinner the next Thursday evening.

She stood waiting for me in the hallway, at the foot of the stairs where I had so fleetingly touched Madelaine's hand. (That recurring theme of staircases?) I shut the front door behind me and walked towards her. Her obvious irritation — expressed by a curious sideways flapping of both arms, fast-twitching eyebrows and sharp nose quivering — resembled a jackdaw whose nest has just been robbed of a prized trinket.

'*That* woman! You'll never *guess*, Mr Corelli.' I arranged my face to look surprised. My gut was already knotted. 'That Ms *Hutchinson*!' Sprayed with emphasis, I waited. 'After all that *trouble* your colleague Mr Stone took as well. She's not only given *notice*. She's gone! Told me her advance payment would take care of things. But that's not the *point*, is it? I've got *another* empty room and all the *bother* of getting a *new* guest. I *checked* her room *very* carefully, I can tell you.' Foolishly, I opened my mouth to speak. But she wasn't allowing that — not yet anyway. 'No *good* saying your Mr Stone might help *again*. Hardly fair, is it? He's already done that once for *free*. I feel duty *bound* to pay his fee next time — either that or get into the *sordid* business of advertising the room *myself*.' Breathless, she stopped flapping her arms, brushed her hands through her hair, made useless adjustments to the neckline of her dress. Nothing could hide the enraged flush rising under her chin.

'I am most sorry,' I said, hiding my satisfaction at the news. 'Indeed very sorry. From her references she was a reliable lady.'

'I'm *sorry* too. I sometimes wonder why I bother with all *this*.' A hand flap at the deep pink carpet, white walls, grey curtains: her world of work. 'You do your *best* for people and then *this* sort of thing happens.'

Momentarily, the pink and the white and the grey blurred together in a kaleidoscope of more exciting colours. But I steadied myself, said what she wanted to hear. As if I cared any more! The date of my execution was fixed. And, yes, by God, that did concentrate the mind! My sole focus now was on confirmation from DS Whiddon.

His report was straightforward. Madelaine Grey had left The Larches at 1600 hours. She had driven her car from the rear car park to the front door, and there loaded it with her suitcase and two boxes of papers. I understood why she had done that. The rear passageway out to the car park was quite narrow. Perhaps more importantly, by not using that rear exit she had avoided passing and repassing an irate Mrs Gridley. But maybe our hostess had been upstairs vindictively checking that Madelaine hadn't stolen a light bulb or lavatory brush.

Then Frimmer came on the line with Whiddon to convey Suzy Green's report that Madelaine had just arrived at Peacehavens where Mr Johnson had volunteered to help carry luggage up to her room.

'So it looks like I die next Wednesday, or the one following. My guess is she couldn't bear to hold back that much longer, sir.'

'Likely enough,' said Frimmer. 'She's no longer resident so unconnected with your fatal accident. All we have to do is keep tabs on her and be sure you know if and when she comes back to Browcaister.'

'The crucial point is that my team pick her up re-entering The Larches,' interrupted Whiddon. 'And safest time for her to do that, as Jake has pointed out, is Wednesday afternoon. That could mean she'll have to lie low in the house until late evening both to kill and to get out. So what sort of woman *is* she, for Christ's sake?'

'One with enough nerve to do that,' I said curtly. 'Don't bother with any labels: determined, mad, ruthless. Just be sure your team picks her up for me — whenever she turns up. And don't bank on that happening when *we* think it most likely. Wednesday's favourite but none of us is ever going to get inside her head.'

'Right,' said Frimmer. 'All details as agreed in orders.' A pause. 'It's still not quite enough, is it?' he added in a peculiarly flat tone.

It must have seemed to the other listeners that he was apparently seeking my opinion. I knew that wasn't what he was after. He wanted me to confirm before witnesses my willingness to die for SIU.

'No,' I said bluntly. 'We go on as planned — all the way. How else can we have an absolutely solid case against her? On top of that her failure to kill me allows us to confront her with my resurrection. That should help break her down!'

Frimmer was too clever to believe I was offering my life merely as surety for his personal advancement and kudos for SIU. Maybe he thought I was just continuing dutiful; perhaps trying to make good again after my part in what had happened to Una and Kathy. But I doubted he suspected other motivations. Fool that I was!

'But there's a new factor come up in relation to Bull's death.' Frimmer hesitated momentarily, but long enough for me to recall his apparent lack of attention during our last discussion. And long enough to register he had used my real name. Then: 'Corelli's dead.'

Somewhere down the connection someone drew in a sharp breath. I knew it wasn't me. I could feel the pain of my upper teeth lancing into my lower lip. Before Frimmer spoke again there was just enough time for me to be surprised at being so shocked by news I had always expected.

'He escaped from the safe house and was found drowned in a fen ditch the next morning. It happened a couple of days ago. We're keeping him on ice. It could be his body discovered in the bath at The Larches, couldn't it? Make use of the coincidence to really get to her?'

'Yes and no, sir,' I said quickly before anyone else got in. 'Yes to making use of his death. No to it being coincidence. I've not the slightest doubt a door or window of your so-called safe house was left open deliberately at a time that suited you. And he fell for it. I don't even want to know what happened when the poor sod reached that ditch. One coincidence is more than enough for this case to bear, don't you think? That I happen to bear a slight resemblance to the man you positioned in front of Madelaine Grey is as far as you're ever going to stretch coincidence with me.' I paused but neither Frimmer nor anyone else jumped in. 'But I guess we might as well use an SIU home-produced corpse now you've so conveniently got one — sir.'

I listened to my four colleagues stuttering, iffing and butting on their phones. I didn't bother. All the practical objections they might raise, and for that matter all the moral ones, Frimmer would have already worked through. No doubt an SIU solicitor had long ago produced all the necessary documentation relating to protective custody instead of kidnap. And all signed appropriately by Corelli himself when offered inducements. Unwittingly signing his life away. Inevitably, it would be an SIU staffed ambulance and an SIU doctor, probably the one who had examined me in the Command Truck, who came for his body after the frantic emergency call from the unfortunate Mrs Gridley. That poor woman's troubles only just beginning! And no problem swapping bodies via the bathroom window; not with Frimmer's organizing skills. Suddenly I had a gutful.

'Right, sir. I take it you want the bathroom sash window greased?'

'Already done, Bull. Sent my man round as window cleaner's helper last week. You just happened to be in the gym that morning.'

I made no further contribution to the

discussion. Last week! But I was in no position to adopt a moral stance, not with that trail of deaths I had left behind me since meeting Molly Poling. And to whatever doubts my colleagues expressed, Frimmer's authority would be more than equal. And that certainty freed me.

Frimmer knew what he was doing but so did I. Plot and scheme as he might choose, I knew the simplicity of my own concern. Whoever else had died or was about to die, it wasn't going to be me. I recalled the woodlouse struggling to climb across the telephone lead. In that struggle he was unaware of any electronic signals passing beneath him inside the lead. Had he been, would he have halted if the lead was frayed?

25

A sullen acceptance of Madelaine's defection now permeated The Larches. Evelyn sulked, betrayed by a new friend who had not bothered either to say goodbye or leave a forwarding address. Mrs Gridley continued enraged at both the manner of Madelaine's departure, and also at the necessity of finding a new paying guest. 'That *woman* had absolutely no thought for others. I suppose I'm *expected* to be *grateful* she gave me back her *keys*. I should have *taken* your advice and interviewed the other three applicants *as well*.'

I had nothing to say to any of that. As for Albert, he was not so much sullen as strangulated at The Larches, able to speak his spiteful satisfactions only when safely ensconced with me in a local pub. Had I cared less about Madelaine's defection, I might have teased him as his splutterings sprayed beer froth into his lap. I had not realized how many ways one man could reiterate the phrase 'The fucking cow's gone!'

I missed her, my murderous companion, especially in the late evening with only the party wall between our solitary beds. And *how* I missed her set me apart from the other residents: her absence enlivened me even as it rendered others sullen and spiteful. That silent, uninhabited room next to mine no longer vibrated with her feminine shufflings as she constructed a temporary life to parallel mine. The still air of that room might resemble that in a sealed sarcophagus, an Egyptian tomb never to be disturbed by hoofs or adze, but I *knew* where the body was.

We had been like two native hunters from different hostile tribes, accidentally cast up in some great modern city: Aboriginals in Sydney, perhaps. And in that alien world of white money and grey souls, as we padded along the parallel skyscraper canyons, we had caught sight of each other only at crossroads: a moment for unspoken acknowledgement that we were both from a much darker world than the enfeebled city inhabitants would ever know. Perhaps I had felt some kind of solace in knowing I was not the sole representative of those encroaching shadows. But what had she felt other than unspeakable hatred?

There is a deeper loneliness than that of missing another's proximity, one that I had gradually come to recognize while still a child. Whatever others had said, however heartfelt their protestations and convincing their lies, they had always slid away from me somewhere along the corridors of time. It was a lesson doubly reinforced in adulthood; firstly in living the life of a policeman who at best only enjoyed the 'official' friendships of colleagues and worse still did so because the uniform precluded much else in the wider world. Secondly, because this other loneliness, the existential one, if you like, proved unassuagable even by women who loved me. No matter how passionately, or even determinedly, they embraced me there was always some unspoken contract I could never elicit and so never fulfil. In their bodies I sought an end to that loneliness, but was forced to own that it was rooted in me. Maybe it was all simple: that I no more liked myself as Jack Bull than I did as Arthur Snell or Jake Corelli.

And always, when this unresolvable loneliness held me, my thoughts turned to my home: the elegant rooms, the pictures, books and music that lay waiting, consolations for the bereft. But the worm was in the rose even there. It was a home left me by a man I despised and who probably despised me equally: his bastard grandson. Worse still, I despised myself for accepting it with the lie that I would take his ridiculous surname.

That I had remained forever Bull and never Postlethwaite was a feeble gesture of independence while wallowing in inherited wealth.

Other justifications were equally pathetic: that my luxurious lifestyle was compensation both for not marrying and for becoming a career police officer. The latter was particularly wimpish since every other officer made that choice without the featherbedding of a service flat overlooking Hyde Park. Ironic that Madelaine, who perhaps lived in a similar ambience, might even have understood my loneliness, was to offer a final 'embrace' that would lead to the deepest loneliness of all — for at least one of us.

In the next few days my perception of her and of me as primitives in a twenty-first century city was not entirely wide of the mark. News of brief 'sightings' by the troubled city population came trickling in. There were DNA links between her and the scrapings from my bedside carpeting. And DNA linked her to two past killings, one of them not even numbered in Stone's researches for SIU. And on the shoe fragment retrieved from Johnson's bonfires were minute traces of limestone matching the bedrock of the abandoned quarry where Madelaine had torched her stolen car. Under the floorboards of Johnson's allotment shed,

314

like fossilized human footprints in mud, eroded and stained by time, lay his collection of press cuttings which related to several of the deaths on Stone's list.

'Still not enough,' said Frimmer. It was not a question. No, I thought. Proof will come only when we fatally confront each other.

It would be too facile to explain away my thoughts and images merely as stilted responses to anxiety. No. They ebbed and flowed naturally within me as I waited for those last days to pass, and sometimes they found logical expression in my renewed ferocity at the gym, in the pool and in my running on the river towpath; like final cockpit checks by a pioneering lone astronaut bound for a previously unvisited planet.

Lift-off came the next Wednesday morning: a message via Frimmer from DC Suzy Green at Peacehavens. Madelaine Grey had not appeared at breakfast, was not in her room, and her car had gone from the car park outside the security fence. She had signed the leave book but informed no one of her intention. Intention was the one thing I had no need to be told.

What I had to tell myself forcefully, was to *get out of the way.* For me to be lurking in or near The Larches when she returned would jeopardize the whole operation. She might be capable of hiding out in the spare bedroom downstairs for several hours but I doubted my capacity for doing so in mine. And I was mindful of her duplicated keys. She could check I was out of the house before locking herself in the spare room. As for Mrs Gridley or anyone else checking the spare room, that was not a problem for Madelaine. The lock could be set from the inside. It was very unlikely Mrs Gridley would discover that and persuade Bernard to come round and sort it the same evening. If I was asked to help with a jammed lock I could plead ignorance, and no doubt Albert would personify it.

My role was clear. Despite churning and contradictory feelings, I had to pretend to live a normal day. Most particularly, I had to return to The Larches at my usual time, dine, perhaps watch TV or go out again for a beer with Albert. All this as if having no idea Madelaine was back in the house silently waiting. And at the end of my day I had to go to my bathroom for the last time. Hearing me, she would stand on a chair in a corner of the room below, retrieve from within the ceiling rose the thread (worm in the rose?) tied to the frayed electric cable, pull it down and listen to me die.

Then, perhaps with feelings akin to satisfaction, or with no feelings at all,

Madelaine would slip from the house into the night. She might draw a deep, steadying breath as she began to walk the neon yellow canyon of that street for the last time; unknowingly committing her every gesture to the implacable cameras in the house opposite. But maybe that deep-drawn breath would have nothing to do with my dying. It might be a first anticipatory tremor at the thought of her next rapist victim, already allocated his place after me in her murderous litany. And could I stay alive to dutifully but so reluctantly save him?

One certainty only: that she, like me, was forever ensnared in Frimmer's clinging and unbreakable web. Until death us do part.

26

'It's 16.00, Jake. Grey's just let herself into The Larches. Jake?' DS Whiddon's voice, unusually high-pitched, slashed at me. Having just completed a fast run along the towpath, the impact of his message into my breathless body collapsed me on to a riverside bench. 'Jake?'

'Yes,' I said, begrudging the exhalation of even that much air. 'Anyone — else in — the house — at that — time?'

'No. All out — as expected.'

'Then we proceed exactly as planned. Out.'

All choices gone.

We had decided to go total: nail Madelaine for every murder, not settle for less. No escape now for her or me. Then a moment of pure terror; something not experienced since that idiot Mahoney, suppurating with fear, had tried to drag me off a sixth-floor window ledge. As he had fallen had there been a similar moment of purity for him? Then my moment passed and I was nearly myself again.

At the front gate of The Larches I suppressed desire to glance across the road at the first-floor windows of the house opposite. Fighting the swelling excitement that stifled lungs and caused my struggling heart to pump harder, I tried to act normally. It was not so hard to hang about in the entrance hall listening for any sounds from the spare room, but achingly difficult to take the necessary shower after my run. I kept my feet in the centre of the rubber shower mat and hoped Madelaine would adhere to what we believed was her plan. If she tried to kill me and get away now she ran the risk of meeting Mrs Gridley or one of her residents returning to the house. But I could not repress a shudder of relief when clear of the shower and drying off.

Back in my room I acted out every element of Corelli's usual early-evening routine, including lying on the bed for half an hour. I had already locked in my car boot those few things which could not belong to Jake Corelli: gun, sketch plans, hair dye, skin toner. But for Corelli all that *mattered* was she was in the room below: the woman Arthur Snell had once gently but so ignorantly held naked in his arms.

And for Bull? However I departed The Larches I would have become myself again at last: dead or alive. If alive I anticipated that Acting Detective Inspector Jack Bull might feel something like the relief and emptiness of a cancer patient pronounced cleared. But how could I be sure? All that I *knew* was that if I lived my rank would revert to DS. I had long abandoned the fantasy that Frimmer might make my acting rank substantive in recognition of exceptional services. And death relieves us of all burdens of rank.

Surrealistically, dinner was a pleasant meal quietly enjoyed. Mrs Gridley was not disposed to chatter as she served us, but whether she was still sulking over Madelaine's abrupt departure, or had failed to win at afternoon bingo, nobody knew. What I did know was that she would have a vast amount to talk about within the next twenty-four hours. Audrey, her fawning friend next door, was going to suffer severely.

I looked in Evelyn's direction and wondered how the approaching disaster would impinge on her. She sat, fat-faced over book and food, swaddled by some kind of bedraggled, grey tracksuit. Perhaps my death in a room just along the landing from hers might excite and enliven her, render her temporarily attractive to some blinkered man. I must still have had a half-smile on my face when I turned away and looked at Albert. For him a smile, however feeble, was a social invitation. Cheerfully, he made the gesture of pulling a pint. I nodded. Drinking with Albert was a fairly regular element in Corelli's behaviour.

As he and I walked into town, summer lightning flickered beneath storm clouds massing to the west, touching the violet dusk with flecks of a pale almost translucent lemon hue. Albert, turned mauve by the light, made some remark about the possibility of us getting wet. I had my own unspeakable thoughts about water and electricity.

I made no attempt to match Albert's guzzling. Nor did I say much; didn't have to. He had received another solicitor's letter on behalf of one of his ex-wives, so my role was inevitably defined as sympathetic listener. But I was amused that on our final evening together my familiar impatience with the man was tinged with something like affection. Perhaps that paralleled the charitable impulse which persuaded mourners to speak only kindnesses across a grave. What might be said over mine?

We left the pub at about 22.00 because I insisted on that, and Albert, staggering, wanted to be accompanied on the walk back. The pavements were black with rain and the sky even blacker, but we had chosen to return to The Larches during a break in the storm. Albert tried to make this a cause for self-congratulation, but dropped that idea when I bundled him through the door and we found ourselves confronted by Mrs Gridley.

'Well!' she said, exasperated as ever.

'Evening, m'dear,' said Albert nervously. Then: 'Excuse me. Need the loo.' He pushed between us and made a kind of shuffling run along the hall and up the stairs. I looked at Mrs Gridley and shrugged with what I hoped was a Mediterranean gesture. We both knew we wouldn't be seeing him again that night.

'Man's an *utter* fool,' she said shortly, snapping home bolts on the front door. 'Good job you're a bit more *sensible* about drink.' She stepped across to the board, and flicked the 'in' signs against my name and Albert's. Those for her and Evelyn were already in place. Against Room 3 there was now a blank space. For the downstairs spare guest room there had never been a space allocated. Wishing Mrs Gridley goodnight and shepherding her along the hall in front of me allowed me to conceal a lurching sensation in my legs which she might have interpreted as the effects of drink. In my room I fell on to the bed to wait out the dawdling passage of Corelli's final minutes.

At 23.00 hours I silently packed the small rucksack: plastic mac, toolkit, pencil torch, toilet bag, rubber gloves, and my mobile still set silent on text. I swung the bag on to my right shoulder, then draped it with the thick bath towel. The towel, rough under my right ear, gave off the familiar furry odours of self and laundering.

I looked round the inhabited room for the last time: toothpaste and toothbrush in the glass above the sink in the far corner, wardrobe door ajar, the few clothes hanging neat in their ranks, open briefcase and faked papers on the tiny desk. The bedside reading lamp switched on, illuminating the small stack of three library books: PD James, *A Certain Justice*, Lawrence Williams, *Images of Death*, Graham Greene, *The Comedians*. Someone, perhaps Evelyn, would either return them to the library or steal them.

The dark pink carpet now scuffed with Wednesday's footprints hid the floorboards and the cavity beneath with its maze of water pipes and electric cables. Below all that Madelaine Grey was silently waiting for me. She had waited for nearly seven hours; perhaps had cat-napped, used the loo, eaten food and drunk water she had brought with her. And no betraying sound after Mrs Gridley had returned. The sheer effort of that: *endeavour pushed beyond all reason!*

As I shut the bedroom door firmly and

finally, I was surprised not by some recollection of Madelaine but by the memory of Suzy Green lightly brushing her hand against the fronds of the cedar tree at The House: that acrid fragrance, and the golden helmet of her hair. But despite that momentary, alerting surprise, I was already drifting dangerously close towards the enervating feeling of surrender which subverts as one is wheeled from ambulance into hospital; passing almost gratefully, into others' control. I shook myself like a damp dog.

In the bathroom I locked the door, hung my rucksack and towel on the hooks on the back of it. I walked to the window and checked that the catch was off. Behind the sash cords traces of grease glinted on the inner edges of the window frames. I raised the lower window a few centimetres. It slid smoothly and silently. A flurry of rain starred the glass panes, confirming the impossibility of seeing any movement below in the car park. But I knew men and vehicles were positioned exactly as planned, that they could see me outlined against the lit window. With them they had the sightless corpse of Jake Corelli.

I urinated; flushed the loo. Then I walked to the sink and stuffed my bath towel into it, turned on the taps. The towel took the water greedily, became difficult to turn over in the sink, but I wanted it as heavy and as saturated as possible, as close to resembling my own body as possible. When it could absorb no more water (like Corelli's body in that ditch?), I turned off the taps. On my mobile I texted the solitary word: Ready.

I never doubted Madelaine was ready.

27

A tremor passed through my body, beginning at my feet, exiting through the top of my head. Then I was myself again: deadly calm. I pulled on the rubber gloves, put the plug in the bath and turned on both taps. Took the screwdriver from the tool kit. This time the side panel screws came out more easily. When I lifted the painted hardboard sheet away from the bath, sweat ran into my eyes, even though the panel weighed so little. I lowered it flat on to the floor, laid on top of it and looked under the bath. The frayed cable was still in position. And so was the black thread, draped over the cable and disappearing down between the floorboards. Down to Madelaine. If she was standing on the chair in the corner of the room below we were now physically closer than when we had lain in our separate beds on opposite sides of the party wall. And she *still* didn't know who I was. I counted to ten on the breath.

Then I stood, reached across the edge of the cast-iron bath, turned off the metal taps. Wasting no thought on the effects of tepid water on a stale corpse, I stirred the water vigorously with the plastic-handled back brush, then dropped it into the water. Another look under the bath: the cable and thread undisturbed.

Silently, I stepped across to the sink and gathered up the saturated towel and flannel. I threw them against the tiles above the bath. They fell from the wall into the water with a satisfying muted splashing. I knelt on the side panel, glanced again at the frayed cable. I wished I could have replicated the farting, slithering sounds made by a body against the sides and bottom of a bath. All I could invent as a further signal was to flick the pumice stone off the bath edge and into the water. The soft splash, and a flurry of rain against the window, were simultaneous.

The black thread jerked. There was a flash and a loud bang from the function box. An extraordinary sensation of heat, the stench of overheated rubber. The thread vanished through the gap in the floorboards. Madelaine had killed me. The shaver light went out but the ceiling lights, on a different circuit, stayed on. I was astounded by my sense of anti-climax. It had all been so simple!

Keeping clear of the bath, I stretched out on the side panel, rested my head on my shaking arms so I could see both my watch and mobile screen at the same time. I had to play dead until Whiddon confirmed Madelaine had left the building. No sound reached me from the room below.

Now was the most dangerous moment for her. No doubt she had done her best not to leave any traces for forensic to discover in the room downstairs. But perhaps she hardly bothered. After so many successful killing years she still had no reason to suspect that a DNA match might exist for her. Even more to the point: why should anyone bother to check the downstairs spare guest room? Corelli had died accidentally in another room on a different floor.

No, the one danger for her was the unlikely possibility of bumping into someone else in the house as she left. Madelaine knew the other guests and Mrs Gridley were in their rooms, and that all their rooms were en suite so no one would be wandering to or from a bathroom. But perhaps Evelyn had remembered she had left a book downstairs, or Albert had decided on some late-night soft porn TV? More dangerously, Mrs Gridley might decide to recheck that she had switched off the TV and bolted the front door when Albert and I had returned.

In my imagination I saw Madelaine step down from the chair, put the black thread in her pocket, move the chair back to its normal position. Very carefully, she unlocked the door, paused before stepping out. Left the room, silently closing the door with the Yale key. Slipped along the hallway past doors to the deserted TV room and the dining room laid for breakfast for three guests. Slid back the bolts on the front door. (The impossibility of closing them again attributable to Mrs Gridley's forgetfulness — perhaps occasioned by irritation at Albert's behaviour.) The familiar Yale turning silently, she stepping — But I was far too slow.

Whiddon's signal on my mobile confirmed she was already walking along Belmont Avenue. We knew where she was going. Her car was parked in the town centre. We would also know her route back to Peacehavens, Whiddon's team having fitted a tracker to the vehicle. But what would she be feeling as the wipers brushed aside the rain almost as easily as she had brushed me aside? Perhaps exultant, celebratory? She believed she had successfully revenged and redeemed another and greater evil. Or was she too mad now to feel anything?

Silently, I replaced the side panel, wiped off the screw heads. Then I repacked my small rucksack but left out Corelli's toilet bag. I sat on the loo and waited for the signal. Only when it appeared on the screen did I realize I had not been as efficient as I had thought; maybe not as calm. I had left my plastic rain jacket in the bottom of the bag, put toolkit and everything else on top of it. But getting wet merely from rainfall was now a triviality. I switched off the light. Then switched on my pencil torch, keeping the beam pointed low. More than my own night vision was at risk. I pushed up the sash window as far as it would go.

They must have been already positioned on the flat roof over the kitchen: three strangers, rain-stained and with a black, wet and shiny body bag. Lit by the refracted downward illumination from my torch, and with their rain cowls raised, they resembled monks carrying an unsanctified corpse to a common burial pit. As they edged towards me, with their own single torch beam also directed downward, shadows were cast against them, rippling like black water as they moved. Like Abercrombie? What had he been spared by that blow behind the ear, snuffing out consciousness of the tentacular arms out of the water dragging him down? Just as electrocution might have spared me the drowning agony? Only Corelli had known the horror of being drowned.

'You out first!' The order hissed through the soft sounds of rainfall, of guttering and downpipes gurgling. I was glad enough to comply, wanted no part in their struggles with Corelli's corpse: of dragging it through the window space without the body bag touching the sill, unwrapping it, lifting and then lowering it into the bath water, getting the bag and themselves out again, mopping the floor as they retreated to the window, which then had to be pulled down from the outside. Most of all I did not want to see the apparition of my drowned self.

I climbed out past them and their burden, silently crossed the roof on the spread rubber mat, slithered down the padded ladder, then took the most enormous breath in as my feet hit the ground. What I needed instantaneously was a moment to be freed of Corelli, to be only Jack Bull. What I got was something other. I was embraced by Thomas as he hissed congratulations in my ear. Later, colleagues might say that was when 'Bull lost it!' Not so. That was when I *found*, and was over-whelmed by, my deepest submarine emotion.

I twisted Thomas and myself round, slammed him against the ladder, pushed my body tight against his, grasped his throat with both hands. I knew I was hissing words into his face, never knew what they were; women's names, perhaps. But I knew I was killing him not just for me.

Then there was a slim steel bar across my throat, pulling me back and away from Thomas. A knee in my back gave an excruciating leverage for that bar crushing my larynx. A voice ordered Thomas to grab my hands. Together, Thomas and his rescuer levered me away from my grip on the Welshman's throat. Then none of us was struggling any more. I was turning round and recognizing Mr Stone. It was not my injury which caused me to vomit over his shoes but revulsion on discovering he had used the steel of his prosthetic right arm to crush my throat.

'Just go home, Jack,' he whispered. 'You're finished here. Absolutely finished.'

28

This final Friday is a flawless morning: England crossing the cusp between summer and autumn. Now, no longer fugitive, and in clothing of my own choice, I walk the driveway to Peacehavens. Behind me lies the respite of a few quiet hours in my own home: safe baths, a flooding of music. And too few hours of sleep. But much else is taken care of: police cars in the car park, and in the gatehouse a uniformed officer sits with white-faced John. And that nice Mr Stone has found a reliable electrician for Mrs Gridley.

As I walk I feel clean, light, as if gravity tugs less powerfully, the straight, tree-lined drive ahead of me a metaphor for this change. No longer fugitive, I am free of old fears about what awaits me round a corner or when crossing a road. Only a bruised throat from a false arm reminds; that, and the faintest vibration sidling the length of every vein. Not hunted now but still haunted.

Lightness is more than things taken care of, terrors pacified. It is also abandoning any belief that I comprehend this work. Rape is shrouded in confusions not only in itself but in attempts to justify punishments; not even execution brings clarity. But Madelaine has thought so and could be right. Perhaps I am too much like the confused and unstable old man who had found a kind of self-recognition in the disturbed world of that young woman.

On the slope to my left, forensically wrapped figures are digging in the muddle of neglected ground, overturning Mr Johnson's improbable secret hopes. And the door of his shed is wedged open. Something must have been said because the men stop work, stare down the slope at me. Nobody waves. Ahead, parked on the gravelled turning circle before the house, are several of our unmarked cars.

The common fate of helpers: to make things worse. I can try to hide my part in Molly's death, bury it in the sterility of necessary procedures. Doing no more than my job. But no such hiding place from Una and Kathy. No petty justifications. And I live in the futile pretence I might eventually be cleansed of the ingrained grime of all this. The bitterest of all police officers' delusions: that they can go home clean.

And I have secrets which continue to entrap.

First secret, never to be disclosed to Frimmer, is that of course I had paid Una and Kathy for time spent with them — and double for the two. Brasses don't give up two working afternoons every week for nothing — however pleasurable. I *know* this secret echoes the infantilism of my original decision to get involved, but I cling to it as if to stay afloat on a sea of blood.

And I have a second secret about woman and her fate, a secret almost hidden from myself: like glancing into a lover's seductively lit bedroom and seeing her only partly reflected in a mirror. My distress at Molly Poling's suicide. I interviewed her and she died. My sorrow reflects that something in me died with her. But I am not yet able to name what that might be, to distinguish between it and a disgusting maudlin senti-mentality. And then there are all those other women, not just the ones I met but the secret army of the abused.

Confusions with the dead and abused are matched by my bewilderment around Madelaine Grey. I say to myself that I have lost neither my sense of duty nor my feelings of repugnance towards her. But she has engaged my emotions in so many different ways that I remain trapped in a maze of ambiguities. Not even the secret that my suit is distorted by the weight of a gun implies clarification.

I push open the main door of the house,

enter the spacious hall where once I sat waiting for confirmation that I, Arthur Snell, could interview Madelaine Grey. And lounging on the same seat is DS Thomas.

'Who's with Madelaine Grey?' I ask.

'Henderson and Green,' sulkily. Neither asks if the other's throat still hurts.

'Not Frimmer or Stone?' Stifling alarm.

'No sign of Frimmer. Stone's through there in the kitchen — our temporary ops room.'

'So what's all the row in there?'

'Dunno. Just started. I'll go see. You wait here.' But as he moves so do I. Propelled by a terrible anxiety, I am already about four steps up the staircase when Thomas pushes his way into the kitchen. Noise splashes out and I identify the sobbing cries of Mr Johnson. Then all last things happen together.

At the top of the stairs stands Madelaine Grey, brunette, totally in white, even her stockings, closely followed by Suzy, blonde in dark blue, and then Paul Henderson, T-shirted in jeans. Even in that crowded micro-second the idiot part of my mind sees a pop group. Instantaneously, I also know it is the grouping of the *four* of us burning into my memory film. But as they step down towards me there is a colour change. Madelaine's face becomes suffused with a sickly yellowish hue.

'Corelli!' She speaks the name as her

doom, presses herself tight against the wall to my right so she is diagonally above me. Suzy, clinging to the banister rail on my left, is now revealed as wearing Peacehavens working overalls. Behind Suzy, following close enough to touch her, Henderson opens and then shuts his mouth.

'Not any more! I am Detective Inspector Bull and I — '

'I admit!' she shrieks down at me, banging the left side of her head violently against the wall. Then, less hysterically, with head still: 'I killed your two vile tarts. Disgusting, evil women!' Then her voice subsides to a hiss as she moves down a step above and against me, almost touching: 'I did nothing else that mattered. Those men never *mattered*.'

Closing behind her, Suzy starts to tell me Madelaine had already been cautioned. But then her voice is drowned by a further bellowing as Mr Johnson bursts from the kitchen with Thomas struggling to restrain him.

There is the briefest sliver of silence as the old man interprets the scene, the dreadful colour of Madelaine's face. Before Thomas, or any of the uniformed officers surging from the kitchen can prevent it, Johnson snatches from his pocket the flick knife I had seen at our meeting on the allotment. Thomas's fist lashes down on to Johnson's arm. Fatedly, the opening knife jumps out of his hand, falls between the banisters and on to the step where Madelaine stands.

She swoops like a ravenous crow, snatches the knife in her right hand, moves more decisively than can either Suzy or Henderson perched high behind her. Madelaine and I realize she had caught up the knife with the blade pointing away from me. With that look of defiling hatred I now begin to understand, and with the impeccable malice of a knowing woman, as if she had stood together with us under the cedar tree, she swings the blade in the direction it points, behind her towards Suzy.

But in this at least, Suzy is a match for her: catches her wrist, twists and the knife clatters back on to the stairs. Then she grabs at Madelaine's right shoulder.

The gun is already clear of my pocket, the barrel rising.

Her right hand released, Madelaine begins to cup her wrists together as if for handcuffs. Staring down into me, her face ebbing from yellow to white, Madelaine speaks to me for the last time: 'Please.'

I fire point-blank a single shot into her chest. She is knocked back against Suzy and together they slump away from me. The shot kills every other sound.

As I kneel beside Madelaine, Suzy crouches forward and, like a canopy, her gold hair seems to caress all three of our faces. I place the back of my left hand gently against the dying woman's cheek. Then her mouth is full of blood. In her closing eyes I see acknowledgement of who touches her, has saved her. A single moment of mutual recognition that will absolutely never be taken from me.

Sequestered from the shouting world around us, Suzy and I stare at each other over Madelaine's face. 'Oh, Jack, Jack, Jack,' whispers Suzy.

We look down again at Madelaine, see that mysterious smoothing out, that emptying away of the person; the look which those who fear emptiness name serenity. I think I was the one who closed her eyes.

Suzy gently releases the dead woman, stands up and clings to the banisters. Henderson puts his right hand on her right shoulder. Temporarily united, they look down on me, on Madelaine. Silent in the hall directly below us stands Mr Johnson, holding Thomas as tightly as Thomas holds him. Behind them uniformed officers are still and silent.

There appear to be enough people to cope. I walk down the stairs and out into the sunlight.

As I step on to the gravel, a familiar large black car swings to a halt in front of me. Hand on his earpiece, Frimmer struggles clear of the rear seats. While he listens I stand. Then he stretches out his hand to me.

'Fucking compassion! The ruin of you. But maybe self-defence. Thomas says something about a knife. Mr Johnson might just have saved your career. I'll take the gun now.'

Surprised to find I am still carrying it in my hand, I give it to him. I lean on the roof of the car. Frimmer had known about the gun; maybe tipped off by Tom at The House. Perhaps my act of free will was really no more than another of his manipulations. He will have proofs for many cases against Madelaine and none of the inconveniences of a trial. Now I know he always gets what he wants. Avoiding my eye, Frimmer gestures at me to join him, and climbs back into the car.

I brush aside a bright yellow leaf settling on the car roof, perhaps the first of autumn. Yellow. I climb in next to Frimmer on the back seat. I shut the door. As I do so my sleeve leaves a broad smear of her blood across the bottom of the window. Frimmer is talking to me but I hear nothing until, as we approach the lodge at the end of the drive, an ambulance swings in from the lane and the siren is sounded against us.

AUTHOR'S NOTE

Mr Stone's researches for SIU were shown to be incomplete. A total of twenty-three murders were eventually attributed to Madelaine Grey. Another twenty accidental deaths were not conclusively attributed, the evidence being insufficient. Detective Sergeant Jack Bull saw no reason to point out to colleagues that the sum total of these two categories of cases was forty-three: the number of deaths in the Moorgate train crash.

We do hope that you have enjoyed reading this large print book.

Did you know that all of our titles are available for purchase?

We publish a wide range of high quality large print books including:
Romances, Mysteries, Classics
General Fiction
Non Fiction and Westerns

Special interest titles available in large print are:
The Little Oxford Dictionary
Music Book
Song Book
Hymn Book
Service Book

Also available from us courtesy of Oxford University Press:
Young Readers' Dictionary
(large print edition)
Young Readers' Thesaurus
(large print edition)

For further information or a free brochure, please contact us at:
Ulverscroft Large Print Books Ltd.,
The Green, Bradgate Road, Anstey,
Leicester, LE7 7FU, England.
Tel: (00 44) 0116 236 4325
Fax: (00 44) 0116 234 0205